THE PERFECT MOTHER

Vivian Simpson hungered to escape the nightmare of her childhood—to forget the hideous violations of her body and her spirit.

She would transform herself into a princess—with wealth, power and pleasure at her instant command.

To make this dream come true, she would destroy anyone—the men she took as husbands or used as lovers . . . or the children who were her helpless, battered puppets in her show of being the perfect mother . . .

BLACK WIDOW

Berkley Books by Christina Crawford

BLACK WIDOW
MOMMIE DEAREST

CHRISTINA CRAWFORD
Black Widow

BERKLEY BOOKS, NEW YORK

This Berkley book contains the complete
text of the original hardcover edition.
It has been completely reset in a type face
designed for easy reading, and was printed
from new film.

BLACK WIDOW

A Berkley Book / published by arrangement with
the author

PRINTING HISTORY
William Morrow and Company edition published 1982
Berkley edition / November 1982

For information address: William Morrow and Company, Inc.,
105 Madison Avenue, New York, New York 10016.

ISBN: 0-425-05625-2

A BERKLEY BOOK® TM 757,375
Berkley Books are published by Berkley Publishing Corporation,
200 Madison Avenue, New York, New York 10016.
The name "Berkley" and the stylized "B"
with design are trademarks belonging
to Berkley Publishing Corporation.

PRINTED IN THE UNITED STATES OF AMERICA

Acknowledgments

My deepest appreciation goes to the following people for their valuable contribution to this book:

Michael C. Agran, Esq.
Gerald Breitman
Peggy Brooks
Donald Fuller, *director, Delinquency Control Institute, University of Southern California*
F. James Gay, M.D.
Jack Raymond
Deanne Tilton, *administrative director, Los Angeles County Inter-Agency Council on Child Abuse and Neglect*
Claudia Walton
Martin E. Weekes, *Chief Juvenile Division, Office of the County Counsel, Los Angeles*

This book is dedicated to my beloved husband, C. David Koontz, whose loyalty, courage and love have been my constant source of strength—without whom nothing would be the same.

Chapter 1

Autumn comes early in the northern Michigan Upper Peninsula. But as hunting season opens, there is a last-minute flurry of activity before snow buries the land deep and cold.

Perched beside swiftly flowing Clear Creek, the seven rough log cabins and main house of Laughing Fish Lodge are a self-sufficient haven in the woods. The country-maintained dirt road ends at the lodge entrance. There are no telephones, no television, no flush toilets in the cabins. The generator in the lodge shuts off all electricity at ten o'clock in the evening. Each cabin has two or three single iron beds complete with coil springs and mattresses. There are wash-bowls, a water pitcher and pegs on the walls for towels. The main house has a single toilet on a septic tank and one shower with hot water.

Breakfast and dinner are served family style in the lodge kitchen at two big tables, but lunch is usually packed to eat somewhere out in the wilderness. Most hunters stay at least three or four days; some remain a full week. One reason weary executives find it a veritable haven is that the only female for miles around is Maggie Owens, the owner's wife and indispensable cook.

On the third day of their week-long vacation Buck Simpson woke just before dawn. His thick gray hair and tanned lean body made him look younger than a man about to turn sixty. The old bedsprings creaked as he turned over and looked across the narrow strip of scrubbed pine floorboards to see if his fourteen-year-old stepson, T.J., was still sleeping. The teenage boy was growing at a rate of nearly an inch a month, all legs and arms and big feet.

This brief vacation was special for the two of them. It was the first time father and son had been together in such a thoroughly rugged adventure, an experience the older Simpson had always wanted to share with a son of his own.

During the past few days in this northern wilderness they had gotten to know more about each other than they had in the six years Buck Simpson had been married to T.J.'s mother, Vivian. Removed from his mother's intimidating influence, young T.J. had responded to the lessons of the woods and of hunting as though he'd been born to them. If the boy had been his own flesh and blood, Simpson couldn't have been more proud of him. He took an enormous satisfaction in being able to pass on to the next generation the information he had learned as a boy.

Simpson had been doing a lot of thinking lately, he realized as he lay quietly in the narrow iron bed. The years were going so quickly. He'd built his family-owned company into a respectable corporate giant, publicly held now and a national leader. But that had taken its toll of his time, his energy, his relationship with the children.

As he studied the sleeping adolescent he'd legally

adopted and grown to love as his own child, Simpson thought also about his daughter, Buckley. What a joy she had always been, the living image of his first wife and the beloved child who came to them late in their marriage as a miraculous affirmation of their devotion to each other. As Buckley matured into womanhood, she looked more like her mother every day. To see the girl become so perfect an incarnation of the woman Simpson loved with such reverence and youthful passion had healed the pain of his wife's sudden death.

He had watched the relationship developing between his daughter and T.J. with fascination. At first there had been the normal sparring for attention, a jockeying for position and the temporarily chaotic competition that broke out in bickering between newly associated brother and older sister. However, once thirteen-year-old Buckley was assured that she was not going to be replaced in her father's heart by the newcomer, a transformation occurred. Simpson watched his daughter assume the role her mother might have played with the new addition to their family. Buckley protected, guided and eventually grew to love T.J. There was no love between T.J. and his own mother, Vivian. T.J. had never experienced the kind of warmth Buckley had known before she learned to speak as she nursed at her mother's breast, or later played by her mother's side, or listened as her mother read to her.

Simpson encouraged Buckley's closeness with T.J., hoping it might divert her jealousy of Vivian. From the moment of introduction Buckley had declared a silent war between herself and her new stepmother. She had begged him not to remarry, not understanding the reason he wanted a union with Vivian so desperately.

Buckley had never been able to forgive his betrayal of her and her mother. They did not speak about it anymore, but he knew the shadow remained between them despite their constant love for each other.

Perhaps it had been folly to name the girl Buckley after himself and to bring her up more like a man than a woman. Fortunately the world had changed in ways that gave her self-assurance and independent spirit great value.

It would have been like old times if she'd been with them now. But at nineteen she was busy carving out her own life. She'd dropped out of college after her second year. Buckley wanted to write, and she landed a job at the advertising agency handling the company account. She was so delighted and so eager to prove herself he'd never had the heart to admonish her for not finishing school. When they'd discussed this trip over lunch last week, she'd promised to come with him next year.

When she was a little girl, he'd taken her hunting and fishing many times. They spent three seasons in a row at Laughing Fish Lodge. She loved Mrs. Owens and followed her around the old-fashioned kitchen, always eager to help. Buckley would listen for hours to the men's exaggerated stories of the hunt, her eyes wide with fascination. When Buckley was old enough, he'd taught her how to shoot a rifle, but she could never bring herself to kill anything. She practiced her shooting out behind the tool shed on tin cans Mrs. Owens saved for her and enjoyed that more. He had always been proud of his daughter. Buckley would have made a hell of a man, Simpson thought with a smile, but she's going to be an extraordinary woman.

His smile faded with the next thoughts that tumbled across his mind in the predawn hours of this morning. He had been unfair to both these children in the past six years of his marriage to Vivian. He had expected them to make adjustments and take care of each other while he allowed himself the luxury of indulgence in Vivian's exquisite face, sensuous body, her courtesan lovemaking. He had taken a strange pride in her beauty, her elegance, the impenetrable quality of her aloofness. She was younger than Buck by fifteen or twenty years, a challenge to his manhood, a victory in the middle age of his life.

It was hard to remember when he first discovered how Vivian deceived him. In the beginning of their relationship it didn't matter if she changed her true age to a more complimentary number or told him that an expensive dress was bought on sale when it wasn't. But eventually he came to understand more fully the scope of her lying.

It was his own daughter, Buckley, who had alerted him. About a year after the marriage Buckley overheard Vivian talking on the phone about boarding schools. When Vivian realized Buckley was in the room listening to her conversation, she became extremely angry with the girl. Buckley announced that neither she nor T.J. was going to be sent away from home, and Vivian slapped her across the face, telling her to mind her own business and stop sneaking around like a spy.

The same night Buckley told her father what had happened. When he confronted Vivian privately, she just laughed. "What nonsense!" she said. "I was talking to my friend Marilyn, who's having trouble finding a suitable school for her girls. It had absolutely nothing to do with either T.J. or Buckley. I'm afraid your daughter's imagination is getting the best of her." That particular incident was simply dropped, unresolved.

It was several more years before it began to dawn on him that everything Vivian had told him about herself or her daily activities was a lie.

She was sick the day their passports had to be renewed. While she was still asleep, he'd taken her personal safe-deposit key out of the locked wall safe and left for the office.

Because he explained his wife was ill, her passport had to be renewed, and Buck Simpson owned a sizable share of bank stock, the teller allowed him to open Vivian's safe-deposit box. In it he found two passports with her photo but different names, a small address book containing a list of men he recognized as judges, politicians and bankers she never mentioned knowing, a bankbook for an account he knew nothing about, as well as a diamond necklace he'd never seen before.

There was another existence, an alternate identity contained in this ordinary safe-deposit box that Buck had never suspected.

He replaced the bank key and never told Vivian what he had done. He had fallen in love with a pathological liar. He had made a fool of himself.

As he looked back over the circumstances surrounding his original introduction to Vivian, his skin crawled with humiliation.

She had been a guest of the man named Benjamin who'd been influential in helping Buck Simpson arrange for a large private loan which made his company's balance sheets look more profitable than they really were just before the family corporation went public.

Benjamin invited Simpson for a weekend cruise to celebrate the success of their venture, and Vivian had made herself subtly irresistible. Shortly afterward they were married.

Simpson never did business with Benjamin again, and the loan was quickly repaid out of his personal finances as the company grew rapidly.

Now face-to-face with Vivian's deception, he felt naïve, betrayed, embarrassed, angry. After his first wife died, he had immersed himself for so many years in his business and self-inflicted loneliness that he'd been easy prey for Vivian. Her physical beauty had aroused his long-dormant sexual cravings. She was such a clever woman.

At first the alliance had seemed ideal. Vivian infused his life with a panoply of parties and romantic vacations. But in return for the undeniable pleasure she gave him, Vivian began spending his money. Her incessant demands became a burden, an annoyance and finally a real financial drain. He tired of her body long before he was able to resist it. In time her voluptuous casualness about sex left him feeling like a whoremonger. There was no tenderness to her, no sweetness. It took him six years to realize the only gift of this marriage he valued was her boy, who had become the son he had never had. He found it impossible to accept the fact that she could hardly stand the sight of T.J.

He tried not to think in terms of regret, but it was difficult at fifty-nine years of age. His sense of shame didn't allow him the freedom to share these thoughts with anyone. The process of divorcing Vivian legally would not be as hard as making the decision had been. The most painful part was over now.

Even his closest friend, Alphonse, didn't know all his plans. Alphonse was the most trustworthy man Simpson had ever known. Not only was he next in line to being president of the company they'd both struggled to build, but he was also Simpson's friend of more than twenty years. Alphonse was the one person with whom Simpson felt completely at ease. Last night they had worked out the final details on a new company acquisition, then sat by the fire and talked over their lives without the usual barrier of professional titles or position.

Simpson had previously asked his friend to be executor of the estate. Tonight he told Alphonse he was going to make him trustee for both his children, not just Buckley. Alphonse showed only mild surprise when Simpson also mentioned changing his will again as soon as they returned to the city. "Vivian and I aren't getting along. I'm afraid it's been a rather expensive mistake," Buck said bitterly, staring into the crackling fire. "I want to make sure both the children are protected just in case anything should happen to me. I trust you, Alphonse. Promise me you won't let her hurt them."

"I promise, Buck."

Alphonse didn't pry, didn't ask embarrassing questions of the man he respected so deeply, but it seemed quite clear to him that Buck Simpson was obviously afraid, perhaps of Vivian, and making all necessary arrangements prior to filing for a divorce.

"T.J.," Buck whispered over to the sleeping boy. "Are we going hunting, or are you just sleeping until noon?"

Instantly T.J.'s eyes flew open. He was out of bed in a second, fumbling around for his clothes, still half-asleep.

"Sorry. I must have overslept," T.J. said, never bothering to notice it was still dark outside.

Simpson and T.J. headed for the main house of the lodge and the enticing smell of breakfast.

"Morning, Maggie." Buck greeted the big woman. "You've got two hungry customers!"

Maggie Owens was way ahead of them. The table

was set and already loaded with steaming biscuits, rosy slabs of ham, a big stack of buckwheat pancakes, golden scrambled eggs, fried potatoes, butter, jam, honey, a pitcher of orange juice and plenty of boiling hot coffee.

"Boy!" T.J. exclaimed as he hungrily filled his plate with a small mountain of north country food. Although he'd been eating like this for nearly three days, his belt hadn't been loosened a notch. The fresh air, the long walks, the excitement of his first hunting trip burned up calories faster than three meals a day provided them. It was like a dream come true. Everything was going great. His dad was real proud of the way he'd taken to shooting and told him so. He hadn't gotten his own deer yet, but his dad said maybe today. T.J. could hardly wait. This had to be the best time of his entire life.

Alphonse pushed open the front door. Simpson knew the minute he laid eyes on the man that he wasn't going hunting with them.

"Oh, brother . . . you need coffee this morning!" Maggie chuckled, recognizing the telltale signs of hangover.

Alphonse made a sour face and slowly seated himself in the nearest chair. "I think it's going to take something stronger than coffee," he mumbled.

T.J. smiled in spite of his compassion for Alphonse's condition. He glanced sideways at his father, who winked back.

"What's got into you, old man?" Simpson asked with a hint of teasing in his voice. "You seemed okay when I left you here last night."

"Yeah." Alphonse tried to nod his head in agreement, deeply regretting the gesture. "But then Owens came in and . . ." Alphonse stared numbly in the general direction of Maggie's kitchen. "What in the hell has your husband got in those jugs anyway?" he asked ruefully.

"I've got just the remedy for you, son, but you best not go huntin' this morning," Maggie said to comfort Alphonse.

Finished with his breakfast, Simpson left the table and stopped near Alphonse. "We'll be back early this afternoon. Hope you're feeling better."

Simpson and T.J. took their rifles out of the long rack near the door. Buck signed the register with their approximate destination for that day, as was the lodge custom.

Just outside the front door Simpson and T.J. bumped into old man Owens himself. His bright eyes twinkling under bushy white eyebrows and the sprightliness of his walk indicated that he was feeling none of the ill effects Alphonse suffered.

"Morning, Simpson. Morning, young man." Owens greeted them. Peering closely at T.J., he continued pleasantly. "Understand today's gonna be your first buck."

"Yes, sir," T.J. replied, trying to keep his mounting excitement under control.

"Well, listen here, boy. Got a piece of old huntin' advice for you." Owens approached the two, lowering his voice. "Remember now, you got to stay real still out there. Real still. Know why?"

T.J.'s eyes were big as saucers. He shook his head no. He was almost afraid to speak.

"Because . . ." Owens said confidentially. "Them deer have tiny ears in their feet. They can hear everything around 'em for miles and miles with them feet. Ever see a deer paw the ground? Ever see 'em set that foot and move it back and forth?" He imitated the action with his snarled hand made into a fist, grinding away at the imaginary earth.

"Yes, sir," T.J. answered quietly.

"Well, boy . . . that's because they've got a little ear right here between their two front toes."

"You mean in their hoof?" T.J. asked politely.

"No, boy," Owens bellowed, startling T.J. "Toes! Horses have hooves." Owens continued. "Now . . . if you move so much as a muscle, well, the vibration goes right through the ground and into that clever little ear. So you mind what your pa tells you . . . and be still!"

"Yes, sir," T.J. said, staring at Owens's back as the old man ambled on to the house.

Simpson smiled, patted the boy's shoulder, and the two of them began the mile and a half walk following Clear Creek to the upper meadow in the woods.

After an interminable silence T.J. could stand the suspense no longer.

"Is that really true, Dad?" T.J. asked, anxiously awaiting his father's answer. "I mean . . . what Mr. Owens said . . . can deer really hear through their toes?"

"That's what they say, son," he answered.

T.J. studied the thin smile on his father's face, wondering why the topic amused him as it did and wondering also if his dad and Mr. Owens were in some kind of conspiracy together.

The early-morning sun held no heat. Walking along the creek bank was easy work. They arrived at the edge of the meadow in about an hour.

"Remember what I've taught you," Simpson said firmly. "The does will come out first. There may be three or four of them. Once the does think they're safe, he'll come out, too. Wait until you can get a clear shot. Take your time. Squeeze the trigger gently." Simpson patiently went over the lessons of the last two days. He couldn't help smiling at the boy's serious face as he warned, "Now don't get buck fever and maybe you'll get your deer."

"Dad, what is buck fever?" T.J. asked very seriously.

"We were talking a little bit about it before you went to bed last night. Remember? When you see that deer, when you finally see that buck, don't panic. I want you to think of him as a target. Otherwise, your hands may start to shake, you'll clutch up and you won't be able to shoot . . . or you'll shoot and miss. You've also got to be careful not to get so excited you accidentally shoot yourself. That's a powerful weapon you're carrying. Just draw down on him slowly, and squeeze that trigger. Buck fever has been known to make people sick. It's the idea of killing a living thing. You have to remember hunting keeps a balance in the deer population and we kill only the buck. Now just relax and make your shot clean."

T.J. settled himself in the best spot from which to watch the empty meadow. This definitely was going to be his day. He could feel it. His excitement was almost uncontrollable.

"I'll be right down there behind that biggest tree, near the fallen logs." Simpson pointed to a spot maybe fifty yards away. Just before departing, he gave the boy a rough, slightly awkward hug. "Good luck, son," he said and then walked off to take up his own vigil out of T.J.'s sight.

T.J. was suddenly alone in the woods. It never ceased to amaze him how quickly everything disappeared in these woods. He'd caught fleeting glimpses of many animals during these last two days, but they vanished before he could raise his rifle. The shadows, the trees, the sunlight played tricks on your eyes, working together to camouflage the deer and rabbits and even the birds.

He remembered everything his father said about handling the rifle safely and found a comfortable place to sit while waiting for the appearance of his long-sought buck. He wondered how it would actually be to see the animal perfectly lined up in his barrel sights. He wondered if he could really pull the trigger when that time came. He wondered how it would feel slowly squeezing the trigger until the bullet fired. Most of all, he wondered how he would feel if the bullet was right on target and the animal fell.

At first T.J. noticed only the silence. Slowly, as he became used to the smaller sounds, the silence disappeared. The air was filled with animal noises, birdsongs, the leaves rustling overhead. The woods became a symphony of noises, some familiar and some strange.

Suddenly, magically, it happened just as his dad said it would. There were the does! Three of them at the far edge of the meadow. When they reached almost the middle of the open meadow, a large buck appeared, raising his head, sniffing the wind. Where just a minute before T.J. had seen nothing but distant grasses, now there was a full-grown buck standing perfectly poised, head up, antlers outlined against a clear blue sky.

Trying not to move one unnecessary muscle, T.J. raised his fully loaded Winchester 30-30 into position. He lined up the sights perfectly. His trigger finger began to squeeze ever so slowly, steadily, carefully.

On a little hill nearly a mile away another hunter also

raised his rifle into position. This man was twenty-nine years old, a veteran of the last terrible jungle war. His name was Sam. The muscles in his body tightened; his hands were steady.

Sam peered through the ten-power scope on his Mannlicher rifle, lining the cross hairs up perfectly with his target. From his hidden vantage point he could see the boy and the deer. He could also see Buck Simpson. He wished the gun in his hand were the M-16 he had used in the Vietnam jungle. The object lined up at the point the tiny cross hairs met was almost a mile distant, only a reddish brown shape, an amorphous blob.

At the exact moment T.J. pulled the trigger on the young buck in the meadow, another single shot rang out. T.J. held his breath, waiting at the ragged edge of his nerves for the buck to drop on the long meadow grasses.

Three does and the young buck fled the meadow with amazing speed. In a few seconds they disappeared into the nearest thicket of trees, and the meadow was empty once again.

T.J., disappointed, realized that his shot had missed entirely. He would not need to track any animal.

Disgusted with himself, T.J. called out to his father.

"Dad? Did you see him?" he shouted toward the pile of logs near the big tree. "Dad?" he shouted again, wondering why his father didn't answer.

The teenager hesitated, looking carefully in the direction he had last seen his father. Slowly, half-crouched, T.J. moved through the edge of the sparse woods.

Only fifty yards away, hidden behind the log pile, Buck Simpson had fallen to the ground. The bullet had ripped through his body, killing him instantly.

Buck Simpson lay facedown. There was a huge hole in his chest where the hollow-point bullet had blasted away his flesh. Blood oozed between the brilliant autumn leaves scattered beneath his body.

T.J. did not see his dead father until he was no more than three or four feet away from him.

When the boy's eyes finally perceived the crumpled body, a jolt of horror electrified him. He stopped, then slowly approached the silent body. Some ancient instinct told him that he was in death's unmistakable presence. For reasons he would ponder the rest of his life, T.J. knew there was no need to hurry. Like a young warrior of civilizations long past, the boy who came into these woods a mere adolescent would leave them a man. He had witnessed death.

T.J. dropped his rifle and knelt beside his dead father. Slowly he reached out to touch the fallen man. There was a lingering sensation of warmth. Carefully T.J. turned him over, face upward.

Buck Simpson's eyes were still open. There was an innocent, almost puzzled expression on his face which belied any comprehension of the tragic and sudden violence. The large gaping hole in his chest still gushed crimson blood. His plaid shirt and heavy wool hunting jacket were torn where the bullet had ripped through with ferocity, carrying his life away on a half inch thickness of shiny metal.

Deep in T.J.'s gut a terrible sound began its journey to freedom. Stinging hot, salt-laden tears streamed down the young man's face as he began gently gathering the limp body in a final embrace, slowly rocking back and forth, holding his dead father in his arms.

The terrible sound rushed steadily upward, racking

every inch of T.J.'s body. He choked on a mouthful of saliva, but the sound broke through. At last it was heard. The sound of T.J.'s mourning cry echoed through the woods. This was a primitive sound close to death itself. It was a raw, powerful incarnation of grief, the sound of one life alone with the dead. The young man was screaming for both of them.

Owens's four-wheel drive pickup truck rattled crazily down the country road. Beside him Alphonse sat grimly, his bloodshot eyes peering through the dirty windshield at the outline of a country store and gas station a half mile farther down the road.

A thousand details flashed through Alphonse's mind. The horror that had darkened this beautiful autumn morning overshadowed his every attempt at precise thought. His best friend was dead, senselessly dead, without warning or reason. He dreaded the responsibility that lay ahead, but Simpson had depended on him for almost twenty years, and he wasn't going to let his friend down now.

Alphonse would never forget the look on T.J.'s face when the boy stumbled into the lodge and fainted. After they revived him, the shock of recalling his father's death seemed to threaten T.J.'s mental stability.

The boy kept mumbling something about buck fever, shaking uncontrollably and choking as though convulsed by a seizure. At first no one realized that it was his father and not T.J. to whom something terrible had happened. His words made no sense, coming in sporadic bursts punctuated by sobbing. There was no focus to either his eyes or his mind. He shrieked and pointed wildly, unaware that nobody understood him. Finally, painfully he told them his father was dead, lying at the edge of the woods near the meadow.

Hearing himself giving the gruesome information seemed to split the remaining thread of consciousness, and T.J. blacked out again.

Alphonse remembered that Maggie Owens managed to catch T.J. just before he collapsed. As he regained consciousness, the big woman gently cradled him in her arms while he wept. Owens and Alphonse went up to the meadow near the woods, covered the body with a blanket and decided to get the sheriff before disturbing any evidence.

Once they got to town, it was agreed Alphonse would call Simpson's wife and daughter, then company headquarters, while Owens gave Sheriff Meader all the details they had.

The county sheriff's office was hardly more than a storefront. Owens and Alphonse entered to find the sheriff eating lunch while doing a crossword puzzle and listening to the CB radio.

Sheriff Meader greeted the two men with his usual cheerfulness. Two years earlier Meader, a man about forty-five, had retired from a city police force and returned home to take on the job of county sheriff. He'd known old man Owens nearly all his life and recognized quickly that the Laughing Fish Lodge owner was in his office this afternoon on serious business.

"Mr. Buck Simpson's been killed," Owens said slowly. "He and his boy were hunting in the upper meadow. The boy may have heard another shot, but no one knows exactly how it happened."

Sheriff Meader lost his pleasant expression immediately. He shoved his half-eaten roast beef sandwich away from him and got to his feet.

"I'm Alphonse Mazzo, with Mr. Simpson's company." Alphonse solemnly shook hands with the sheriff. "May I use your phone to notify his family?"

Sheriff Meader pointed to the phone on his desk as he flipped the CB radio over to the emergency channel and began to alert his deputy.

Alphonse hesitated momentarily as though trying to decide which call to make first. He went over the words he would use once more, knowing it was hopeless to expect anything other than chaos these next few hours. He started to dial Vivian, then put down the receiver and hesitated. He couldn't explain even to himself why it seemed right to call Simpson's daughter, Buckley, before anyone else.

He thumbed through his personal phone book for her number and dialed. After several rings the girl answered.

"Buckley . . . this is Alphonse." He took a deep breath, gathering his courage and fortitude.

"Alphonse!" Buckley sounded surprised. "How are you?"

"I'm afraid I have some very bad news. There's been an accident." Alphonse felt his resolve draining away. His voice cracked. He braced himself against the edge of the sheriff's desk.

"What?" Buckley asked urgently. "Alphonse, what's happened?"

"Please sit down," Alphonse said, stalling against that dreadful moment he knew was immediately upon him. "Your father is dead."

There was a terrible silence. Buckley felt her legs go weak, her heart nearly stop beating.

"No . . ." Buckley moaned. "Please God . . . no!"

"I'm sorry. I'm so terribly sorry. I'm making arrangements for you to be picked up. In about an hour. One of our planes will bring you up here."

Buckley felt her world going blank. She hung up the phone. The news of her father's sudden death made her feel as though her own life were ending with his. She was just nineteen years old, but she felt her youth draining from her with the flood of tears that flowed down her face. She couldn't think. She braced herself weakly against an unknown piece of furniture and sank down into an unseen chair. She was plunged into a bleak chasm of despair.

Alone in her apartment Buckley buried her face in her hands and wept. "Daddy . . ." she moaned. Out of the mist of her grief, her father's face appeared in her memory. Vividly she saw his gentle smile, his strong features, his unruly gray hair and his deep brown eyes. He had been her source of wisdom and strength, her friend and protector. She couldn't imagine life without him.

"Daddy . . . I love you!" she cried out as though hoping to catch his spirit before it departed earth forever. "I love you!" She wept in anguish. "Don't leave me, Daddy . . . please," she begged, never realizing in her sorrow that it was too late for him to grant her another wish. "Oh . . . my God . . . please . . ." She could not continue her prayer. Her long auburn hair slid damply across her face as Buckley wept.

Slowly a dullness began to displace her tears. Her breathing returned to normal. The agonized gasps subsided. She sat quietly, crying but attempting to collect her thoughts.

"Daddy . . . is . . . dead," Buckley said aloud as though hearing the words would help bring relief or at least reality. "Daddy is dead," she repeated.

She sat staring into space, trying to comprehend the enormity of what had just happened, then dried her face with shaking hands and walked unsteadily down the hallway to her bedroom.

There was no reason to change her clothes. The slacks and sweater she was wearing would be all right for the country. She threw a few personal belongings into an overnight bag and grabbed her coat. On her way downstairs she stopped to ask the building manager's wife if she'd feed the cat for a few days.

Sheriff Meader and his deputy studied Simpson's body where it had lain undisturbed since T.J. ran from the woods several hours earlier. The afternoon sun cast long shadows which partially camouflaged the large pool of human blood. Sheriff Meader shook his head.

"Some asshole hunting without an ounce of common sense," he said in disgust, pointing to an immense hole in Simpson's body where the bullet exited. "Even if the son of a bitch was lucky enough to hit a deer, he'd blow half the meat clear into the next county!"

"City machos." The young deputy nodded his head in agreement. "Come up here for the weekend with enough firepower to hunt elephants." The deputy kicked a stray leaf in frustration. "But what the hell can you do? It's legal." Almost as an afterthought he asked, "What time is your man from homicide arriving?"

Sheriff Meader checked his watch. "Anytime now. We'll just wait here." He was grateful to have his old buddy visiting again during hunting season and felt lucky to have found him still at home on Sunday afternoon. He was convinced that John Needham would help handle this properly. Needham still served as a police detective in Simpson's hometown. He would command the necessary respect and credibility. There was going to be plenty of excitement around here once the press got wind of the accident, and Sheriff Meader didn't want any of the usual "country shit kicker" barbs surrounding his handling of the case.

"That kid going to be all right?" the deputy asked conversationally. He'd been thinking about how T.J. was the same age he'd been when he learned to hunt.

"Doc says the tranquilizer will help calm him down," Meader replied.

"Any chance he did it?" the younger deputy inquired.

"Unlikely," Sheriff Meader replied with just the right amount of authority. "All he had was a regular thirty-thirty," he said, pointing at the rifle T.J. had dropped on the ground near them.

"Yeah," the deputy answered, staring at Simpson's large wound, knowing that no Winchester 30-30 had made that hole.

"Terrible shock for a fourteen-year-old. His first hunting trip." Sheriff Meader spoke the thoughts both men shared.

Vivian Simpson had just returned from a sauna and a swim at the health club on the top floor of her apartment building when the call from Alphonse came through early Sunday afternoon. She faced the next hour with absolute clarity, her mind feverishly planning, making a hundred small decisions.

What she felt for her dead husband could never be called love, but the realization that he had gone from her life affected her more than she might have expected. As she caught a glimpse of herself in the antique French hallway mirror, Vivian realized she had tears in her eyes.

"Jesus . . ." she said, staring at herself almost

detachedly. "When was the last time I cried?" Her mind refused an answer.

She busied herself with the details of departure. When the small piece of monogrammed luggage was packed and sitting in the front hallway, Vivian emerged from her room, dressed and ready to face whatever awaited her. She looked around at the elegant surroundings that life with Buck Simpson had provided. The carefully chosen antiques, the Chinese porcelain bowls filled with peony-sized fresh pink roses made her feel serene and secure.

As she waited for the company limousine to arrive, Vivian began mentally to add up her share of the proceeds from Buck Simpson's estate.

She knew he carried a personal life insurance policy in the amount of $250,000. There was no doubt in her mind that he had named her as the beneficiary because she'd gone through all the papers in his briefcase the night he'd signed them at home.

In addition, she would probably get the apartment and all personal possessions, including the antiques, the silver, both cars and the securities in their joint account.

Vivian picked up Friday's copy of the *Wall Street Journal* and thumbed through it to the composite stock transactions page, running her index finger down the long list of closing quotes until she located the company stock. To her enormous pleasure she saw it had last traded at just under thirty-eight, up from nineteen only a year earlier. Buck Simpson had been an excellent businessman.

Several years ago Vivian had overheard a brief discussion regarding the number of company shares held by Simpson after the business had gone public. As she remembered, it was an extraordinary number, but was it the same today as when she'd originally found out? Locating the small hand calculator usually kept in the upper right-hand desk drawer was irresistible. She decided to figure the stock value at Friday's quote and multiply by 500,000. As the digital display flashed a series of little red numbers, Vivian's heartbeat increased rapidly.

"Nineteen million dollars!" she said aloud, devouring the information from the calculator. Quickly she repeated the multiplication process, and the result was exactly the same: $19 million.

If only she knew all the details of his will. To judge from the honesty and fairness of his business reputation, the most probable disposition would be the division of the estate in three equal portions. Simpson had told her a year ago that Alphonse was his executor and Buckley's trustee. Vivian assumed she had control of her share plus T.J.'s inheritance until her son became twenty-one years old. Buck's gesture in adopting T.J. would pay off handsomely.

Perfect, she thought, unable to resist a private smile. It wouldn't be difficult to prevent a teenage boy from ever seeing a dime of the money. The only obstacle might be T.J.'s close relationship with Simpson's daughter, Buckley. However, Vivian found it hard to imagine the nineteen-year-old girl as a competent adversary. Buckley was too involved with herself, her career and her own future to pose much of a threat. Appeal to the girl's innate selfishness, Vivian thought, and she'll choose to mind her own business.

The first step to controlling T.J. completely would be to remove him from Buckley's influence. Buckley's interference had prevented Vivian from sending T.J. away earlier, but the girl could not stop her plans now. Once the two adolescents were out of constant communication, their relationship would diminish rapidly.

Alphonse might cooperate voluntarily. Surely he wouldn't risk an entire career and position of company president over a family squabble. Vivian didn't concern herself with the man she considered Simpson's flunky. If he stood in her way, she knew enough about him to bring him to heel.

Satisfied that she'd covered all bases for the time being, Vivian relaxed enough to relish the idea of being a millionairess who must temporarily act the part of a bereaved widow.

She doubted whether any of Buck Simpson's friends knew how close to divorce they had recently come. Her abundant female intuition had ferreted out the stray signs that her husband was secretly planning his escape. Neither of them had said a word about divorce. There hadn't been the usual bickering couples go through before making these decisions. She and Buck had never quarreled. But Vivian knew. She knew he had been planning to divorce her and was going to tell her very soon. Death unalterably changed all his careful plans. That same death had set her free.

Of course, there would be funeral arrangements, the will probated, and a perfunctory waiting period of dutiful widowhood, but after that Vivian would be free.

Free. The very thought of total freedom excited her. It was the closest she'd been to sexual arousal in years. She felt a sudden rush of greed and pleasure flow through her.

All the way to the airport, settled comfortably in the back seat of the company limousine, Vivian decided she would have to be on special guard with Buckley and the meticulous Alphonse. She'd been handling T.J. so many years he had no response left beyond submission. But Alphonse and Buckley were different. Perhaps they would be so enmeshed in their personal grief they wouldn't focus on her. That would certainly make the next few months easier. She could position herself solidly in control.

For the first time in her life she'd have all the money she wanted and wouldn't have to answer to another soul. It was extraordinary to contemplate. She was very careful not to smile in case the driver was watching her through the rearview mirror.

Vivian arrived at the general aviation terminal before Buckley. She did not welcome this final hour of their flight together. Immediately on board the sleek company aircraft, Vivian fixed herself a drink from the well-stocked bar and assumed an expression of dignified sorrow.

Buckley hurried from the car, ran across the narrow airstrip and put her arms around the regular copilot, Sandy, who stood at the bottom of the airplane stairs, waiting for her. She could see that he'd been crying also and had protected his red eyes with dark glasses.

"My condolences, Buckley. We all feel . . ." Sandy's voice dropped into silence.

"Thank you, Sandy." Buckley nodded, brushing a strand of hair back from her face and hurrying up the short stairs into the cabin.

Buckley deposited her shoulder bag in the luggage closet and entered the compact seating area where Vivian sat facing her, drink in hand. She felt a chill go through her as she realized the woman's immaculate makeup was untouched by even a single tear. She would never have known anything had changed from looking at her stepmother.

"Buckley, dear . . . I'm so sorry . . . such a tragedy." Vivian's voice faltered as she extended her hand in a gesture of communion.

"Hello, Vivian," Buckley said coldly. She made no attempt to touch her.

A stranger witnessing this meeting of the two women would think Buckley rather rude. Even Buckley marveled that Vivian's behavior today was so exemplary. It had taken years for her to discover that Vivian wasn't real flesh and blood; she was only a perfect imitation.

As the plane began its final journey this afternoon, each woman assessed the other in her own way. Toleration was the most they could expect from each other.

Vivian observed Buckley's obvious grief with dispassionate appraisal. She did not fully comprehend the depth of emotion the younger woman experienced and was suspicious of it.

Vivian had long ago suppressed her own rage of jealousy over the bond between young Buckley and her father, between Buckley and T.J. She had used every opportunity to create subtle misunderstandings, distrust and estrangement between father and daughter but had never been more than momentarily successful.

Buckley had not seen Vivian in months. It was no secret between them that they put on a façade only for the sake of keeping peace with her father. Since Buckley started work and moved into her own apartment, it had become easier. She and her father met regularly for lunch, and once in a while she accompanied him on short business trips. Buckley and T.J. still went to movies and soccer games together, but the whole family came together only on holidays.

Sometimes a flash of understanding comes in a single second. Such was the case for Buckley this terrible autumn afternoon. As she sat in Vivian's cool presence, Buckley suddenly knew for the first time that the woman had never loved her father. In that same moment Buckley felt a surge of indefinable superiority over Vivian. All these years the woman she'd alternately feared and hated had actually been jealous of her, jealous also of the friendship between brother and sister. In the presence of love Vivian automatically became an outsider. It went a long way toward explaining why Buckley had felt so much anger buried behind Vivian's chilling smile. She would have to tell T.J. to be on his guard. Buckley knew instinctively that without the safe haven of her father's presence, Vivian would try to separate T.J. from her, and she was determined not to let that happen.

Buckley stared in amazement at the beautiful woman, so perfectly attired. She felt as revolted as if she'd been condemned to travel with a rotting corpse. My God . . . poor Daddy, was her last thought before the copilot, Sandy, announced they'd be landing immediately.

Alphonse, Sheriff Meader and John Needham filled the available chairs gathered around the fire in the iron Franklin stove at Laughing Fish Lodge. Maggie Owens was in the kitchen, crying as she prepared extra food for the unexpected influx of people.

Old man Owens had elected to stay with T.J. in his cabin. The doctor said the sedative might last until morning, and Owens was fully prepared to keep faith with his vigil all night if necessary.

Sheriff Meader, Alphonse and John Needham sat in conference. Meader's deputy had already taken Simpson's body to the county coroner.

"Just luck we found the bullet," John Needham said quietly. He was about the same age as Sheriff Meader but a thinner man with muscles taut and sinewy. His hawkish face was not handsome but significantly tough and razor-sharp. Ten years ago he'd been transferred from the vice squad to homicide and excelled as a career officer.

"The lab will confirm it in a few days, but I'm sure it's a .308-caliber hollow-point bullet," Needham continued in a monotone. "Unless I miss my guess, we're going to find out that the weapon was one of those Mannlicher SSG sniper rifles."

"Sniper rifle?" Alphonse exploded. "What the hell has a sniper rifle got to do with deer hunting?"

The sheriff stepped in to answer quickly. "It's a long-distance gun. Capability of more than a mile with a ten-power scope. We try to discourage them here because novice hunters don't always follow up their shots, but the rifle is a perfectly legal weapon purchased over the counter without special permits."

"Jesus Christ." Alphonse sighed, sinking back into his chair. He was exhausted, and this day wasn't over yet. Alphonse, Sheriff Meader and Needham had driven over half the county. They'd located the little hill from which another hunter had shot at the deer T.J. saw in the meadow. They'd finally found the casing and even the bullet shell itself. There was no trace of the other hunter, the man Alphonse now identified as the owner of the Mannlicher sniper rifle.

"What about the roadblock?" Alphonse asked in a tired voice.

"I don't have any real hope we'll find him," Sheriff Meader responded. "We don't have enough men to check all the country back roads, just the main highway. Who knows where he is by now. Chances are he never knew where his bullet finally hit its mark."

"Sheriff Meader . . ." Alphonse began slowly, his

words dry, his throat parched. "What am I going to tell Mr. Simpson's family?"

Meader shot a glance at his friend John Needham as though mentally checking his reply with the expert before answering. Needham shrugged his shoulders in a resigned fashion.

"The truth, bizarre as it may seem," Sheriff Meader said evenly. "Mr. Simpson and his son were in the woods hunting. The boy and another hunter nearly a mile away shot at the same deer simultaneously. T.J.'s shot missed entirely, but the other hunter's shot went wild and killed Simpson. It was one of those freak hunting accidents. That's all we know."

Alphonse looked from Sheriff Meader's face to John Needham. He could understand their lack of emotional response and wished desperately he were able to imitate them for the next few days. But every time he managed to get himself under control he saw Buck Simpson's bullet-torn, bloodstained body lying in the woods. Fortunately he had a lot to do. He was, after all, executor of the estate, in addition to his company responsibilities. Alphonse determined that the finest tribute he could give his dead friend was to carry out those responsibilities in a way that would have made Simpson proud.

Alphonse was so engrossed in his own private thoughts that he didn't hear the lodge station wagon pull up in front.

As he saw the front door open, Alphonse stood. Vivian Simpson entered first, looking for all the world like visiting royalty. Her immaculate city clothes, her scarlet polished nails and perfectly styled hair seemed out of place in these primitive surroundings.

"Vivian." Alphonse went to her, extending his hand. "I'm so terribly sorry. He was a great man . . . a great friend."

"Thank you, Alphonse," she replied demurely.

"Vivian Simpson . . . Sheriff Meader and John Needham, homicide detective." Alphonse finished with the introductions as Buckley came through the front door, looking just as distraught as Alphonse himself felt.

"Alphonse!" Buckley exclaimed, deeply grateful to see his familiar, trustworthy face. She put her arms around the man she'd known all her life as her father's best friend, feeling a momentary security in his embrace. Alphonse kept a protective arm around the girl as he introduced her.

Vivian shook hands with both the sheriff and Needham. Immediately she realized that coming to this outpost in the wilderness was a mistake. She loathed the rustic homeliness of Laughing Fish Lodge, right down to its ridiculous name. She decided she must return home tonight. Her mind raced to find an acceptable means of rescuing herself.

"How is my son?" she asked solicitously, feeling no personal compassion for the boy but shrewd enough to know that was what would be expected of her as T.J.'s mother.

"He's sleeping," Alphonse replied, then added quickly to avoid misunderstanding, "The doctor gave him a sedative."

"Oh." Vivian dabbed a handkerchief gently at her tearless eyes.

"Sheriff, where's my dad?" Buckley inquired in a small voice so filled with sorrow that both the sheriff and Needham turned immediately toward her.

"Coroner . . . down at the county," Sheriff Meader said kindly. "We're all very sorry."

"I'd like to see T.J.," Buckley said to Alphonse flatly.

"Second cabin on your left," Alphonse told her. "But I wouldn't try to wake him, Buckley."

"I won't," she promised, sounding like a child responding to parental authority.

Vivian watched Buckley leave the room, her responses so natural and uncontrived, so devoid of guilt. It was then that Vivian felt the first twinges of panic. This place, this terrible place reminded her of the girlhood she'd been desperate to escape. The old iron stove, muddy boots lined up in one corner, the mismatched wooden chairs around a long dining table, the smell of home-fried potatoes and the sight of a large ketchup bottle with its top oozing sticky, dried redness sent cold chills down Vivian's spine.

With outward calm Vivian neatly set her pale leather purse on a table, opened it and lit a cigarette.

"Sheriff, please . . . could you tell me how my husband died?" Vivian asked, looking directly at Sheriff Meader. Something about the man called John Needham warned Vivian not to deal directly with him.

"Far as we can determine, it was a hunting accident, Mrs. Simpson," Sheriff Meader replied, feeling a vague discomfort in her presence. "I'm not sure this is the right time for all the details, unless you prefer."

"No," Vivian said. "You're right. The details can wait. Thank you, Sheriff. I'm sure you've done everything you could."

Sheriff Meader took her statement as a signal to depart. He stood somewhat stiffly. "My condolences, Mrs. Simpson." The sheriff put on his hat and headed for the door, followed by John Needham. It had been an unusually long Sunday, and tomorrow would be worse. Tomorrow the news media and the reporters would be all over this county. He was going to need a good night's rest before he could deal with them.

Just outside the car Needham stopped with a puzzled look on his face.

"What's the problem, John?" Meader asked, getting into the driver's seat of the vehicle plainly marked as property of the county sheriff.

Very thoughtfully, as though flipping through a mental filing cabinet, John Needham said, "I could swear I knew that woman from somewhere, but I'll be damned if I can place her."

"You probably saw her picture in a newspaper. Simpson was a real powerhouse. They used to appear at all the big society parties," Sheriff Meader answered, turning the key in the ignition.

"That's not what I mean," John Needham responded with a touch of irritation in his voice.

When she was sure that the two officials were sufficiently out of earshot, Vivian turned to Alphonse.

"When is the will being read?" she asked without a trace of emotion.

Alphonse stared at her. "Customarily after the funeral."

Before he had a chance to continue, Vivian issued her orders. "Meet me tomorrow afternoon at the apartment. We can settle the details of the funeral, and you can proceed to make arrangements immediately. At the same time you can bring whatever forms you need to begin the legal process. I'll also need some money next week." She picked up her purse. "I'll have the company plane take me back tonight. There's obviously no reason for me to stay.

You can handle the details here and return to the city in the morning with the children."

It was Wednesday afternoon before the funeral was over and the family gathered with Alphonse at the lawyer's office for a reading of Buck Simpson's last will and testament.

Vivian had initially wanted them to meet in her apartment but dropped the request when she realized the others felt it was in poor taste.

Alphonse was first to arrive. He was still wearing the black suit, starched white shirt and a subdued tie bearing the company logo that he'd chosen for his funeral attire. It seemed to him the weight of his financial and personal responsibilities lay heavily upon his body.

Buckley walked into the large paneled office several minutes after Alphonse. Her long hair was pulled back into a single twist held securely with a tortoiseshell clip. Wisps of auburn strands floated softly around her cheekbones and down the back of her neck. Her large eyes had deep circles unhidden by makeup. The lines of her young mouth were firmly set against crying. She greeted Alphonse warmly, shook hands with the attorney who stood in courtesy and sat again after she found a chair close to his desk. Buckley felt no sense of anticipation about the contents of her father's will. Her confidence in him was so complete and her trust in his judgment so absolute that she never doubted for a moment that he had taken care of her in the best way possible. She wished only for the power to turn back time, to return to last week and see her beloved father's face again rather than endure this awful task of hearing his final wishes read from a sterile piece of paper.

Lost in her own thoughts, Buckley was visibly startled to hear Vivian's composed voice announce her arrival with T.J. As she turned to face Vivian, Buckley narrowed her eyes ever so slightly as though avoiding a suddenly harsh light.

Vivian had changed her clothes after leaving the cemetery. She was now dressed in a salmon-colored light wool suit with a beautifully ruffled silk blouse and pale lizard shoes. The fragrance of her expensive perfume filled the entire office and drew everyone's attention to her.

Poor T.J., pale and ghostlike, shuffled behind his mother silently. His eyes never left the floor, and he kept his hands shoved deeply into the pants pockets of his blue suit. Now and then he shifted his neck muscles, trying to ease the discomfort of wearing the unfamiliar shirt and tie. He had the appearance of a sleepwalker, as though the prescription ordered by a country doctor that first terrible afternoon had never quite worn off.

There was no denying Vivian's excitement. Her eyes sparkled behind the tinted glasses she wore, and her hands fidgeted with anticipation. Buckley was revolted by Vivian's inability to disguise her mercenary nature. The woman seemed barely aware of her son's physical presence, treating him like a shadow. It was clear to everyone that she had no sympathy for the boy's anguish.

The attorney announced quietly that it was time for him to read the will, and Alphonse finally sat down. A silence fell upon the room, with only the crackling of paper to break the stillness. After the normal preliminary declarations and bequest of personal property to Vivian, the attorney reached Article Three, which read:

* * *

> I give the sum of $100,000 to T. J. SIMPSON; provided, however, if he is under the age of twenty-one (21) years, then such gift shall go to my Wife, as Trustee, to be held, managed and distributed as the T. J. Simpson Trust for the benefit of T. J. SIMPSON.

The terms of the trust revealed that T.J. would receive his inheritance at age twenty-one, but if he did not live that long, Vivian would be the beneficiary.

The attorney proceeded:

> I give, devise and bequeath all of the rest, residue and remainder of my estate, both real and personal . . . to the Trustee hereinafter named, . . . who shall divide the trust estate into two separate and distinct trusts, the Marital Trust for the benefit of my Wife and the Residuary Trust for the benefit of Buckley, to be determined as follows and to be disposed of as hereinafter provided. The Marital Trust shall consist of such property which qualifies for the marital deduction in an amount equal to one-half (½) of the trust estate. The Residuary Trust shall consist of the balance of the trust estate.
>
> The Marital Trust shall be held, managed and distributed by the Trustee for the benefit of my Wife in accordance with the following provisions: The net income of the trust estate shall be distributed to my wife, during her lifetime, in monthly or other convenient installments, but in no event less frequently than annually. . . .

* * *

> The Residuary Trust shall be held, managed and distributed by the Trustee for the benefit of Buckley in accordance with the following provisions: While Buckley is under the age of twenty-one (21) years, the Trustee may distribute to or for the benefit of Buckley so much of the net income and principal as the Trustee, in its discretion, deems necessary or advisable for her reasonable care, comfort, support and education. The Trustee shall distribute the trust estate to Buckley, and the trust shall terminate, when she attains the age of forty (40) years.

What shocked Buckley was that T.J. had been left nothing now. His immediate future depended solely on Vivian's goodwill. It didn't seem right that her dad could have been so naïve, so blind about Vivian. T.J. was completely at his mother's mercy for the next seven years. The beaten look in his eyes told Buckley that he knew it, even though he may not have understood all the legal language. He realized his fate was sealed and delivered into Vivian's hands without hope of benevolence.

The lawyer continued:

> I nominate and appoint ALPHONSE MAZZO as Trustee of the Marital Trust and the Residuary Trust. If he shall for any reason fail to qualify or cease to act as Trustee hereunder, then I nominate and appoint my Wife and such bank with a net worth in excess of $100,000,000 as my Wife may nominate from time to time as Co-Trustees. If my Wife should fail to qualify or cease to act, then the bank that she nominates

shall serve as sole Trustee. My intent is that my Wife shall not serve as the sole Trustee hereunder.

That initial sparkle of excitement in Vivian's eyes had turned to steel. She took no pleasure in the words that profoundly affected her personal plans. Buck Simpson had boxed her in a corner. He'd allowed her to retain decisions over her son, but he'd removed access to the millions of dollars she'd get from selling the stock and left the voting power with his trusted friend Alphonse. That effectively kept Vivian impotent to exert influence or gain independence. She'd be totally dependent on handouts from Alphonse, whom she loathed. It meant she would have to be charming when all she felt was contempt; she would have to ingratiate herself when she really wanted to annihilate him as an obstacle. It also meant she would have to be very careful. Damn that Buck Simpson, she thought. He let me think I was really winning the battles so he could keep the ultimate victory for himself.

Buckley was not surprised that Alphonse had been named executor and her trustee. In fact, she was grateful to her father for anticipating her need of assistance and guidance.

The attorney turned over the last page and laid the document on his desk, then folded his hands carefully.

"You are probably concerned to know how long the estate will be in probate. Normally it would take about a year, but in the case of a large and complex estate such as this one, considering the tax planning opportunities available, I think you should expect the probate to take as long as two years."

"Two years?" Vivian repeated aloud before she

had a chance to mute her inner thoughts.

Alphonse and Buckley knew this information came as a most unwelcome surprise to Vivian, with her heart so set on power over Buck Simpson's money. T.J. cast a look of hatred at his mother. Before Vivian noticed him, T.J. returned his eyes to the pattern of the carpet, methodically counting its dark green rosettes to keep himself calm.

"Of course," continued the attorney, "there are insurance benefits and Mr. Simpson's company pension to help the family in the meantime." He turned to Alphonse. "Perhaps you'd explain those details, Mr. Mazzo."

Alphonse nodded his head and reached for a sheaf of papers in his briefcase. He cleared his throat, hoping his voice sounded more composed than his mind felt.

"Mr. Simpson left a ten-thousand-dollar GI insurance policy naming his daughter, Buckley, as beneficiary." He closed the policy and picked up a second folder. "In addition to the two hundred and fifty thousand dollars' life insurance, there is a hundred thousand dollars of company group life insurance with Mrs. Simpson and Buckley named as equal cobeneficiaries."

Vivian's emotions swung from annoyance to anger. That miserable skinflint, she thought. It's not bad enough that he left me crawling on my hands and knees to that flunky Alphonse; now he's made sure I don't even have a good time waiting for the bastard to dole it out!

"Finally," Alphonse droned on, shuffling papers, "there is a three-hundred-thousand-dollar company pension death benefit to be paid to Mrs. Simpson as a monthly annuity for the rest of her life."

"May I see that?" Vivian asked, trying to keep anger out of her voice.

Alphonse handed her the policy, appalled at Vivian's callousness.

Quickly Vivian found the schedule of monthly payments. It took several moments for her to figure out that $300,000 would produce a monthly payment of approximately $1,900, which would not support her present life-style even with the insurance money thrown in. This was not the outcome she'd expected.

Buckley couldn't stand the tension any longer and gathered her courage to be the first to leave. The basic information had been transmitted. The process of dividing her father's estate would now begin. She knew there would be endless discussion of technicalities and fees. But as Buckley looked at T.J., her heart ached for him. What strange turn of fate had plucked a boy from his childhood and thrown him headlong into tragedy? Why had he been singled out for the blood and the terror and the agony? She felt his silent pain and, in a peculiar way, shared his sense of guilt. T.J. held himself responsible for Buck Simpson's death, even though he'd been told by a dozen different people that he hadn't caused it and couldn't have prevented what happened. It was an accident. But T.J. couldn't shake the feeling that his presence had made him responsible. If only he could have done *something*, maybe Buck Simpson would be alive today. No one was able to change his feelings.

That his stepfather had left T.J.'s immediate future totally in the hands of Vivian only confirmed his sense of guilt and the ensuing punishment. His stepfather hadn't left him even a small personal token to hold onto as a talisman against the hostile world. He felt bereaved and strangely rejected for a second time in his life. His own father, Josh Marks, had deserted him when T.J. was almost four years old, never to be seen or heard from again. Today his stepfather's will told him clearly that for a second time he was at his mother's mercy. Neither of the men he'd loved as a father had been able to change that. They both had left him prisoner of a woman who hated him. T.J. tried numbly to force his shame back into the darkness of forgotten memories.

It embarrassed Buckley that she and T.J. had been so unequally treated. She needed to find a way to make it up to him somehow. But at this moment all she wanted to do was get out of this room, which was slowly suffocating her with the unavoidable details of death. She stood to take her leave rather unceremoniously.

Vivian expected no display of affection from Buckley, and she got none. The two women simply exchanged empty words of parting. Buckley leaned over to embrace T.J. briefly, trying to express her compassion with the gesture. She then shook hands with the attorney and thanked Alphonse.

Chapter 2

One month following the reading of Simpson's will, Vivian sent T.J. away to boarding school. He was unable to adjust, and Vivian was forced to find another. She managed to enroll him at Crestview during mid-semester break.

On this cold Friday afternoon the exclusive upstate boys' preparatory school buildings looked bleak and dreary surrounded by dark obelisks of leafless trees.

Even after an hour of playing soccer, T.J. Simpson, recently turned fifteen, could still feel a stinging sensation from the subfreezing wind on his face. It was too cold to sweat. The opposition Blue team won by a narrow margin. It was days like these that made T.J. wonder if all the legendary eastern prep school "spirit" held in such esteem by soccer coaches wasn't just sadistic bullshit.

Cooper, six months older than T.J. and captain of their team, let them all know how worthless he considered them. Willie had missed every shot, and Hank had nearly knocked himself out in a collision with one of his own players. Cooper said it was thc turning point in their team's losing.

T.J., Cooper, Willie and Hank jogged back to the gymnasium locker room while Cooper nagged at them the entire way. T.J. wished he were already sixteen. Cooper lorded his age and size advantage over the rest just like an army sergeant. Hank and Willie never argued with the older, taller boy, but T.J. was constantly at odds with him. It wasn't just Cooper's natural advantages that irritated him; it was the way he took it for granted that he was simply superior to the rest of them in every way. Yet he was grateful to Cooper's mother, who had gone out of her way to ask T.J. for the weekend whenever he was allowed to go.

But now, in the middle of February, T.J. had been restricted to the campus grounds for the past three weeks because of a fight. He hated boarding school and hated Vivian for sending him up here after his dad had died. He never felt comfortable. He had more unchanneled nervous energy than any Friday afternoon game of soccer was ever going to use up.

The steaming hot shower felt good beating down against his skin. He stayed under the steady stream of comfort longer than did his three buddies, soaping himself up twice just for the excuse of feeling a few more minutes of pleasure.

By the time he got dressed and finished drying his unruly brown hair, Cooper, Willie and Hank had left. T.J. studied himself in the long mirror above the row of sinks, putting a final stroke of the comb to his slightly damp hair. With a certain pride he noticed the fuzz beneath his sideburns beginning to turn into a real beard. Soon he'd begin shaving. He'd always considered himself lucky not to have as many zits on his face as most of the other guys.

"T.J.!" Cooper's voice yelled outside the gym. T.J. turned away from the mirror, shoving the comb into his back pocket and swinging a winter jacket over his shoulder.

As he opened the gym door, he saw Cooper sitting behind the wheel of Mr. Williams's brand-new car with Hank and Willie in the back seat. "C'mon!" Cooper called out. "We're all going to town!"

"Cooper . . . what the hell are you guys doing?" T.J. shouted. He knew perfectly well that the school's headmaster was nothing short of fanatic about anybody's messing with his car.

Cooper stuck his head out the window, grinning. "Well, get the hell in . . . we don't have all day."

For a moment T.J. hesitated on a gut hunch that Cooper was bullshitting again. The guy had a way of cooking up trouble, then bailing out at the last minute, leaving everyone else to take the rap. "What cock-and-bull story'd you give Williams?" T.J. asked suspiciously.

Cooper laughed. "Made him an offer he couldn't resist."

"I'll bet," T.J. replied sarcastically. Cooper had a nasty habit of letting you know just how rich he was, how much money his dad made and how easily he conned his father into buying him anything he wanted.

"I did. All I said was that when the new Porsche my dad's getting me arrives next month, I'd be glad to let Williams drive it anytime he wants." Cooper laughed again. "You should have seen his face! You know what a nut he is about cars. Well, the old fart damn near turned green with envy. Yes, sir . . . he just about shit in his prep school drawers at the thought." Cooper snickered, and the other boys, including T.J., laughed with him. "The rest was just a piece of cake! Will you get in this damn thing! I'm freezing my ass off."

What the hell, T.J. thought. If Cooper's lying again, it's his butt, not mine. He opened the passenger door and slipped into the front seat.

The country road from Crestview Boarding School to the small village they all jokingly referred to as town was very slippery. The afternoon sun had thawed patches of frozen ground, but it had suddenly turned cold again, and ice was invisibly forming, making driving conditions hazardous.

T.J. and Willie had learned to drive, but Cooper was the first one in the group with a driver's license, passing the test on his sixteenth birthday only a month before. He's sure as hell no expert, T.J. thought as he held onto the side of his seat, trying to appear calm.

They stopped in town for a couple of minutes. The rest of the guys wanted to get some hamburgers and shakes at the coffee shop, but Cooper said to order them to take out. After some grumbling they agreed. Eating in the car was better than missing out altogether. Every one of them was sick of the boring food at school.

When they were all reassembled, Cooper took a different route out of town.

"Hey, Coop . . . you're going the wrong way, man," T.J. said after a couple of minutes. He'd been so busy juggling the food in his lap, trying not to spill all over the floor of Mr. Williams's immaculate car, that he hadn't noticed immediately.

"Just stuff your mouth and let me do the driving, okay?" Cooper said in a surly tone of voice. T.J. was used to the guy's somewhat shitty attitude, but this sounded different.

Cooper opened the pack of cigarettes he'd gotten in town, shoved one into his mouth and lighted it with the car lighter.

From the back seat Willie piped up. "Coop . . . lemme have one of those."

"Sure, kid." Cooper joked, flipping the pack over his shoulder.

T.J. stopped eating his hamburger, glancing first at the speedometer, then at the countryside racing by. Cooper was going nearly seventy miles an hour.

At just that moment the car hit an unseen ice patch and went out of control, skidding and careening around in almost a full circle.

"Jesus Christ!" Hank screamed from the back seat.

Willie had slid onto the floor with a frightened groan.

"You crazy asshole . . . you're going to get us all killed," T.J. yelled, grabbing the dashboard.

Cooper tried desperately to get the car straightened out. His hands were clenched around the steering wheel so tightly his knuckles were turning white.

The car finally came to a stop facing the wrong direction halfway across the road with its front two wheels in the dirt. Willie crawled onto the back seat from the floor, shaking from head to foot. Hank's unlit cigarette dangled from his mouth, crumpled in three pieces from his face hitting the seat in front of him.

"Cooper . . . you're a jerk. You could've gotten us killed . . . you know that!" T.J. said unsteadily.

"You guys sure scare easy." Cooper laughed mercilessly, covering up his own fright. "I saw that stunt in the movies last week and just tried it out to see how much you pussy-footed zit pickers could take." Cooper laughed again.

T.J. was so mad he hauled off and smashed Cooper right in the face with his closed fist. Cooper yelped like a mongrel dog. Seconds later, blood smeared across Cooper's nose and upper lip as he drew his hand away. His eyes sprung tears of pain. In a rage Cooper opened the car door and leaped out, slamming the door behind him.

"You're so goddamned smart . . . *you* drive back!"

"What a mess," T.J. said in despair. We've all got our asses in a sling now, he thought as he slid over into the driver's seat and started the engine. Very slowly and carefully T.J. turned the car around and headed it back in the direction of Crestview.

As they passed Cooper walking alongside the road, T. J. stopped.

"Get in . . . you'll freeze walking ten miles."

Cooper gave him a dirty look and flipped him the finger, then continued walking without paying attention to any of them.

T.J. shook his head, wishing he'd never come along. "Bastard," he muttered under his breath, and turned his full attention toward driving.

They hadn't gone five more miles before T.J. heard the sound of a police siren despite the blaring car radio.

He looked in the rearview mirror and saw the flashing lights behind him. The color drained out of his face.

"Oh, shit," T.J. muttered as he pulled the car off to the side of the road and came to a stop.

Chapter 3

The two great industrial rivers with their ancestral Indian names, Monongahela and Allegheny, formed the land into a slender triangle where they joined to flow together through western Pennsylvania. Since the Industrial Revolution this city had become the hub of commerce and manufacturing serving a tristate area. Most people believed that all the steel, all the commerce and banking and trade were still controlled by the same seven families who earned massive fortunes out of oil, timber, mining, railroads and modern food processing. Grandsons, nephews and cousins, with Buck Simpson among the most ambitious, continued to run the elaborate interconnecting networks that bound Pittsburgh to a world of power far beyond its boundaries. Only two generations ago the black grime of the steel mills had forged an ominous city of constant midnight, with murky streetlights turned on before noon. Today those same mills, troubled by international trade, were slowed, now only occasionally lighting up the evening sky in an eerie reminder of their prime years. New buildings replaced the old; parks shone brilliant green, dappled with tall trees; the stately mansions fell temporarily from grace only to be renovated as colleges and museums, provided through the seven-family philanthropy. Slowly there evolved the modern renaissance of a major metropolis.

A freezing wind blew steadily, howling through the downtown of steel and glass. On the river sturdy tugboats slowly pushed heavily laden barges, relentlessly crushing bits of ice as they chugged downstream. The winter sky was brilliantly clear this Saturday morning.

As Buckley awoke, she was surprised to find herself alone. She turned over and saw a note on her bed table which said: "You are a delight. Have to catch an early plane. See you in the office Monday." It was signed by Tony Marshall, the man with whom she'd experienced her first serious love affair. He was extraordinarily handsome, a former champion skier and now senior art director at the Henry Advertising Agency. Recently the office grapevine had been betting on his promotion to vice-president.

Less than eight months ago Buckley had arrived at the agency, scared to death of the responsibility of her first real job but determined to prove she could do well and be valued in her own right instead of just being known as the daughter of one of this city's most influential men.

Yesterday Mr. Henry had given her a promotion. She knew that her father would have been very proud of her. For the first time since his death she had a sense of well-being about her entire life. Her affair with Tony left Buckley with more ambivalent feelings. Despite the fact that he was egotistical and a hopeless perfectionist, it was impossible to overlook his deep blue eyes, his incredible body and undeniable talent. Last night they'd had a wonderful time at Zelda's, the most popular gathering place after work for the young professionals and singles crowd. Making love with Tony was glorious. Why, then, did she feel so awful afterward when she was alone? She got the impression he thought of her as being too easy, not as demanding as she should be, not requiring enough respect.

She decided that last night marked an end to this unsatisfactory relationship. When Tony returned to the office Monday, Buckley resolved to make it clear to him that she was no longer interested in his one-night stands.

More than anything in the world Buckley would have liked to stay in bed this morning. She had promised herself a quiet Saturday after a long, hard week. She needed time to sort out her feelings about Tony, about her father's estate being settled and about the overall direction of her personal life. But the phone call from Vivian's housekeeper, Estelle, telling her T.J. had been arrested and his mother was away on vacation, changed her plans instantly. Unfortunately her car refused to start, Alphonse was away on business, the Auto Club said it would take several hours before it could get her assistance and her friends were unavailable, so she was forced to take the bus. It never occurred to her not to try to help T.J. immediately.

"Where to, miss?" the ticket clerk's grumpy, disinterested voice inquired.

"Which bus to Grasslands?" Buckley asked politely.

"Gate twelve at ten-forty," was the curt reply.

Buckley took her seat in the front of the bus next to a window. Only minutes later the huge half-empty intercity bus lumbered out of the terminal. It was so early that traffic was still light.

They drove along the river road for a while; then the driver turned onto the main highway instead of taking the turnpike. It was a two-hour trip to the juvenile detention facility at Grasslands according to the crisp schedule card she'd gotten with her ticket. It would be afternoon by the time she arrived.

Mile after mile of countryside rolled by, mesmerizing Buckley as she stared out the window, trying to marshal her thoughts into a plan. She had very little information about what had actually happened to T.J.

Her father had taught her not to rely on secondhand facts, and his advice had saved her from making mistakes many times in the past.

This vivid recollection of her father triggered a resurgence of her feelings on the day he had first told her of his decision to marry Vivian. It was one of the most painful events of her life. She saw an invisible curtain go down just behind her father's eyes as he looked at her that day. The two of them had been so close, inseparable since her mother died. They had shared a love and friendship Buckley assumed would continue the rest of their lives.

But on that day when she was thirteen, her father shut her out with such subtlety she almost refused to believe it was happening between them. Her immediate instinct was to scream with horror. She wanted to throw herself on the floor in front of him, begging him not to do this to them. Buckley felt real panic for the first time. She wanted to pull at him, shaking loose that terrible curtain across his eyes. She wanted to rip and tear at that dreadful aloofness, shredding it in her hands. The room spun around her, enveloping her in a frenzy. She couldn't bear what her father was doing to her, to himself, to the memory of her mother, to their closeness and oneness.

The agony of his pushing her away in favor of Vivian turned the girl quite mad for a moment. She was temporarily in touch with her own primitive being, devoid of thought, carried on a tidal wave of passionate love and desperate need. There was no reason to this moment, only terrible feelings. There were no words for it, only anguish and shivering. In that moment she was every terrified baby coming out of its mother's safe womb, she was eons of daughters adoring their father's strength and command over the known world, she was every woman abandoned and bereft. She felt herself drowning in tears she couldn't cry.

It took several years before the relationship between them resumed its former closeness. Eventually Buckley learned to adjust. But she blamed Vivian, not her father, for what had happened. She soon learned to fear Vivian's coldness, her cunning and anger. Someday, Buckley vowed, she would pay her back.

When her father died, there was no longer any need to put up a front, not for Buckley and not for Vivian. Her feelings about Vivian did not, however, apply to T.J. Buckley realized he had never known the kind of closeness with either of his parents that Buckley had shared with her father. He saw himself as an outcast, almost an orphan. Though he barely remembered his real father, he felt a sense of betrayal and a deeply buried outrage that the man had deserted him. Then, too, he had been right there the terrible day her father was killed. Nothing could erase the compassion Buckley felt for him as T.J. tried to recover from his shock, horror and guilt.

T.J. had a tendency to have his feelings hurt too easily, to take offense too quickly, to be overly dependent on what other people thought of him. He felt abandoned. He saw himself as the victim of circumstances, as though what happened to him were always someone else's fault.

Despite all that, her stepbrother was capable of being charmingly funny, a good friend and a loyal companion. He was like a stray puppy with big, sad eyes that needed a good home and lots of love. Although she knew he'd hate her for it if he ever discovered the truth, Buckley felt deeply sorry for him.

As the rolling hills and small-town shopping centers passed her window, tears welled up underneath Buckley's closed eyelids. The little girl of her childhood years was suddenly crying out for help. Daddy is not here anymore. He never will be able to talk to me or hold me close ever again. I will not hear the sound of his laugh, smell his cologne, watch him walk just as confidently through the woods as down the office hallway. Lord, how I wish he weren't dead. Maybe there never is a training ground for loneliness. You just face it and do the best you can.

The rumbling bus ground to a jerking halt. "Grasslands," the driver bellowed, jolting Buckley upright. She grabbed her purse, tightened the belt of her trench coat and descended the steep bus stairs.

It was not a large station. Not much more than a shed with a ticket window and a snack stand. On the quiet street Buckley saw a single taxi waiting. She shared the cab with two other passengers from the bus.

The county juvenile detention facility sat on a treeless knoll overlooking a small town as though it were the primary industry or perhaps a major tourist attraction.

How strange, Buckley thought. Here we are, three people sharing a taxi, scared to death about someone we love, and no one says a word. As if reading her mind, the woman sitting next to Buckley turned and asked, "This your first time?"

Buckley was surprised to find herself embarrassed by the question. Only a moment ago she was wishing for some companionship; now she yearned for anonymity again. She stared at the woman who'd spoken to her. There was a beaten look to her dark eyes. It brought back the terrible wave of loneliness Buckley had experienced on the bus. For a split second she thought about asking the cabdriver to take her back to the bus station. She wanted to go home. Even in the coldness of this unheated taxi she felt perspiration on her skin, soaking into her sweater.

The woman knew her answer. She nodded with a resignation that contained more than sadness. There was a weary rage lying just beneath the surface of those dark eyes, a lifetime of hardships and disappointments written on her face.

The woman followed her out of the cab and walked silently beside her toward the imposing front entrance. As they reached the door, she turned and said to Buckley in a whispered warning, "Just don't let them con you—they'll get to you if they can!"

Buckley stopped. The woman entered without her. "Damn it," she said aloud with a growing anger, "why the hell can't people mind their own business?" She hesitated on the steps, desperately wanting to turn and run away.

Chapter 4

The brilliant Caribbean sun had already consumed nearly a bottle of her special tropical tanning oil. Vivian Simpson looked with frank admiration at her bronzing skin as she gently stroked more oil onto each outstretched leg. She was in amazingly good shape for being forty-six years old.

Vivian adjusted her wide-brimmed straw hat slightly, watching the dappled bits of shade sprinkle a pattern across her gold waist chain and the bottom of her emerald green bikini. She wiggled her toes in sheer pleasure, feeling a breeze off the water brush past as the boat moved forward. Sailing delighted her.

Living on St. Croix was her idea of perfection. If she had her choice, this was where she would stay until the estate was finally settled. It had come as a shock that she was not in total control of Simpson's money, but Vivian had never shirked the excitement of a challenge. She'd initiated a full-scale investigation of Alphonse, seeking to discredit him as trustee.

In this tropical paradise Tony Marshall, who just arrived this Saturday morning, was her weekend lover and sailing companion. He was sixteen years her junior, had a voracious sex drive, was immorally ambitious and managed to be well dressed even in swim trunks, sandals and beach shirt.

Vivian knew the moment she met him at the Henry Advertising Agency party three months ago that he was an ideal component in her human chess game. In return for access to her personal influence with the agency, Tony kept her informed about the company's marketing plans, and because Buckley had a job at the same agency, Tony enabled Vivian to keep track of her stepdaughter without personal contact.

"How are things at the agency?" Vivian asked casually.

"Great—couldn't be better, thanks to you." Tony smiled appreciatively.

For Vivian, Tony was delightful weekend amusement. She looked at him sipping his rum drink as though watching an animal being fattened for slaughter. It was having control over him that Vivian relished, not the man himself. She smiled with a little sigh of contentment. Tony's eyes twinkled, knowing he had pleased her.

"Ever see Buckley?"

"Occasionally . . . at the office . . . we work on several of the same accounts."

"How's she doing?"

Tony measured his words. "At the moment she's got more enthusiasm than talent. She's immature."

Vivian tilted her head back, taking a long, hard

look at Tony. "Are you saying you prefer older women?"

"I prefer women, not girls," Tony responded easily.

Vivian laughed.

She and Tony returned that afternoon to the condominium Vivian had leased for six months on a lovely hill near Frederiksted, overlooking the pale green ocean and surrounded by flaming red bougainvillaea vines. Vivian went to her bedroom and immediately undressed.

Tony was pleased. One more day alone with Vivian and one more night in bed with her would be just the insurance he needed to secure his future career moves.

She was still in the shower when Tony knocked on the bathroom door. "There's a long-distance phone call from your housekeeper."

Vivian quickly wrapped a towel around herself and took the phone in her bedroom overlooking the beach. Her first thought was that the woman was calling to say her apartment in the city had been robbed.

"Estelle?" she answered, thoroughly annoyed.

The housekeeper's voice sounded muffled. Vivian could clearly understand that the woman was agitated at being unable to contact her earlier and that the problem was with T.J. As she listened, Vivian's eyes turned cold and still. Her face perceptively hardened. The tiny lines of forty-six years stood out unmistakably for the first time in the late-afternoon sunlight. She seemed to age several years as her expression lost the gentility she normally imposed upon it for the sake of sociability and public appearance. The corners of her mouth turned downward like an animal about to snarl. Then almost magically a dark glimmer flickered in her eyes.

"Tell them you were unable to reach me," she said. Slowly and deliberately she settled the receiver back in its cradle and returned to her shower.

"Shit and two is eight!" T.J. spat out in a rage as he watched his buddies Willie and Hank leave the cell this Saturday morning with a burly uniformed guard. The heavy metal cell door clanked shut with a thud that echoed down the hall. It was a hollow, empty echo that seemed to fill T.J.'s whole body as he turned and threw himself down on the thin bunk mattress. He lay there only a few minutes, feeling his heart pounding, tears beading on his eyelids and a sense of panic filling his body. He had to get up again and pace.

The cell in this ancient wreck called the county juvenile detention facility was intended for only two boys. Last night all three of them had shared the cramped quarters. There were only two steel bunks, three thin mattresses, no urinal, one tiny sink, no window. One of them had had to sleep on the floor, and they all had had to bang on the door, yelling for someone to unlock the cell when they had to go to the john.

T.J. had to keep moving. Every muscle in his lanky six-foot body was tensed. He wanted to pound his fist into the wall but restrained himself at the last moment.

Last night Willie had been so scared he'd thrown up twice. He had also pissed in the sink. Hank had tried to bull his way through by bragging about how he was going to be a big man at school when the guys found out how great he handled being busted. T.J.

said he was full of shit because he wasn't acting like any big man until *after* his dad had promised to get him out first thing in the morning.

T.J. could feel his pulse racing as he recalled the results of his own phone call Friday to the outside world. The housekeeper answered at his mother's apartment. She said Vivian had left for a vacation in the islands and wouldn't be back for a few weeks. He begged the woman to call his mother down there immediately. Estelle told him it might take a couple of days to reach Mrs. Simpson.

"You ignorant bitch—don't you know this is a fucking emergency?" T.J. swore at her. "Just call Buckley then. She'll know what to do!" T.J. hung up.

Why did he do that? Why did he fly off the handle so fast? He knew it never did any good in the long run, but for the moment it made him feel better.

T.J. cringed when he realized what his mother was eventually going to say. He knew she didn't give a shit about him or anyone else, for that matter, but she was going to make one hell of a scene. After his stepfather had been killed last fall, she'd never shown any real emotion toward him. She sent him away to boarding school and made excuses not to see him except briefly over Christmas vacation.

He loved his stepfather, even though they'd gotten to know each other only toward the end. The man was kind and fair. He'd shown a real interest in T.J. But since his death T.J. knew he'd failed the man in some unspoken way. He had terrible nightmares about being accused of killing his stepfather, of being on trial for murder and unable to speak in his own defense.

T.J. wished like hell his stepfather were alive

today. Vivian couldn't do this to him if Buck Simpson were still alive. Someone would rescue him, someone would care. But each time T.J. started thinking this way, all he could see in his mind was that blood-soaked autumn day, and the throbbing headache that had plagued him ever since would begin again.

He sat down on the edge of a bunk, dejected and confused. God, he hoped Buckley had got his message and showed up. But what if Buckley didn't come? What if Buckley didn't really give a damn about him either? T.J. shuddered. Maybe he would just die here. Maybe no one cared. Maybe everyone in the world would just forget that T.J. Simpson had ever existed.

He got up and paced around the small empty jail cell, feeling alone and scared. It was hard for him to believe that the other guys were on the outside and he was the only one left here. Worse still, he was being charged with a felony. When they arrested him and read him his rights, he heard an officer say, "Grand theft auto." No one had to remind him that he was also driving without a valid license.

T.J. should have known Mr. Williams would never lend his car to anyone. "I was just a jerk, that's all," he said. "Now who gives a shit? Who's going to believe me?" Those guys are all right back where they started, safe and sound, T.J. thought. They're probably having a great time, telling the rest of the school about how brave they were, what a game it all was. Mostly that damn Cooper. I'll bet he's turned himself into a hero by now. King Kong of the car snatchers. So who cares if my whole life goes to hell? Nobody.

T.J. flopped down onto the hard bunk, feeling

terrible. He listened to the hollow sound of the jail. "This is one hell of a fix, all right. If I get out of here with all my marbles, I'm going to be one lucky sucker," he said out loud.

The guard's keys made a clanking noise as he thumped down the hall. T.J.'s ears picked up the sound instantly. That dumb tin rattle meant hope. Hope that maybe Buckley was here. Hope that maybe T.J. could get out of this stinky cell. As bad as he'd thought boarding school was just yesterday, what a paradise, what a garden spot it would be this afternoon!

Sure enough, it was T.J.'s turn. Some of his natural spunk returned with the sight of that key turning in the lock. T.J. pulled himself upright, brushed off his clothes, tried smoothing his thick brown hair and walked to the cell door.

"You got a visitor," the guard mumbled routinely.

Inside the prisoners' visiting room, Buckley leaned her elbows on the counter. The thick window in front of her was reinforced with wire mesh. She looked at the speakerphone provided each cubicle, then down the row of friends or relatives sitting hunched toward the wired pane of glass, trying to communicate with people on the other side they could neither touch nor hear clearly. The booth opposite Buckley was still empty, although the guard had definitely indicated where she should sit. Each small booth was numbered, so she assumed there was a corresponding set of numbers on the prisoners' side.

Prisoner. What a dreadful sound the word had. Her father would be turning in his grave if he'd known his stepson was imprisoned even for one night. If only he were here, this would be over immediately.

In spite of the grim circumstances, Buckley remembered when he took her on a fishing trip with a friend from Texas. The two men, reminiscing about their past, started talking about what the word "if" really meant. The Texan listened for a while, then replied seriously: "My daddy once said, 'If a bullfrog had wings, he wouldn't bump his ass when he jumped!' "

Caught in this brief memory of a happier time, Buckley didn't realize she was smiling as T.J. sat down on the other side of the partition.

T.J. felt enormous relief at the sight of his stepsister. He thought the smile on her face was a weird reaction, but then Buckley didn't always do what you'd expect. Maybe that was why they got along so well.

"I hope you don't think this is fun-and-games time," T.J. said to open their conversation.

Buckley couldn't hear a word he said and motioned for him to talk into the speakerphone beside him. It wasn't easy. You had to lean forward, talk into the phone while pressing the button down, trying simultaneously to keep eye contact with each other through the wire mesh in the glass.

"How are you?" Buckley asked, any hint of a smile gone.

"Terrible!" T.J. snapped back. "Can't you get me out of here?"

Buckley sadly shook her head. "No."

"Why not?" T.J. leaned forward anxiously. "They let the other guys go."

"They weren't charged, T.J., and you are."

"But I didn't take the damn car. Cooper did."

"Can you prove that?"

"Sure. Just ask Cooper. Or better yet . . . ask Willie or Hank; they were there the whole time."

"T.J., I want you to know I tried to get them on the phone. No one answers. The officer at reception says you'll be held forty-eight hours until they can schedule a preliminary hearing on your case. There's nothing I can do to make them let you go today."

"Damn." T.J. looked bleakly down at the counter. Without raising his eyes he asked, "What about Vivian?"

"She's out of town, that's all I know. I tried to reach Alphonse, but he's on a business trip and won't be back until late tonight. T.J., listen, I'll get either Alphonse tomorrow or someone at the company on Monday. There's nothing I can do today. See, I thought maybe they'd release you in my custody, but . . . they won't."

He leaned very close to the window, barely whispering into the speakerphone. "Buckley . . . you got to help me! You've got to get me out of here! I'm innocent . . . Cooper stole the car . . . I didn't have anything to do with it! Please . . . I'm *suffocating* in this place."

T.J. was pale, his eyes brimming with tears. He was scared, a haunted look on his young face. His hands were trembling, and his voice cracked.

"Buckley, what about the insurance money?" he asked desperately. "Can't you just pay someone to let me go?"

She leaned very close to the speakerphone and whispered. "T.J., listen to me carefully. We may as well face it. You're going to be here for the next two days. I'll get Alphonse and a lawyer, but nothing can be done now. As for the estate, until the will comes out of probate, every single dollar is frozen. No one can touch it, not even Alphonse. But of course, I have the money for a lawyer if you need one."

"So I sit here, right?" He lowered his voice. "They treat you like a convicted criminal in here, Buckley. Please, think of something! This place is awful. You know I don't belong here!" he pleaded.

Buckley's heart nearly broke for him. Their relationship had been so filled with good-natured teasing and sibling competition that she hardly knew how to cope with seeing T.J. like this. He suddenly looked older to her, yet at the same time he seemed so young, so vulnerable. "T.J., you've got to tell me everything . . . right from the beginning."

T.J. cleared his throat and began slowly. "Yesterday I walked out the gym door and saw Cooper sitting behind the wheel of Mr. William's new car with Hank and Willie in the back seat. I got into the front seat next to Cooper."

"Go on," Buckley said with a heavy sigh. Such a dumb prank, she thought. Cooper Havenhurst is a spoiled brat. He's the one who should be locked up, not T.J.

"Well," T.J. continued, "the car hit an ice patch and went out of control. Cooper and I had a fight—I punched him, and he got mad and stormed off. I swear, Buckley, I was taking the car and the guys back to school. Next thing I heard was the police siren." T.J. took a deep breath and sat very still.

Buckley hoped with all her heart and soul that he'd told her the truth.

"I can't stand it," T.J. said desperately. "I didn't do anything wrong. Why the hell am I the only one left here? Damn it! It's not fair!"

"Of course, it's not fair. But that's not our biggest problem right now." Buckley put her hand out instinctively to comfort him, but the glass and wire mesh stood coldly in her way.

"T.J., just tell me straight: Did you have *anything* to do with stealing that car? I mean, did you know Cooper stole it, did you think it was funny, did you go along with it in any way?"

On his side of the partition T.J. shook his head vigorously. "*No!* For God's sake Buckley, you don't think I'm lying, do you?" His voice was a hoarse whisper.

She studied him carefully. More than he knew, she wanted to believe in his innocence.

T.J. felt uncomfortable but didn't turn his eyes away from her. Buckley was his only hope, his single, fragile link with the world outside.

"What are we going to do now, Buckley?" T.J. asked tentatively, not quite daring to hear the answer.

"All right, as soon as I reach Alphonse, he'll figure a way out for us. I know he will, T.J. Today is Saturday. Just try to get through tomorrow . . . somehow . . . and Monday they'll schedule a hearing. I'll explain everything to Mr. Williams. He'll probably drop the charges, and it'll be all over."

Even as she formulated their plan, Buckley felt unsure it could work as quickly as she tried to encourage T.J. to believe it would. Alphonse was going to be very upset when he found out, Mr. Williams might be tough to convince and whether any of them could circumvent Vivian was yet to be seen.

"Why can't I just go home with you like I did all those times from school?" T.J. asked, desperately seeking a way to freedom right now. He was scared to death of being left alone with these street-tough strangers here another day.

"I told you," she answered with patience and care. "They say I'm not old enough, I'm not your legal guardian and you're charged with a felony. They have the right to hold you for an investigation."

"Damn!" T.J. muttered angrily. "You're the only one who gives a shit . . . did you tell them that?"

"Not in those exact words . . . but I told them. It just doesn't fit their rules, T.J. What else can I do?"

They were caught in an impasse, and they both knew it. On one side was the labyrinth of official red tape, complicated by circumstantial evidence; on the other was Vivian's impenetrable disdain for her son and her apparently cruel disregard of his predicament.

The guard arrived at that very moment to announce visiting time was up for them. T.J. became frantic. He tried to cling to the booth, clawing at the window.

The speakerphone was off. She couldn't hear his voice, but he was begging her to get him out. Buckley half stood, putting both hands on the glass, trying desperately to let him know she'd help. She grabbed the phone at the last moment. "Don't worry, T.J. I love you—I'll get help—I'll be back! I promise."

Chapter 5

"What do you mean, you've been trying to get this phone call through for two hours? It's now only seven o'clock Sunday morning!"

Vivian's anger was in sharp contrast with the peaceful surroundings of her island condominium bedroom.

"Of course, you woke me up! Listen, Alphonse, I couldn't care less if T.J. rots in that country slammer for the rest of his worthless life, and I'll be damned if he's going to order me around! He brought this on himself, and now he's going to suffer the consequences," she said in a quieter but no less furious tone of voice.

A soft breeze caught the sheer open robe she slipped on, revealing her suntanned naked body underneath. The gold waist chain she wore loosely around her picked up rays from the brilliant sunlight streaming through a nearby window and glistened against her well-oiled skin.

"And I'm telling you to stay out of this! I'm his mother, and I'll decide what's going to be done. If you so much as make one phone call on his behalf, I'll see to it you regret doing it for a very long time."

Vivian's impulse was to hang up on Alphonse, but she restrained herself. She wasn't due back for another week, and she was determined her vacation would not be cut short.

"The flights are booked solid until next Sunday," she lied. "Meet me at the airport for the six-thirty flight. We'll discuss it further then." And with that she finally slammed the phone down.

Vivian paced angrily back and forth across the pretty bedroom. She was alone. Tony had evidently gone for his usual morning swim.

For the first time in years Vivian's mind flashed back to the hatred and contempt she'd felt toward her own parents.

Since emigrating to this country more than a hundred years ago, her ancestors had been farmers, prosperous on paper but miserly. They clung to their backcountry values, a cheerless religion and collective gratitude for a chance at a better life.

Vivian, originally named Sissy, was the youngest and very first child in her family of eight to express discontent, to feel confined by the miles of open space. She needed people; she wanted to see lights, buildings and the rush of things happening.

For most of her life she felt like an unnoticed servant in her own house. There were two older sisters who cooked and sewed and understood farm life better than she ever could. There were also three boys, her brothers, who got everything: food, attention, clothes, spending money and recognition. She walked through her early years a stranger in her own world. Once she'd read a story in one of those true romance magazines about a family that had one child different from the rest because the mother had an affair with the town doctor, became pregnant, had the baby, and no one ever knew except the woman and the doctor. Would that explain why she didn't fit into her own family, why she always felt so out of place? But then she studied her mother and couldn't imagine the woman having an affair with anyone. How would she meet another man? She never went anywhere, never said more than three words at any given time and managed with fewer than those if she could.

Vivian couldn't remember exactly how she had created the person she eventually became. A good part of it was gleaned from magazines she furtively read at the little country store where her father went every few weeks to buy the meager staples he begrudgingly supplied for running the farm.

He told everyone his youngest daughter was allowed to come with him because she was strong enough to help load some supplies but not a valued farm worker and her presence would be missed the least. The truth was that these excursions provided her father with the only sexual partner he could coerce without spending money.

Halfway to town there was a deserted horse barn. Every trip they stopped at the barn, where he mauled his daughter's body crudely, quickly, never even seeing her completely naked, just pulling down her handmade muslin breeches and plunging himself inside her. Only once, the first time, did she have either the courage or the stupidity to refuse him. That day her father beat her with his fist until she cowered before him tear-soaked, bloodstained and vulnerable. She vaguely remembered being just twelve years old.

Back home she went over the magazine stories and photos in her memory a thousand times. She imagined herself dressed in the fine clothes, decked out in sparkling jewels, going to all the exotic places she saw in the color pictures. Through long hours of household drudgery she amused herself by pretending she was already one of those perfectly gorgeous women. In her mind she transformed herself from a skinny country farm girl into a big-city beauty.

At about thirteen years of age she'd begun experimenting with a rearrangement of reality. She figured, quite correctly, that since no one in her family cared much about her, no one would notice if she changed. She started by saying everything exactly the opposite from what she really meant or felt. If she liked a particular thing, she'd announce without provocation that she hated it. If events happened one way, she'd say they happened another. If she felt happy, she'd force herself to frown and sulk. When she was angry, she'd smile. No one noticed. No one cared. No one paid any attention to her.

One by one she chose to deal with all the things that scared her. The hardest to overcome was her fear of blood.

She was also nauseated by the sight of death, so she offered to slaughter the small animals used for dinner. The first time she volunteered, her mother glanced sideways at her. There was a glimmer of surprise in the woman's eyes. But as usual her mother said nothing. She simply nodded her head and handed over the heavy, sharp butchering knife.

By the time the young girl reached the rabbit hutch

her hands were shaking violently. She couldn't even feel her legs, but her bony knees knocked together as she walked forward.

The rabbits she usually visited to pet and feed perked up their ears as she neared the cage. She stopped in her tracks. As though sensing she was not on one of her usual visits, the rabbits seemed to freeze, only their long ears flicking back and forth like white furry antennae. From that moment she went through the motions in a trance. It was as though she were standing outside her own body.

First she laid the butcher knife on the ancient tree stump where killing was done. Then she saw herself reach into the cage, deftly snatch a rabbit by the back of its neck and drag it out. She reached up with her free hand and grabbed the big stick which hung by a leather thong from the side of the rabbit hutch. Rabbit in one hand, stick in the other, she moved to the tree stump, where she set the struggling animal, holding it as steady as she could. For a moment she hesitated. Then she raised the heavy stick in the air and brought it down across the back of the rabbit's neck with a cracking thud. The animal lay silently next to the old butcher knife.

She replaced the killing stick carefully and returned to the tree stump, never quite daring to turn her back on the dead animal. She lifted the rabbit, turning it over and plunged the butcher knife into its neck, drawing a bloody line down its entire soft body. She lifted the knife again and whacked off the rabbit's head. Now the two severed pieces lay next to each other. The knife was dripping blood. She felt the acid taste of bile rising in her throat. Her stomach convulsed, and a retching gag shook her whole body.

She raced for the edge of the clearing to vomit into the long grass.

When it was over, she returned quietly to the tree stump and her dead rabbit. Very slowly she reached her hand in the rabbit's gut and cleaned out the cavity, dumping the refuse into a tin pail. Carefully she skinned the small creature, cleaned up the area and returned to the house with meat for dinner.

It was dusk. She stood at the squeaky screen door for a minute. The rabbit still felt warm in her hands. The next time it wouldn't be so hard.

When she finally told her mother about her plans to leave the farm, the tired woman looked as though the girl had used forbidden swear words. The shock on her mother's face was unexpected because, after all, there were five other children to carry on the family traditions.

At dinner that evening her mother said, "Your youngest girl wants to go live in the city."

Everyone at the long table stopped eating and stared. She felt her skin go cold. Her heart was pounding, but the rest of her body felt dead. Her father looked up from his mountainous plate of food and stared at this daughter on whom he'd vented his monstrous sexual needs. He had never felt a sense of kinship toward her. She was frail, not of their stock or strength. Since he did not identify her as his flesh and blood, he felt strangely vindicated as he found secretive opportunities to fondle her, silently assaulting her, spewing forth his semen into her young, ill-prepared body. She possessed none of the common family traits.

"You eighteen yet, Sissy-girl?" he growled, never raising his piggish eyes to a confrontation.

"Yes, sir," she mumbled.

He finished chewing the mouthful of food, swallowed hard and washed it down with a long drink of homemade cider. "Go, then," her father said, and returned immediately to the more important business of finishing his dinner. If he tried to stop her, she might retaliate by saying something about what had gone on between them. Everyone else at the table resumed eating. The clicking of knives and forks was the sound Vivian remembered most about the day she left home. Not even her mother said good-bye. She would never know if the silently resigned woman suspected what had taken place between her brutal, ignorant husband and her youngest daughter or if her mother even cared.

She'd never seen any of them again. From the day she left that farm, walking down the dirt road to the bus station, she concentrated solely on the woman she renamed Vivian.

When she left home, she discovered she had taught herself the skills she needed most. She had conquered her fears and learned to lie with such control it didn't seem like lying anymore. She was perfectly disciplined and completely devoid of moral restrictions. She was a living canvas upon which any picture could be painted.

Vivian's anger subsided. "Sissy-girl" was gone forever. Standing near the window, Vivian took a deep breath of clean salt air. She wanted a drink.

She opened the bedroom door and walked through the living room to the bar. After rummaging around for a minute, she came up with all the components for making piña coladas.

"Need some help?" Tony's soft voice said from

immediately behind her. He was dressed in swim trunks and a beach shirt.

Vivian looked up, a seductive smile edging its way across her mouth. "What do you think?" she asked, running her tongue across her lips. She watched curiously as Tony looked appreciatively at her naked body underneath the open robe.

Tony took the bottles she held in her hands. He walked to the counter, opened the lid of the blender and then got a bag of crushed ice from the freezer.

Vivian sat on one of the wicker barstools, robe draped casually over her crossed legs as Tony made their drinks.

Tony handed her a large glass filled with the cold, frothy rum drink. At the last second he expertly flipped a straw in the middle of it. Then he poured his own, and they clinked glasses in a toast.

"To the most beautiful woman in the world," he said with genuine admiration.

After taking a very long and deliciously welcome drink, Vivian smiled. "You do that so well anyone would mistake you for a professional bartender."

Tony laughed. "Years of experience. The talents of a perennial guest." He glanced at his watch as he walked around the counter to sit next to her. "Bit early, though."

"Not really." Vivian uncrossed her legs, allowing the robe to fall completely open. Pretending she didn't notice being naked, she returned to her drink, finishing half of it in a few long swallows.

"It's really glorious here," Vivian said, staring out the nearest window.

"Certainly is," Tony replied, running his hand across her knee and up her thigh.

Without responding to his caress, Vivian continued. "Could you ask for more than this?" she said, gesturing toward the island paradise visible outside the window.

Tony laughed. "Yes," he said, leaning forward to kiss her.

Vivian tipped her head back, tossing her hair freely. "Sure you have to leave tonight?" she asked, taunting him.

"Positive," Tony replied with just the right note of regret and disappointment in his voice.

She laughed deep in her throat. "Well then, what are you waiting for?"

Tony put his glass down on the counter and easily lifted Vivian off her barstool perch to carry her into the bedroom.

Chapter 6

After Buckley left T.J. on Saturday, she made numerous attempts to reach Vivian in St. Croix. Finally, she phoned Alphonse, who promised to keep calling until he reached T.J.'s mother. As her next step Buckley made an appointment with Mr. Williams, the headmaster of T.J.'s school, for Sunday afternoon. She then called the Havenhursts, Cooper's family. Mrs. Havenhurst answered the phone. Her voice sounded reassuringly sympathetic.

"I'm so sorry about all this, Buckley," Mrs. Havenhurst said. "If you're going to be out this way, why don't you come over here for cocktails on your way back to the city?"

"Thank you," Buckley replied. "I'd like that. Will six o'clock be too early?"

"No. That'll be fine, dear," Mrs. Havenhurst said sadly. "We're all most distressed about T.J. He was Cooper's best friend."

Buckley remembered that Cooper had invited him for many weekends when T.J. was unable to go home, but she never thought they were exactly "best friends."

She was nervous about her meeting with Mr. Williams. He was such a pompous man, so filled with an overblown sense of his own importance. Williams carried his position as headmaster of a prominent school like a badge of knighthood. It's a wonder we don't all have to call him sir, Buckley thought.

Sure enough, at Crestview Sunday afternoon, Mr. Williams ushered her into his office with all the formality of a member of some royal household.

"Mr. Williams, I've been to see T.J.," Buckley began carefully. "He swears he didn't take your car. Cooper Havenhurst did. Both Hank and Willie can corroborate that. If you'll just drop the charges against T.J., there's a good chance we can get him released tomorrow."

Mr. Williams did not look pleased. He did not look sympathetic. In fact, this meeting with Buckley seemed to make him more nervous than usual.

"Surely you won't continue to press charges against a boy you know is innocent!" Buckley insisted, trying to get Mr. Williams to say something.

"I'm not aware that Cooper Havenhurst has come forward to take responsibility, nor am I at all prepared to take T.J.'s word regarding his own innocence."

"Then would you please call Willie and Hank into this office and ask them?"

"Neither of them has returned to Crestview as yet."

"They both have telephones, don't they?" Buckley asked sarcastically.

"Cooper is, of course, one of our most valued

boys,'' Williams said in a slightly nasal, mincing voice.

And, thought Buckley, Mr. Havenhurst is one of your most generous benefactors as well as a trustee on the school board.

''Mr. Williams, let me ask you this: If we can prove that T.J. is not guilty of stealing your car, will you allow him to return to this school?'' Buckley asked directly, feeling her dislike of the headmaster growing stronger by the minute but realizing she needed some kind of commitment from him.

''Miss Simpson, I am responsible for both the administration and the reputation of Crestview School.'' Mr. Williams stood up from behind his desk and faced the window, now clasping his hands together behind his back. ''You must understand that I cannot become directly involved in decisions regarding T.J. personally. It is the responsibility of his mother to make those decisions.''

Buckley forced herself to hold her temper, realizing that if T.J. was going to return to this school, it wasn't constructive to alienate the headmaster.

''If you don't press charges, Mr. Williams, then there's no reason for Crestview *not* to take him back, is there?'' Buckley asked as politely as she could.

''There are a number of very good reasons not to readmit T.J. Simpson,'' Williams replied. ''I understand from his mother that you prefer to overlook his antisocial behavior, blaming his problems on her.''

''What?'' Buckley sputtered in astonishment. ''All I have ever done is ask the school to treat T.J. fairly. Mr. Williams, you know perfectly well T.J. recently suffered a terrible tragedy. For God's sake, don't you have any compassion?"

"If Mrs. Simpson wishes to discuss the matter of T.J. with me, I'll be happy to talk to her."

Buckley stood, knowing that any further conversation was useless. "Thank you for your time, Mr. Williams," she said, extending her hand as he turned to face her.

"We're always happy to see a boy's family here at Crestview," Mr. Williams replied, sounding more like an undertaker at a funeral parlor than the headmaster of a fashionable prep school. Buckley was furious with him, but she realized Cooper's father was one of the most important men in the whole state. Of course, there would be no charges against his precious son. If Cooper had totally demolished Mr. Williams's car, there would still be no charges. Williams would be paid off, shut up, and life would continue as usual.

Still in a rage over Mr. Williams, Buckley drove to the Havenhursts', taking the longest way she knew. She needed time to calm down, time to think.

When Buckley finally arrived, Cooper's mother answered the door. Normally it was a rather rowdy and raucous household, but this evening there were only three of them in the living room. Cooper was nowhere in sight, nor was he mentioned. Mr. and Mrs. Havenhurst were unusually subdued and formal with her. Clara Havenhurst had a drinking problem. Mr. Havenhurst smiled benevolently at his wife, pretending everything was in perfect order at the other end of the couch.

Buckley was very uncomfortable. Everyone was acting as though she were here for a purely social evening, as though nothing had happened.

"I don't know exactly how to ask this," she began, "but I need some help. T.J. is the only one left in jail, and he's innocent. Your son took Mr. Williams's car out of the school parking lot on Friday afternoon as a joke, a prank." Buckley looked anxiously from one end of the coffee table to the other, hoping to find a hint of encouragement. Mrs. Havenhurst stopped eating her delicate tea sandwich. Her face filled with a sort of distracted sadness. Mr. Havenhurst looked directly at Buckley.

"Go on," he said without indicating emotion of any kind.

"Well, I know Mr. Williams wouldn't press charges against Cooper if he told the truth . . . and if Cooper admitted taking the car, T.J. would be released from the detention facility at Grasslands. My stepbrother *is* innocent, and all I'm asking is for you to help me prove it."

The silence that followed her request was nearly deafening. Buckley hardly dared breathe. She could hear her own heart beating.

Mrs. Havenhurst suddenly blurted out, "Buckley, dear—"

"Clara!" Mr. Havenhurst reprimanded her swiftly. The commanding tone of voice let his wife know that she was to keep her mouth absolutely shut for the duration of this conversation.

With a note of superior righteousness that made Buckley's skin crawl, Mr. Havenhurst began speaking as he poured himself a second drink. "Now, Buckley . . . you know things are never quite as simple as you'd make them out to be. My son has a brilliant future ahead of him. I wouldn't want anything to jeopardize that . . . you understand?"

Buckley was angry with herself for being such a

fool as to think these people might help.

"I'm quite surprised at you, Buckley. You're from one of the most prominent families in the state. Of course, you're still young, but skulking around like this and going behind Vivian's back, asking for charity, are most unbecoming to a woman of your upbringing."

Buckley felt her face going crimson with embarrassment. He was purposely humiliating her. She wished she could get up and run from this horrible living room without saying another word. But she'd started the whole thing, and she was going to have to get through it now as best she could.

"What would your father have said? You know what a man of pride and principle he was. He would not have approved such behavior. He believed, as I do, in keeping private doors closed and taking care of one's own."

"I'd appreciate it if you left my father out of this." Buckley had hardly touched her small plate of food. She neatly folded her cocktail napkin. She couldn't bring herself to be humiliated by Mr. Havenhurst any longer.

"If you'll both excuse me, I'll be going now. I have to be at work early tomorrow, and it's rather a long drive back to the city."

"Of course, dear." Mrs. Havenhurst spoke for the first time since her husband's reprimand.

Mr. Havenhurst walked a silently raging Buckley to the front door.

"Buckley," Havenhurst almost whispered, "give up this sordid business; let time take its course." He put his unwelcome hand on her shoulder in what was intended as a fatherly gesture. "You're in way over your head, my girl. Keep out of things you'll never understand. After all, you're young . . . you have your whole life ahead of you. Don't ruin everything with blind stubbornness." He smiled as though assured she would respond favorably to his impeccable logic.

"That's easy for you to say, Mr. Havenhurst, because Cooper is free. But what about T.J.? He's locked up in jail for something he didn't do! You just don't give a damn that your son caused all this trouble, do you?" Her eyes were blazing with anger; the personal humiliation of minutes earlier had vanished.

Havenhurst shook his head sadly, opening the front door. "There's nothing more I can say."

"Good night, Mr. Havenhurst," Buckley replied curtly, and left.

As Havenhurst closed the door behind her with a solid thud, Buckley suddenly knew this rejection was symbolic of the way she and T.J. were being locked out. No one wanted any part of them or their trouble. They were a problem with no easy solution.

Chapter 7

Alphonse impatiently awaited Vivian's arrival at Gate 41 of the airline terminal. The past week had been one of the most unpleasant in memory, and this next week wasn't starting better.

The Tuesday before, against Vivian's specific instructions over the phone, Alphonse and Buckley had returned to Grasslands, spoken once again with the juvenile authorities and come away thoroughly disheartened.

He was astonished to discover the cold reality facing young T.J. It was impossible for Alphonse to believe that after a preliminary hearing the authorities still had the right to hold T.J. up to thirty days for further investigation. All the sympathy and good intentions in the world didn't matter if they weren't also specified by the lumbering, antiquated code of juvenile justice. Since Vivian refused to return immediately and take custody of her son, Alphonse even offered to be personally responsible for the boy if the facility would release T.J. into his custody. It wouldn't.

More disturbing still was the news Alphonse had received on Thursday afternoon. He was having lunch with a member of the company board of directors, a personal friend of Simpson's for many years and one of the three outside directors. After careful discussion about the upcoming vote on Alphonse's becoming president of the company, this director casually inquired whether or not Alphonse knew of any reason why he should be under investigation. Was there, the director put it discreetly, any past impropriety in Alphonse's business or personal life which might surface at this inopportune time and render the board's current decision impossible?

Alphonse kept his composure. "Nothing," was his unequivocal answer.

Immediately after lunch Alphonse returned to his office at company headquarters, where he left strict orders not to be interrupted. Within an hour he had obtained the information he sought.

Vivian Simpson had requested, and the board had granted, a thorough investigation of Alphonse. This was not just the normal run-through. Vivian made sure the information would cover Alphonse from the time he was born.

Beads of sweat formed on Alphonse's upper lip and at his temples. He knew perfectly well what such an investigation would uncover. Thirty years ago, when he and Buck Simpson first met, Alphonse had been completely candid. Later, when Simpson offered him a job, the company was still family-owned and -operated. Buck Simpson dismissed as the indiscretion of youth what would now surely be part of the evidence used as adequate grounds for the board to refuse Alphonse his long-sought promotion.

As a young man Alphonse had barely graduated from high school. He came from a coal-mining region in the eastern Pennsylvania mountains. No one in his family had ever attended college. Every male descendant, including Alphonse, had gone to work in the mines. Determined that life would hold something better for his own children, Alphonse cheated on his entrance exams and won a scholarship to the state university. While in college, he made living expenses by working nights as a bouncer for a small-time racketeer named Damian, who ran a private gambling club on the city's outskirts. It was through Damian that Alphonse met a man named Benjamin who, among other services, had begun to specialize in lending large amounts of money to otherwise-legitimate businesses in return for future favors. Eventually it was Alphonse who put Buck Simpson in contact with Benjamin when his boss and mentor needed a discreet loan to tidy up company losses.

As Alphonse sat in his office overlooking the gleaming city and both its rivers, those days seemed a million years ago. But if Vivian intended to use the information to ruin his professional career, Alphonse knew without a doubt that she would. He was the major obstacle standing between her and the power that came with voting shares of stock from Buck Simpson's estate. Alphonse had previously opposed her efforts to get actively involved in corporate policy on more than one occasion. Now she would try again, armed with additional ammunition. She would discredit him as trustee, name her own bank and become a formidable adversary.

As long as he had the backing of the board of directors and a publicly unblemished record, Alphonse could prevail. However, Vivian was now calculating her move to unseat him permanently. Something told him he might be in real danger of losing this round to her. If he did, that was the end of his career at the company. He would be forced to resign in disgrace.

His ability to protect T.J. and Buckley according to Simpson's last wish would also be denied. Alphonse was trapped. If he persisted in helping Simpson's children, Vivian cleverly threatened to remove the tangible rewards of his entire life's work.

"Alphonse, I'm at my wits' end with that boy." Vivian began her conversation the minute she spotted him at the airport. "No matter what school I put him in, he either runs away or gets himself expelled. Now he's been arrested! He's simply too much for me to handle."

Alphonse took the carry-on luggage from her. He led the way briskly through the crowded terminal while her voice hammered at him. The way Vivian treated him, you'd think he was her chauffeur, not the acting president of her late husband's corporation and executor of his estate. But Vivian had an annoying habit of treating everyone around her like a servant. On more than one occasion Alphonse had seen her reduce competent executives and grown men to groveling attendants. Despite a growing fear over his personal future, he was deeply annoyed with her irresponsible behavior during this past week.

Alphonse studied Vivian as they made their way down the escalator. She was astonishingly beautiful in a carefully managed way that women with money can be after they turn forty. She was slender from hours spent at the gym and under the hands of a most capable masseuse. Her face showed no sign of tension. Even after a vacation, the color of her hair was perfect, no gray, no dark roots. Simpson had spent too much money on her jewelry, but she wore it very well.

"Buckley and I have been deeply concerned. She's . . ." Alphonse began.

"This is none of Buckley's business! Nor yours, I might add," Vivian snapped viciously. "You'd better remind her of that fact. She's not to interfere with my son in any way, Alphonse. Believe me, that girl pretends to be sweet and concerned, but all she really wants is to make trouble."

Alphonse hated confrontations and wished he were safely at home with his wife, Carolyn.

"You know he's sitting in *jail* right this minute! What concerns me is the newspapers' getting wind of it. They love that sort of tawdry gossip. Neither you nor I nor our company can afford a stupid, petty scandal right now," Vivian continued.

"I know that, Vivian. But what is it you expect me to do?" Alphonse asked quietly.

"I want your help, Alphonse."

Vivian's voice sounded sincere, filled with genuine concern. Alphonse could actually hear the tears begin. It was a warning to him. He knew to be very careful.

"T.J. has to have a completely different environment."

Alphonse waited for her next sentence until he realized she wasn't intending to be so transparent. She wanted him to fill in the blank spots. If he did, Vivian would behave as though the solution were his idea, absolving herself of responsibility.

Alphonse had been this route with Vivian before, particularly during conversations which dealt with getting control over company stock. She always started with a seemingly innocent statement, but he'd learned that Vivian was never innocent.

Alphonse was determined not to do her bidding unwittingly. For once he was going to force her out in the open, even if it had to be with silence. He wished he could see into that brain of hers. If only he could ferret out what she was up to. His instinct told him it involved her husband's entire estate as well as her son. In his will Simpson had left equal shares of his majority holding of company stock to Vivian and Buckley. At present Buckley was no threat to her because she couldn't vote or sell her shares. At this time Vivian knew Alphonse was the key since he was trustee, controlling all their stock.

The company limousine and driver were waiting for them immediately outside the airport baggage claim area. Vivian realized Alphonse was not going to cooperate easily. She would have to handle him carefully.

As she gracefully settled into the limousine, she said, "You know T.J. . . . you've know him since he was a little boy. You're executor of the estate, trustee, practically his guardian. Even before this incident he was having a terrible time . . . trouble at school, poor grades. He needs the influence of men . . . real men." Her voice wavered. "You can understand how badly I feel not being able to give him that. Even though my husband was only his stepfather, he loved that boy like his own. T.J. can't seem to adjust to losing him." She turned her head toward the window, putting on a very good impersonation of the grieving widow.

Alphonse still said nothing but sat staring straight ahead as the limousine pulled out of the airport and onto the highway.

"The fact is that T.J. has become increasingly unstable. The school sends me reports of his violent behavior and even suggests the need for psychiatric treatment. Alphonse, I don't want to have T.J. committed to a mental institution, but if this continues, I may have no other choice." Vivian continued in a direct manner. "But there may be a better way. If he could be sent quietly out of the country—put in one of those Australian mining camps for five years or maybe signed on one of those merchant ships going around the world. A structured environment, the company of men—I'm sure it would do him a world of good." She smiled. "Of course, he mustn't have his passport, and we wouldn't say it was for a long time; you could just tell him it was a spring vacation . . . an adventure." Vivian leaned toward him seductively, fully expecting his acquiescence.

"Je-sus!" was the only word that escaped Alphonse as he listened in morbid fascination. If Vivian could figure out a way secretly to eliminate T.J., she would never have to share any of the estate with him. The boy would simply disappear, and there would be no possible chance for a future alliance between Buckley and T.J. Vivian would ensure her base of power.

Without giving him any more time to think the situation over, Vivian moved closer. "Alphonse, it's important. This isn't just my personal problem, you know. Do you think I'd be talking to you if it was? If that boy causes any more trouble or hurts someone during one of his idiotic pranks, which seem to happen with alarming regularity these days, it would be terrible; it'll reflect on all of us. As trustee of the estate you should feel at least partially responsible. Think of your own future, your lovely family. Don't forget, you're next in line for company president. Maybe even chairman of the board someday. I might be able to give you just the support you need in return for a small favor right now."

Alphonse stared at her, feeling angry frustration welling up in him. He wondered if she knew he had already been told about the investigation she ordered. He felt paralyzed by her ability to lie so perfectly.

Reluctantly he had to admit that in a perverted way she was right. As deeply as Alphonse cared about the two kids, he couldn't risk losing his job over them. After a lifetime of hard work he was on the verge of tremendous success. Running the company had been his dream of many years. At the annual board of directors' meeting only a month away, that dream could easily become reality. Only Vivian could stop him. Alphonse knew she would not hesitate to use both the investigation threat and her personal influence with the board of directors to get what she wanted from him. He must take a strong stand now. He couldn't let her know how threatened he felt. He needed time to find his way around her, a plan to alter her destructive course.

"Vivian, he's your son," Alphonse said in a steady, firm tone. "You can't simply decide one day that you don't want him around anymore and discard him. If I had anything to do with this madness, I'd probably be arrested for kidnapping! What will happen if he can't take it? If he jumps ship or runs away from the mines, what chance do you think he's going to have alone in a foreign country at fifteen without even a passport?"

"That's his problem. If he won't obey the rules, he's got to learn the world will punish him." Her voice was cold as ice.

"No, Vivian. I will not be a part of this. It's barbaric. I won't have anything to do with it."

She was furious, but her voice remained remarkably calm. "You'll be sorry, Alphonse, and that's *my* promise."

The long black limousine sped noiselessly through the darkness toward the distant city lights. None of them noticed the undistinguished blue sedan that had been following them since they pulled out of the airport terminal.

Chapter 8

Across the sparse but tastefully decorated law office reception room, an antique clock chimed six times. Buckley folded her magazine and put it back on the large wooden coffee table.

It seemed to Buckley as though she had lost her bearings in her own world. At work following the weekly staff meeting, when she tried to confide in Mr. Henry, her boss and her father's longtime friend, he became visibly nervous, saying that he preferred to keep personal problems out of the office environment. Over dinner the next evening Tony Marshall advised her pointedly not to meddle in other people's business if she wanted to advance her career. He said that nothing ruined your chances faster than becoming known as a troublemaker. Buckley decided that was their last date. Not even his incredible body, bronzed by a recent Caribbean holiday, could make up for the distaste she felt toward him. He had no right to give her orders.

But it was Alphonse who puzzled Buckley most.

Alphonse, her trusted and loyal friend, had become sullen, nervous and distant. Although he vowed his only concern was for their wellbeing and safety, he, too, warned Buckley to drop the pressure she was putting on everyone to help T.J. and to stop demanding intervention in a situation which was not her concern. Alphonse had taken a decidedly hands-off attitude toward both of them. He was quite firm in his decision that Vivian should handle the juvenile authorities. When Buckley angrily accused him of not caring about T.J., the look on his face confirmed her suspicion that she was absolutely correct. He wanted nothing to do with the problem. He made it clear that he did not wish to be placed in the middle of a confrontation between Vivian and Buckley.

She remembered staring at him in disbelief, feeling that he'd turned into an enemy before her astonished eyes. "It's a damn good thing my father's not alive to hear you talk like that, Alphonse," she'd told him, feeling her temper flare. "He must be turning in his grave!" were the last words she said to Alphonse before leaving his office.

Never before had Buckley realized what a temper she possessed. The first time occurred when the attorney she offered a retainer fee to handle T.J.'s release told her he couldn't accept the case.

"Why not?" she'd asked.

"A conflict of interest," he replied.

"What does that mean?"

"We've done legal work in the past for both the company and Crestview School," he said impersonally. "It's strictly a matter for the school's headmaster, the boy's mother and the juvenile authorities. Miss Simpson, I realize you have a deep emotional involvement here, but my law firm has a practice to maintain in this city. I'm afraid we'd appear rather foolish to our fellow professionals if we took a case against our most prestigious prep school, the widow of a leading businessman philanthropist and the state juvenile justice system . . . particularly a case without merit."

"Where did you get the idea this case was without merit? My stepbrother never took that car. Everyone knows it, and no one will do anything!" Buckley demanded with growing irritation.

"Well . . ." He hesitated briefly "This is really a small community. The parties involved are not exactly strangers to several of our senior partners and their wives."

Without giving him an opportunity to insult her further, Buckley gathered her belongings and stormed out of his office.

Her anger was followed by a tiredness she'd never known before either. It was as though she were becoming a stranger to herself, undependable and irritated. There was something missing in her everyday exchanges with other people. She felt a growing distance between herself and her friends, including the men and women with whom she worked. Intuitively she sensed even her job was now precarious. Her anger and frustration were building an invisible wall around her she couldn't reach beyond. She wasn't able to free T.J. or get help herself. There was no doubt that she hadn't been an efficient employee or pleasant company during these last two weeks, but it disappointed her to see people she'd considered friends, like Alphonse, so quickly absent themselves.

She stared at the reception-room clock in disbelief and, with a sigh of exasperation, walked over to the receptionist. The woman was covering her typewriter for the night. She had a pleasant plain face. Buckley guessed her to be about fifty.

"Excuse me, but could you check again for Mr. Stevenson?"

The receptionist finished smoothing the typewriter cover and smiled. "Of course." She pressed a single button on her telephone. "Miss Simpson would like to know how much longer before Mr. Stevenson is free." As she listened to the reply, a flicker of surprise crossed her face. "Thank you," she said, replacing the receiver slowly. When she turned to face Buckley, it was with reluctance.

"Miss Simpson . . . I'm very sorry . . . but, Mr. Stevenson has left for the day."

"What!" Buckley gasped. "He's gone? But . . . but I left work early to see him. I had a four o'clock appointment . . . I've been waiting *two hours*!"

"I know. I'm terribly sorry."

"Damn it!" Buckley exploded. "How could he do that? He knew I was here waiting . . . we had an appointment."

"I'm very sorry," the receptionist repeated.

"Sorry doesn't do me much good, does it?" Buckley snapped. The receptionist shrugged her shoulders, reaching in the bottom drawer for her purse.

"I'm sorry. I didn't mean to be rude," Buckley apologized. "It's not your fault. It's just that for the past two weeks I've been turned down by every other law firm I've called. I didn't expect this. Mr. Stevenson and my father were good friends . . . for *years*."

Sadly the receptionist nodded her head. "I know."

"What am I going to do now?" Buckley sighed deeply as she turned away from the older woman and walked to the chair where she'd left her purse. She was exhausted. She just didn't seem to have the strength to fight this wall of indifference, this barricade of rudeness.

"Have you by any chance tried legal aid?" the receptionist's kind voice asked quietly.

Buckley picked up her purse, fighting back tears of discouraged embarrassment. "Legal aid?"

"There are some fine younger attorneys who volunteer their time. Maybe someone there could help you." The receptionist scribbled information on a piece of paper and offered it to Buckley.

So it's come to this, Buckley thought as she stared at the well-meaning woman and took the piece of paper. Buckley Simpson, daughter of the wealthy and powerful chairman of the board, reduced to begging for handouts. She felt thoroughly humiliated. Buckley could feel tears welling up in her eyes, blurring the handwriting.

"Thank you," she said quietly, stuffing the piece of paper in her purse. Before the tears started falling down her face, Buckley turned and quickly left the office.

Fortunately she found herself alone in the elevator. In the building lobby there was a small newsstand. She bought a packet of tissues, opened them immediately and blew her nose. The old man shook his head emphatically.

"Bad day, huh?"

"Terrible!" Buckley muttered and left immediately.

As he watched her walking quickly away from him, the old man shook his head. Such a pretty young thing, he thought. Much too young to be having terrible days. Seems like this world just gets harder and harder for folks. The old man began closing up.

Buckley hurried to her car in the underground parking garage. She barely noticed the man sitting in a dark sedan several spaces away from her car. She was cold, hungry, discouraged, and wanted to get home.

After driving several blocks, Buckley stepped on the brake, swerving to avoid a large pothole she saw in the road at the very last moment. Automatically she checked her rearview mirror to make sure she wasn't going to cause an accident in the process. A thought flashed across her mind that the blue sedan directly behind her was very similar to the car she'd seen in the garage several minutes earlier.

Buckley didn't know that this same blue sedan had also followed Vivian and Alphonse as they left the airport, nor could she know that the rather muscular man in his late twenties who was driving the car had been responsible for changing her life.

That's odd, she thought. Could that man possibly be following me? She tried to dismiss a creeping feeling of discomfort. After all, this was a main street in town. Lots of people used it instead of the expressway on their way home to the suburbs. Just to be sure she was imagining things, Buckley turned quickly onto a side street without signaling.

The blue sedan expertly turned the sharp corner. Sam couldn't resist a smile of admiration as he spun the steering wheel rapidly. This girl was a good driver. Spunky. She was going to be amusing, might even turn out to be pretty.

Buckley was now convinced it was not imagination. Someone was actually following her. She tried to think where the nearest police station was located. Her hands began to shake as she clutched the steering wheel. She tried to note any significant details about the car behind her, but it was too dark. All she could see was that it was a blue sedan, nondescript and standard.

Buckley drove faster, trying to lose the blue car behind her in the rush-hour traffic. She was no match for the man following her.

As traffic thinned out, the blue sedan began closing the distance. When there were only the two cars left on the road, the blue sedan accelerated, but to her enormous relief Buckley saw the bright lights of the police station and a line of parked squad cars in front of her.

"Damn it!" Sam muttered to himself as he saw her head for the safe haven of the police station. He floored the accelerator and sped toward the darkness. She must not be the one I want after all, or she'd never go to the cops. It must be the other one, he concluded as the blue sedan raced along the two-lane road at high speed.

As Buckley pulled into the police station, she saw the blue sedan speed past her. Before the car disappeared, the rear plate was momentarily illuminated. She took a pen out of her purse and quickly jotted the information on the back of a deposit slip in her checkbook.

Buckley pulled into the precinct parking lot and sat thinking for a few minutes, trying to sort things out in her mind and calm down.

She wasn't sure just what to do next. How could she report something like this? She had no description of the man.

She gathered up her courage and decided to talk to

an officer inside the station. Even if they couldn't do anything, maybe the lunatic who followed her was wanted on some other charge and the license number would help track him down.

The desk sergeant was a woman. Buckley walked up to her, took a deep breath and began.

"I'd like to report that someone was following me," she said quietly, still feeling unsure of herself. "I got the license number. It was a man in a blue sedan," she continued while searching her purse until she located her checkbook. Buckley opened the checkbook and showed the scribbled information to the sergeant.

"There's not much we can do about your allegation; it's just a suspicion unless you were accosted in some way. Were you?" the sergeant inquired.

"No," Buckley said, feeling sheepish and instantly paranoid.

"I'll take the license number and run a check on it. If you'll answer the questions on these forms, I'll register your complaint for the record."

"Thank you," Buckley mumbled, and dutifully began responding to the impersonal questions regarding time, place, car make and model. It suddenly seemed like such an unnecessary waste of time. With everything else the police had to do, who in the world cared about some girl being followed?

"Evening, Mary," a strangely familiar male voice said.

Buckley turned toward the door to see a tall hawk-faced man dressed in regular street clothes enter the station with two uniformed officers.

"What are you doing out here, John?" the desk sergeant asked.

"Homicide near the river," John Needham replied, noticing the young woman standing at the counter. Needham remembered her vaguely. It suddenly came to him. Laughing Fish Lodge. Hunting accident. Simpson's daughter. Needham had become rather famous within department circles for solving impossible cases with the help of his phenomenal memory.

"Miss Simpson?"

Buckley looked at this stranger half in apprehension and half with curiosity. Who was he? How did this man know her name? She didn't recognize him as a familiar person, but he must be with the police department from the way he spoke to the desk sergeant.

"John Needham," he said by way of explanation. Realizing she didn't associate his name with their previous meeting, he added, "I was one of the investigators at the time of your father's accident."

"Of course . . . I'm sorry I didn't place you."

"Understandable," Needham replied. "What's the problem tonight, Miss Simpson?" he inquired politely.

"Mr. Needham, I'm sure someone was following me. I took down the car's license plate number and wanted to report it."

"Hmmm . . . Sergeant Jameson, may I have a look at the report?" he asked the desk officer. She obligingly handed him the paperwork.

John Needham rarely took written notes. He never willingly created the impression of seeming overly curious. But tonight he took out his small note pad and wrote down a description of the vehicle and its license number. In less than a minute he returned the report to Mary Jameson.

"Miss Simpson, this is not the safest area for a

young woman alone in her car at night. If you'd like, I'd be glad to see you home."

"Thank you, Mr. Needham. I'd appreciate it," Buckley replied gratefully.

After these past few weeks she was quite willing to accept whatever assistance might be forthcoming. She had no reason to be afraid of a police officer and appreciated his gesture of kindness.

"Good night, Mary . . . Steve . . . Jim," Needham said to the sergeant and uniformed officers standing near the desk.

As she watched Needham leaving the station, Mary Jameson wondered at his suddenly humanitarian behavior. He was as tough and callous a man as the police force ever turned out.

"How's your brother doing?" Needham asked as he and Buckley descended the precinct house steps. "I remember he took your father's death very badly."

"Mr. Needham, it's been awful," Buckley replied, with an openness resulting from days of rejection. "He's up in Grasslands right now."

"Grasslands? What for?"

"It's a terrible foul-up in the system I don't fully understand. Two weeks ago he was a passenger in a car one of the boys took from boarding school without permission. They had a fight, and my brother was returning the car when they were arrested. All the other boys have been released. But T.J.'s mother, Vivian, won't sign the papers taking responsibility for him, and I can't seem to get anyone else to help us."

It seemed so natural to pour out her troubles to John Needham. Perhaps it was his fleeting association with her father, perhaps it was his status as an officer of a legal system she wasn't yet willing to abandon that made him appear to be the perfect listener.

"I'm very sorry to hear that," he said, removing a business card and offering it to her. "I'm not involved with the juvenile division, but call me if you continue to have problems."

"Thanks," Buckley responded with gratitude. Right at that moment she made the decision to pursue the possibility of legal aid.

"By the way, was Vivian Simpson ever a model or an actress before she married your father? Her face seemed familiar," Needham asked casually as he watched Buckley unlock her car door.

"I only know that she was divorced, had lived in California for a few years and seemed to be independently wealthy. I don't remember Vivian's ever mentioning a job or career. All T.J. ever said was that she traveled a lot."

Needham nodded thoughtfully. "I'll follow you," he said, and walked quickly to his unmarked police car.

As Needham got back into his car, he made a mental note to run a quick check on Vivian Simpson. He had remembered something about the woman that triggered an old grudge.

Chapter 9

It took Needham several days to locate the long-buried information and arrange a meeting with Alphonse. They agreed on lunch at the newly opened Grand Concourse restaurant. It was near the company headquarters and a great favorite of Alphonse's in recent months.

Needham descended the stairs into the glimmering baroque restoration of what had previously been the downtown railroad station. After years of neglect this relic of the heyday of railroad travel had been turned into one of the city's most spectacular eating establishments.

The popularity of the Grand Concourse was evident. It was not quite twelve-thirty, and already the place was full. Needham announced himself to the headwaiter and was taken to a small booth to await Alphonse.

After ordering coffee, John Needham took a moment to study his opulent surroundings, so different from the environment normally encountered in the daily round of a homicide detective. John

Needham wondered if he looked as out of place as he felt. He'd preferred to have ordered a drink along with the rest of the clientele, but if he drank, it was on his own time late at night and usually alone. The years of being suspicious and cautious had not permitted him to let his guard down with other human beings. He was not aware of being lonely. It was just a way of life.

Alphonse checked his watch, annoyed at being late for this meeting. He'd been taken by surprise when the call from Needham came through two days ago. Not once since that afternoon six months ago in the north woods had Alphonse even thought about the hawk-faced detective. Alphonse had his hands full now running the company while trying to defend himself against Vivian's attempts to discredit him as trustee. His patient wife, Carolyn, was complaining that she never saw her husband anymore, that work was all that seemed to interest him. It wasn't that Alphonse loved his work so much as that he had to spend the time just trying to stay even with it. The organizational genius of Buck Simpson was sorely missed, as were his good judgment and ability to see priorities so clearly.

With minimal apologies Alphonse sat opposite John Needham and ordered a double scotch on the rocks.

"This is quite a place." Needham opened their conversation casually. "I haven't been here since the old days when it was still the train station."

"They've done a fantastic job." Alphonse nodded appreciatively. "Our company was one of the private donors."

The waitress brought Alphonse's drink and the menus. Both men ordered quickly, knowing that they didn't have much time.

"Why did you want to see me?" Alphonse asked the detective.

Needham leaned toward his companion slightly, intending to lower his voice from its normal conversational level.

"It's about Vivian Simpson. I couldn't quite place where I'd seen her before. Then last week I saw Buckley Simpson again, quite by accident. I was reminded of her father's death and remembered something didn't quite match up."

Painful as it was for Alphonse to remember the specifics of his first meeting with Needham, the man now had his complete attention.

"I started checking with some old sources and came up with a couple of things I wanted to discuss with you."

"Such as?"

"How long did you know Mr. Simpson?"

"Over twenty years."

"Do you know how he met Mrs. Simpson?" Needham's eyes narrowed as he waited for the answer.

"Yes. He met her on a yachting vacation with some business friends."

"Was one of those friends a man with the first name of Benjamin?"

"Yes, as a matter of fact, it was."

Needham nodded his head with satisfaction. So far the pieces fitted. "Did Mr. Simpson know that she was working for Benjamin?"

"No, I don't believe he did," Alphonse replied quietly as the waitress brought their lunch orders. "What did she do?"

Needham smiled sardonically. "That would be hard to prove after all these years, but my suspicion is that she was his primary courier, among other things."

"Courier?" Alphonse asked cautiously.

"Benjamin was a high-class smuggler in the old days. Dealt in drugs and classified information. My hunch is that she did most of the traveling and delivered the stuff personally. She used to be considered part of the international jet set, which would fit in with the little information Buckley Simpson gave me about T.J.'s never knowing what his mother did to earn a living but remembering that she used to travel all the time."

Alphonse leaned back in his chair. So, he thought, I'm not the only one with a skeleton in the closet. Little did John Needham know that he'd just given Alphonse the edge he needed in his present battle with Vivian over control of the company voting stock. If she continued to threaten him with exposure, he wouldn't have to bend over and take it. He could strike back.

"What does this have to do with Mr. Simpson's death?" Alphonse asked Needham.

"I'm not sure yet. It's a long way from having a highly questionable past to being implicated in murder."

"Murder?" Alphonse said almost too loudly, sitting upright and at full attention. "Are you talking about Buck Simpson?"

Needham's look cautioned him to speak quietly. "At the moment all I have are the slimmest pieces of evidence and some nagging suspicions. However, I think they're worth pursuing, and I wanted to find out what you knew."

"My God!" Alphonse exclaimed. "If there's any doubt that Mr. Simpson's death was not an accident

. . . I'll help you any way I can!"

"It might be best if you didn't say anything about our meeting to anyone. There's no use alarming the family or the company, and I wouldn't want the press to get wind of this right now. There's no substantial evidence yet."

"Of course," Alphonse agreed.

"By the way," Needham asked casually, "do you know if Mrs. Simpson ever had a separate checking account of her own?"

As executor of the Simpson estate Alphonse knew the answer immediately. "Yes," he replied. "In fact, she had both a checking and savings account. When we began work on the estate, I was rather surprised to learn that they were more substantial than even the generous household allowance she received during the time of her marriage would have accounted for, unless she'd come into the marriage with money of her own, and I never remember Mr. Simpson saying anything about that."

"I see." Needham nodded thoughtfully. "Could you tell me which bank?"

"First City," Alphonse replied without hesitation. "But I don't understand what Vivian's bank accounts have to do with this."

"Maybe nothing, but thank you for your cooperation, Mr. Mazzo."

Now it was Needham who looked at his watch. "I'll have to be going. Thanks for lunch." Needham stood, making no attempt to pay his share.

"There is one thing . . . the night before Mr. Simpson died he told me of his plans to change his will. I got the impression he was also going to divorce Vivian. But he was killed the next day."

"Are you sure about that?" Needham asked.

"Absolutely."

"That might be enough to reopen this case," Needham replied seriously. "Call me if you think of anything else."

"I will," Alphonse assured him, shaking hands.

Needham quickly disappeared into the crowd of luncheon guests now departing the huge restaurant, leaving Alphonse to ponder the impact of their strange meeting.

As much as he disliked Vivian, it was still hard to imagine that beautiful, composed woman could have been involved in murder. Vivian had proved easily that she was in her apartment building at the time Buck Simpson died. There had been a dozen witnesses who saw her at the health club that day.

Alphonse wasn't sure he could trust John Needham either. He was arrogant in an uncomfortable way. Why in the world should he be interested in an accidental death case that had only peripherally involved him in the first place? None of this was making sense. The only useful piece of information Needham seemed to have was about Vivian's past with Benjamin. The more Alphonse found out about Vivian, the less he understood why Buck married her. However, if he stood in her way, she could jeopardize his current career. Fortunately, there was a temporary stalemate. No major changes could be undertaken at the company until the estate came out of probate. Alphonse knew that Vivian was working ceaselessly behind the scenes to achieve her goals, and it wouldn't be long before she let him know exactly what they were. He would have to be careful. The worst thing in the world right now would be a family scandal or an open confrontation with her. He was not yet prepared to go to war with Vivian Simpson.

Chapter 10

Buckley made an excuse to leave work on Thursday to go to the legal aid office. Just two days from now T.J. would begin serving his third week in jail.

The dingy building was in a terrible section of town. The streets were dirty. Even in the cold weather there was the lingering smell of garbage. It was a decaying melting-pot neighborhood, and Buckley sensed she stuck out like a sore thumb.

During the long days since Buckley last visited T.J. at Grasslands, she had found herself consistently feeling out of place. What shocked her most was the indifference she encountered in the people she asked for help.

How could they turn their backs so calmly? How could they live with the knowledge that an innocent boy was in jail? It was beyond Buckley's ability to comprehend.

The elevator door creaked shut. Buckley pushed the button for what should be the fourth floor. The number on the button had worn off long ago. She noticed the empty space where inspection certificates are usually placed, which brought forth a resurgence of her terrible fear of elevators. Alone in this old elevator right now, she could feel her heart beating faster. Her hands turned clammy. She had to take a few deep breaths, hoping the doors would open immediately at the fourth floor.

She was so intent on getting off she nearly bumped into the two elderly women who were waiting. She barely noticed them except for the dark clothing and shopping bags.

Down one corridor and halfway along the next, she found the room marked "409—Legal Aid." She stood for a moment, gathering her courage. When she opened the door, it was like walking into bedlam.

The small space was crammed with people. The air was stale, smelling of nervous sweat. She heard the sound of crying mixed with an argument. Old people, young people, the desperate and impoverished. There were no private offices, only a reception area with a multilingual girl giving out numbers. Buckley took an information card which she was to fill out and stood inconspicuously against a far wall.

She felt dazed, descending into a kind of terrified stupefaction. She felt an enormous urge to bolt for the exit door. Did her face have that same hollow, cornered look of the other people waiting for help?

Through the fog of her own anxiety she listened to muffled conversations. The drone of human confusion and misery was endless. This place was a hospital for the invisible injuries of civilization, an emergency ward for social casualties.

As she stood leaning against the once-green wall, Buckley saw the looks of helplessness on lawyers' faces each time the door opened and another group of walking wounded arrived.

Just as she was about to give up and leave after

waiting two hours, Buckley heard her number called. A rather disheveled young man with a shock of curly black hair stood and repeated the number she held clasped in her hand. Buckley waved it at him as a reply, and quickly gathered up her purse and coat.

"Sit down, I'm Seymour Feinberg, what's the problem?" he said without pausing in the usual places. His shirt was rumpled from being worn too many hours; a heavy beard had grown visibly since he shaved this morning. He was tired but evidenced an interest that might be pure nervous energy but passed quite well for genuine concern. His pencil was held at attention, a clean yellow sheet of lined legal tablet waiting for the information.

"Why don't you just start at the beginning and let's see what we find?" Seymour asked with surprising gentleness. He guessed she was about twenty, from a good family and in some sort of trouble she couldn't tell her parents or friends. He took time to study her pretty, clean face, her long, shiny hair. In the temporary silence between them, he found himself wishing they'd met under different circumstances.

Buckley looked up from studying her nervous hands, clenched tightly in her lap. She thought Seymour's face not particularly attractive, but it seemed intelligent. His olive skin in the harsh fluorescent overhead light had visible signs of past teenage acne. His dark hair was a tumble of tiny curls, unruly and receding from his forehead, making his face seem longer and more serious than it must have been when he was younger. Buckley guessed him to be about thirty.

"Mr. Feinberg, I need help," she began hesitantly.

Seymour wondered how often he'd heard those exact words, seen that look of embarrassed desperation. "Please, just Seymour."

"Seymour . . . what I mean is . . . my stepbrother, T.J., needs help, and I'm able to pay you for it."

"Where is he?" Seymour asked, ready to write down the information.

"In Grasslands," she replied quietly. "For two weeks and I can't get him out."

Seymour looked up at her with an expression of surprise. "Why is he there?"

"It's a bit hard to explain, but . . . he was in a car with a group of boys from boarding school. T.J. didn't know it, but Cooper Havenhurst took the headmaster's car without permission. Sort of a prank, I guess . . . a joyride. T.J. and Cooper had a fight, Cooper stormed off and T.J. was arrested for driving a stolen car. Well, T.J. and the other two boys were taken to Grasslands. But Hank and Willie were released to their parents the following morning."

"And T.J.?" Seymour asked, still writing. "Why didn't your parents do the same?"

"My father's dead," Buckley answered. "My stepmother, Vivian, T.J.'s mother, was away on vacation. I tried calling after she returned, but she doesn't return my calls. Mr. Williams won't agree to drop the charges. I tried to get Cooper's parents to help, but they don't want their son implicated. Hank and Willie are too scared of Cooper Havenhurst's family to open their mouths without being forced by the court, and Vivian won't cooperate with the court to set a final adjudication date."

Seymour looked directly at her. "Why not? T.J. is her responsibility."

"Of course, I know that . . . but she doesn't seem to!" Buckley replied angrily. "The only reason T.J. isn't back at school right now with all the other boys is that Vivian won't do anything!"

"Wait a minute . . . calm down. Getting angry all over again isn't going to do any good." Seymour studied his notes while Buckley took a deep breath, trying to get control of her anger.

"Under ordinary circumstances this matter wouldn't require an attorney," he said evenly. "Usually it's quite routine. Everyone agrees to cooperate, the charges are dropped, the juveniles are released and the incident is forgotten unless there's damage of one sort or another. Particularly in cases when the families have influence and all parties know one another."

"But these aren't exactly ordinary circumstances, are they?"

"It wouldn't appear that way . . . no."

"Do you think there's anything you can do to help us?" she asked, almost holding her breath for fear of hearing another rejection. "I told you, I'm not asking for a favor—I'm willing to pay your fee."

Seymour stared thoughtfully at his notes, then checked his watch. "It's nearly five o'clock. Too late to reach any of the probation or social workers up at county," he said. "Look, I know you're very upset, but why don't you just try to see this through the weekend? It's very likely that Vivian will arrange for his release tomorrow or Saturday. If she doesn't . . ." He paused long enough to reach into his pocket and pull out a business card. "Please call me on Monday," he said, handing her the card. "I'm in practice with my uncle. I'll speak to him about this, see if he has any further suggestions."

Buckley smiled gratefully, tucking the business card into her wallet. At least he hadn't said no.

"But . . . I don't want to give you false hope. Juvenile justice is not exactly my field of expertise. If we can't get this cleared up informally, we'll have a real mess on our hands. Have you ever been involved with juvenile court?''

She shook her head no.

''Well, let me warn you . . . it can be a real labyrinth.''

Buckley stood, not wanting to hear any more bad news today. ''Thank you, Seymour. I'm really grateful. I'll tell T.J. we've finally got some help.''

''I hope it'll all straighten itself out. If it doesn't, call me Monday.''

''Thanks . . . I will.'' She smiled and left.

Seymour quickly packed his briefcase and hurried out of the crowded office before he was handed the insurmountable problems of another client.

Rain came down in sheets against the windshield of his old green Dodge. Seymour was on his way to have dinner and spend Friday evening with his mother, Uncle Zachariah and Aunt Mina according to established family tradition. Zack and Mina had no children of their own. Seymour was like a son to them.

Something about these Friday nights together maintained a bond between Seymour and a world of orderliness that he didn't feel anywhere else. Seeing Aunt Mina light the candles, smelling the always-familiar kosher food, hearing the ancient prayers grounded Seymour in a sense of continuity, purpose and rightness nothing else matched.

As he drove through the downpour, Seymour wondered about the last client he'd seen today, the young woman named Buckley. It was so clear to him. Those two kids simply had nowhere to turn when trouble came. Every system with which they were now forced to deal held a basic assumption that there was an underlying family unit gluing together the complicated fabric of society. Without that family the system had very few alternatives.

Seymour had been reared in a strict, religious family. His father, named Isaiah, after the prophet, was a man whose only dream in life was to be a rabbi, but his dream was beyond the reach of a young immigrant struggling to earn a living in a new country.

Growing up, Seymour wondered if there was ever any real love between his father and himself. Try as he might, he was not able to pierce the barrier of stubborn righteousness with which Isaiah surrounded himself.

After graduating from public high school with honors, Seymour went to the city college on a scholarship, working nights and weekends for one of Uncle Zack's partners in a warehouse. Seymour wanted to follow in his uncle's footsteps and become a lawyer. He had seen Uncle Zack use his knowledge of law to make the world work for him, not against him.

It was a crushing disappointment to Isaiah when Seymour told his father that he was not going to be a rabbi. But the final break between father and son came when Seymour told Isaiah of his desire to enter the field of criminal law.

"You tell me you want to defend criminals?" Isaiah asked with despair. "How can a man be proud to have a son who takes up with criminals! Is that what they teach you in these colleges? You should be as ashamed of yourself as I will be of you. You disgrace us. We believe in the law, but you . . . you want criminals free."

Seymour swore at his father for his ignorance and refusal to listen to anyone else's opinion. Isaiah struck Seymour across the mouth. "Out of my house!" his father screamed. "I have no son."

From that day until three years later, when Isaiah died suddenly of a heart attack at the age of fifty-two, father and son never spoke to each other again. Although Seymour had written a long letter of apology, asking forgiveness, the letter had been returned unopened. To his horror, Seymour found out that his father had even followed ancient Orthodox custom and for seven days had sat *shiva* for him, as their religion required when someone died, ritualistically mourning the death of his only child.

The world is a very strange place, Seymour thought, peering through the rain-splattered windshield into the night. He was glad it was Friday. He was glad he was going to Zack and Mina's. He was glad to be with family.

He remembered what Uncle Zack had said to him not long after the funeral. "You have to have a passion for life. If you lose that, there's nothing but problems to face. That's the key to everything. Open up your mind, boy!" Uncle Zack had shouted at Seymour. "Think of the possibilities. If you live with passion, everything you do is worth the effort."

The windshield wipers seemed to be losing their battle against the pouring rain by the time Seymour pulled his rattling car into his uncle's driveway. The lights in the living room glowed warmly as beacons welcoming him in from the storm. Inside the house he knew the table was already set. Friday night dinner was waiting to be served. Aunt Mina would say the prayers of thanksgiving, and Zack would launch happily into one of his many tirades against complacency.

Chapter 11

After meeting with Seymour and his uncle Zack twice during the week, it was decided that both Buckley and Seymour should visit Grasslands. Seymour drove them there in her car so erratically that Buckley sighed with relief when he pulled into the visitors' parking lot at Grasslands and found an empty space at the far end. He grabbed the briefcase and locked the car, looking at the huge detention building carefully for the first time. He wondered if there was a separate branch of architects that specialized only in ugly institutions.

Inside, where they had to register, the visitors' area was already full, even though it was not quite noon. Buckley and Seymour got coffee out of a machine and found a place to wait.

A deputy appeared at the desk. "Simpson?" her voice boomed loudly.

Buckley's head turned immediately. She put down her coffee and walked quickly to the information desk.

"Probation officer Watkins wants to see you. Follow me."

"I have a lawyer with me. We'd both want to be there."

"That's fine," the deputy answered without any hesitation.

Buckley hurried back to where Seymour was sitting. "We're to see T.J.'s probation officer."

They gathered their belongings quickly and followed the deputy out of the visitors' area. The woman walked with an almost military gait, keeping her jumble of keys ready for each door they went through, unlocking and locking carefully every time. Finally, she led them into a long corridor with doors on both sides.

"Second one on the left."

Buckley and Seymour continued walking until they came to Watkins's office. Seymour knocked, and a man's voice told them to come in.

"I'm Buckley Simpson." She introduced herself, holding out her hand. "This is our attorney, Seymour Feinberg." The two men shook hands.

The small office was piled floor to ceiling with folders, books and memorabilia. Watkins's desk was barely visible under the stacks of paperwork, files, coffee cups and two giant ashtrays filled to overflowing.

Watkins was about forty-five. His face was lined and weathered, but his eyes flashed and sparkled under bushy eyebrows. He was in good physical condition for a man who sat behind a desk most of his life.

"We have some problems." Watkins unceremoniously opened the conversation. "T.J. is not making life here any easier for himself. Apparently he has quite a history of difficulty with rules and authority."

Watkins spoke slowly. "First of all, as you know, Mrs. Simpson did not appear in court for the preliminary hearing on Monday, three days after T.J. was arrested. Since there was no one willing to corroborate his story, the arresting officers requested additional time to obtain at least one friendly witness. At first none of the boys was willing to make a statement, and their parents were uncooperative. Finally"—Watkins paused to check the notes in his file—"I think Willie Tilton will give us a statement substantiating everything your stepbrother originally told us."

"Then why can't you release him?" Buckley asked, realizing her voice sounded belligerent.

The probation officer looked weary, as though he'd been through this same conversation a thousand times before. "But even if Willie clears T.J., we are still required to return to court for a final adjudication. I'm afraid the court calendar is momentarily jammed. We've just had a series of gang-related arrests . . . all criminal charges and one murder. Judge Harding, who's presiding in T.J.'s case, has required a more complete investigation. However, T.J. is scheduled to return to court in about ten days. That's the best we can do."

Buckley took a deep breath, feeling herself shaking with anger. "So, if I understand correctly, Mr. Watkins, you're telling me that there's a way to prove T.J. is innocent of the charges against him but the system is in such a state of confusion that you can't let him go? Is that right?" Without waiting for him to answer her rhetorical question, Buckley continued. "Now that he can't be punished for any crime, he's being punished instead for the shortcomings of the court personnel! That's great! If he were an adult, if he were just two years older, we could get him out on bail. But because he's a kid, he sits here at the mercy of total incompetence and bureaucratic red tape. I'm not asking you to let a hardened criminal loose on society . . . I'm only trying to help an innocent boy!"

"I understand your anger, Miss Simpson, but I'm afraid the situation is even more complicated than you realize."

"More bad news?" Buckley asked sarcastically.

Watkins nodded. "According to the rules, we are supposed to release every juvenile to either a responsible adult or another institution, such as a correctional facility or alternative home placement. Lately we haven't always been able to do that, but we keep trying."

"I don't follow you. What's the problem?" Seymour asked.

Immediately Buckley felt her anger rising. Who had already gotten to this man? Who had been talking to him about T.J.?

"I want you to know from the outset that I'm on T.J.'s side," Watkins assured them. "He shouldn't even be here, in my opinion."

"If he shouldn't be here, then would you please explain to me why you've already detained him for nearly three weeks?"

"After several conversations with Mr. Williams, the headmaster at Crestview Boarding School, I have learned that the school is not going to readmit T.J. Mr. Williams wouldn't be specific; he simply stated it was not in the school's best interest and refused to elaborate further. So that option is closed," Watkins concluded bluntly.

Buckley was stunned by this new information. She'd never expected the school to do that. Havenhurst must have put a lot of pressure on Williams. Maybe Vivian had refused to pay the tuition. In any case, Mr. Williams had now assumed an active role in the conspiracy against T.J.

Watkins continued. "Mrs. Simpson does not want T.J. to live with her because she claims the boy is too difficult to handle all by herself. She insists on a complete psychiatric evaluation before T.J. is released."

"In short, it's an impasse," Seymour said, voicing Buckley's exact thoughts. "T.J.'s mother wants the state to take responsibility, and the court doesn't have any place to put him. Right?"

Watkins answered quickly. "She refuses to do anything constructive to help the situation. Instead of visiting him herself, she sent one of the lawyers from her husband's company to talk with him."

Watkins closed the file and folded his arms on the desk, studying Seymour and Buckley for their reaction. "It was the next day after that visit that T.J. began evidencing serious behavior difficulties."

"I'm not surprised," Buckley responded, showing her agitation. "How the hell would you feel?"

"The same way he does, I'm sure. But that's not what I hope you'll talk to him about. I know he trusts you, Buckley. He feels that you are the only person in his life who really cares about him. He may listen to you. *Please*, try to impress upon him that we're trying to do the best we can. We have very few alternatives. But he must try to cooperate with us, work *with* us to solve this, or it's going to get worse."

Watkins leaned toward them, speaking quietly. "Institutions don't have the same leeway, the same tolerance as the outside world. T.J. has to be careful, or things will go against him. His misbehavior here will become reason enough to hold him longer."

"Mr. Watkins, I know I'm a novice when it comes to understanding the process of juvenile justice, but it seems to me that there ought to be some reasonable alternative to holding an innocent boy for nearly a month!" Buckley said, trying to remain logical and calm.

"It's not that simple. I must remind you that although T.J. may not fit the category, we do have many juveniles in here who've committed felonies, everything from grand theft to murder. The community wants us to get tough, to prosecute more, spending less time and money on the frills."

"What frills?" Seymour inquired sarcastically.

Watkins understood the criticism but continued without giving Seymour the satisfaction of a debate. "Rehabilitation, long-term foster care, counseling."

"Mr. Watkins," Buckley interrupted, "I fail to see how that relates to T.J."

He studied her carefully as though evaluating one of his regular delinquents, deciding what part of her was true and what part was playing the inevitable con game the kids put him through.

"You may choose to overlook the fact that T.J. had quite a serious history of trouble before he ever got here. Unless I'm mistaken"—Watkins flipped through several pages in T.J.'s file—"the previous incidents include truancy, drug addiction, running away from school, acts of violence toward other students and now grand theft auto."

Buckley's eyes widened with horror as she heard

Watkins intone the official litany of offenses T.J. had supposedly commited.

"*That's* how you're trying to help him, Mr. Watkins?" Buckley said in moral outrage. "Where did you get those ideas? Did you bother to check any of these charges against T.J., or did you just swallow this horseshit whole?"

Seymour put his hand on Buckley's arm, trying to warn her not to cause a scene. He didn't know her well enough yet to realize it would be a futile gesture.

"I mean, did you ever ask T.J.? Did you listen to his side? Did you ask *anyone* else if this garbage you were so damn quick to enter in your file was true? Or doesn't truth matter to you either, Mr. Watkins?"

"Buckley, I think . . ." Seymour tried to intervene.

"Please, Seymour." She flashed him a plea for silence. "Even if you're not interested, Mr. Watkins, I'm going to fill you in. T.J. witnessed my father's death and nearly had a nervous breakdown because of it. There was never any doubt that T.J. had absolutely nothing to do with the accident because the bullet that killed my father could not have been fired from T.J.'s rifle. But it's haunted him ever since. Furthermore, T.J.'s running away from school occurred on a weekend when he couldn't go home with his mother because Vivian had other plans, and he came to see me. It was Vivian, not the school, who accused him of running away. As for the alleged drug addiction, T.J. and some other boys at Crestview got caught smoking pot—nothing more serious than that. Sure, he's been in some fights; how many boys haven't? As you can see, Mr. Watkins, we're not talking about a person who's dangerous to society. T.J. is not a delinquent, a felon or a murderer. He had nothing to do with any grand theft auto except be gullible enough to believe that spoiled brat Cooper Havenhurst. But I don't see Cooper in this medieval hell hole with a file on him, do you?"

She was shaking with anger when she finished, furious with the injustice heaped upon T.J. and frustrated to the point of tears by her inability to effect any change for the better.

Seymour had been trying to think of some solution. "Mr. Watkins, I'm sure you realize the boy is under a terrible strain. He's high-strung, but he's no juvenile delinquent. T.J. is not the sort of young person that can hold up under sustained pressure for very long." The trouble is, Seymour thought, T.J. can't fight this place all by himself.

"What's the best way for us to help T.J. right now?" Seymour asked Watkins in a professional tone of voice.

Mr. Watkins thought for a moment, looking from Seymour and Buckley to the closed file on his desk. His thumb flicked the edge of that file as though he were mentally clicking off possible answers. When he looked up, it was with candor and directness.

"First, try to find a relative or responsible adult willing to take custody of the boy. If you succeed, please remember that we will still have to obtain Mrs. Simpson's consent. Second, talk some sense to him. We've all got to help him see his way through these next ten days. He's going to be thoroughly evaluated by a county psychiatrist, Dr. Tanner. The better he conducts himself, the better his chances are." Watkins lowered his voice but spoke with some compassion. "It's really not such a terrible place if people cooperate. Believe me, we're not all monsters."

Buckley felt a cold shiver run through her body. How in the world was she going to convince T.J. that these people were here to help him? The place was a damn rat's maze, and T.J. was the rat. Like it or not, he would have to play their game, go along, not cause any trouble. In the meantime, she and Seymour had to work like hell to find a way to get T.J. out of Grasslands before he broke under the strain.

"Thank you, Mr. Watkins. We'll do everything we can." Seymour stood up, and the two men shook hands again. Buckley and Watkins looked directly into each other's eyes. She didn't trust him, but she had no choice. There on his desk was T.J.'s file. What Watkins entered in that file was going to affect T.J. for a long time. Buckley manufactured a smile and held out her hand.

"We depend on you, Mr. Watkins. I know you'll help T.J. Please call me if there's any emergency." Quickly she wrote her phone number on the front of T.J's file. "I love him very much. I'm sure you'll do everything you can. It's all right to visit him now, isn't it?"

"Of course. I'll call over and let them know."

Watkins studied the girl carefully as she and her attorney left. Her attitude toward T.J. was so unlike his mother's, Vivian Simpson, who had been in this office just three days before. The picture emerging from this meeting with Buckley and Seymour was completely different from what he had been led to believe previously. Maybe T.J. wasn't just another delinquent teenager. Maybe there was more to him than the unmanageable, violent-tempered young doper his mother had described with such desperation.

Watkins looked over his notes of their meeting carefully. At the time this distraught mother had elicited his sympathy. He was all too familiar with the unnervingly dispassionate criminals among many of the juveniles with whom he dealt.

In contrast, Buckley seemed genuinely concerned about T.J. There was a good relationship between the two. Maybe Watkins was wrong to write the boy off so quickly. After all, he'd been around too long to believe every good story he was told. He didn't want to fall into the trap of first impressions.

This was going to be a tough one, Watkins thought. Something didn't add up, particularly since T.J. had no previous record. It disturbed Watkins to think of what was ahead for the boy if he became part of this system's responsibility by sheer default of the world outside. Or worse, if finally they had to let him go, forcing the boy to make his own way alone on the streets.

Watkins shoved T.J.'s closed file to one side and took the next case folder off the top of the huge pile on his desk.

Seymour and Buckley drove halfway back to the city in silence, each trying to arrive at a workable plan.

"That son of a bitch Watkins! I can't believe he's doing everything he could." Seymour finally exploded. His normally placid face was crimson with anger.

"Now you know what I've been going through," Buckley answered with a strange feeling of relief that someone finally understood. "Could you stop somewhere along the river? I need to get out and walk."

Seymour pulled off the river road at the first spot marked "Scenic turnoff."

Buckley leaned her elbows on the heavy guard railing. She stared out across the silvery gray river.

Behind her the river park's trees were gently swaying in this afternoon's brisk wind. The sun was shining for the first time in days. Even the dark tugboats and somber river barges looked cleaner than usual. Across the wide river, row upon row of neatly painted houses stood out clearly, their windows catching an occasional glint of sunlight.

She felt strangely peaceful walking here, even with Seymour's indignation making him talk in a steady stream. Seen from this vantage point, the city didn't look so old, so industrial. She'd often wondered what it had been like to live here before the smoke, the constant rumbling of industry and the faint smell of chemicals intermittently filled the air.

"I'm hungry," she said suddenly. "Let's drive across the bridge. There's a great little Italian restaurant in the hill district."

Seymour looked at her strangely. "You weren't listening to me."

"Yes, I was. I heard every word. But I'm hungry. Can't I listen and be hungry at the same time?" She smiled.

Seymour shrugged his shoulders and shook his head in confusion. He put his arm around her lightly as they walked back to her car.

As Seymour negotiated the rather steep hillside streets, Buckley listened carefully to what he was saying.

"I talked to my uncle after calling the court yesterday. He agrees with me. The judge assigned to T.J.'s case is being unusually difficult, even though Zack doesn't have any great affection for judges," Seymour told her with a smile. "He suggested that Vivian may have contacted the judge herself."

"That would make a lot more sense than Watkins's mumbo jumbo . . . which makes me want to scream!" Buckley said as they trudged up the hill to the restaurant entrance.

Quickly settled into a corner booth, Buckley ordered soup, pasta and a side order of broccoli sautéed in oil and garlic. Seymour asked for sausage and peppers. They also decided on a bottle of red wine.

"What are we going to do?" Buckley asked. She felt oddly distracted, as though she couldn't quite grasp what was going on around her.

"Remember what Watkins said? The part about finding a relative . . . well, what about T.J.'s real father?"

Buckley's eyes brightened with interest. "Do you think we could find him?"

"How much do you know about the man?"

"Only that his name is Josh Marks and he used to live in California. But if he'd take custody of T.J., it might solve all the problems at once."

"Would Vivian ever consent to that?" Seymour asked skeptically.

"Good question," Buckley answered. "But if we don't find him, we'll never know the answer. Right?" She smiled with a faint glimmer of hope in her voice.

They sat in silence for a few minutes as the waitress poured the wine into two small glasses.

"Buckley, it's time we thought this whole thing through again." Seymour hesitated, not at all sure how she would react. "You mustn't take on more responsibility than you can handle. You've done everything you could." He emptied his glass with a couple of swallows and refilled it.

"Maybe that's what makes me feel so bad. Nothing I've tried to do has helped!"

"But that's not your fault!" Seymour said emphatically.

"Fault?" Buckley repeated, appearing strangely amused. "Fault? What does fault have to do with any of it? Is T.J. at *fault*? Mr. Watkins?"

The waitress brought a tray with their food and plunked everything down on the table in front of them.

Buckley looked across the table at her new friend, feeling overwhelmingly lonely again. When this feeling came over her, it almost seemed as though she couldn't breathe. She felt disconnected, even from Seymour, who was about as close to her as anyone right now.

"Buckley," he said gently, "I want you to spend the next couple of days thinking. I'll do everything I can to help you find Josh Marks, but if we can't locate him, we're at a standstill." He held up his hand as though asking her not to interrupt. Gathering momentum, he continued. "I care very much what happens to you. I don't want to see you screw up your whole life over something you can't do anything about. Unless Vivian decides to cooperate, you may have to face the fact that you can't help T.J."

"Jesus . . . what do I do? Just turn my back and walk away? Sorry, T.J., you're a pain in the ass to my rosy future?"

"You're being dramatic, Buckley. You're confusing your love for T.J. with a sense of responsibility for changing an entire system."

She thought over what he'd said for several

minutes. He was right. Ever since this thing started, she'd put T.J.'s problems before her own. She'd neglected her work and her friends. Now it was turning into a mess. But she thought about T.J.'s hollow, bloodshot eyes, his scared face, and her heart started pounding with anger.

"I'll think about it . . . seriously, I will," she said.

"Yeah, sure you will." Seymour smiled, shaking his head in disbelief.

"I mean it." She managed to smile back, not wanting to ruin these few hours together. Seymour was the only person left that she could talk to without having to put on an act. It was hard to remember back just a month ago. The happy days with Tony seemed like another lifetime.

Seymour slipped his hand gently over hers. "It's probably very selfish of me, but one of the reasons I wish this were over is . . . so you and I could just be people."

She smiled at his kindly face, welcoming the warmth of his hand on hers. "I know."

"I'm not complaining," he added quickly. "If it weren't for all this trouble, we'd probably never have met. Strange, isn't it?"

"A little." Buckley nodded.

Seymour motioned to the waitress for their check. "Let's go."

She pushed her plate away, having eaten little of her dinner. She swallowed the last of her wine. "We can have coffee at my house."

"Fine," he said, pleased at her suggestion.

As they drove back to her apartment, Buckley was so preoccupied with her own thoughts, she didn't notice the silence between them. She and Seymour had instantly developed such a comfortable relationship that she never considered him a date. He was just Seymour, her friend and loyal companion in the toughest battle of her life.

When they walked into the large old-fashioned living room furnished with an eclectic mixture of very fine antiques next to junk store treasures, Seymour looked around appreciatively and said, "What a nice place."

From the kitchen Buckley laughed as she quickly opened a can of cat food and heaped several spoonfuls into the pet dish. "The fireplace works now, but the landlord still has a thing about central heating. He's quite a character. Had a running battle with the building and safety people for months. He says it's a plot to ruin fine old architectural features. This is one of those historic monuments from the eighteen nineties. Only the bedroom and bath have central heating."

She tried not to make it sound like an apology because Buckley had fallen in love with this eccentric building from the moment she answered the newspaper ad for a one-bedroom apartment in a restored mansion. She adored the heavy paneling, the marble fireplaces, the French doors and carved banister leading from the entrance foyer to the second floor. Each room had a high ceiling and classic proportions. It suited her period of transition from living at home to being on her own because it had such character and charm.

"All I have is instant," Buckley called from inside the kitchen.

"Fine," Seymour called back, taking off his coat and neatly folding it across the back of a chair in the living room.

"What do you want in it? All I have is milk."

"Milk's fine," Seymour said, walking to the kitchen door.

"You're easy to please, aren't you?" Buckley laughed.

Seymour nearly blushed. "Sometimes."

As she handed him a cup of coffee, she knew he was going to kiss her before he actually did. Although Buckley was almost ten years younger than Seymour, in this instance she was more sophisticated. She had her passionate but brief love affair with Tony to thank for that experience.

Seymour was hesitant and tentative in the way he touched her. He didn't have the finesse for which Tony was so well known.

Buckley slipped her arms around his back, gently caressing him as they kissed. She made no move which would indicate resistance to him; she responded but did not lead. She was enjoying the feeling of being important, of being wanted and needed by him. She was glad to be able to give him something in return for everything he'd done for her. But she knew their feelings for each other weren't equal. He was falling in love with her. She cared deeply about him as a person and friend, but she felt no romantic attachment. It was not like being with Tony. But then, she thought, it's not necessary for every time to be the way it was with Tony.

When they entered her bedroom, she purposely didn't turn on the lights. They took off their clothes in the dark. Buckley sensed that Seymour was shy. He was a gentle, sweet lover. He was giving and considerate.

In the darkness she could imagine Seymour was anyone in the whole world. In that sense he was the perfect lover. Tonight he was any man she wanted him to be. While they made love, she let the fantasies and the physical sensations kaleidoscope across her mind without censorship. She was having an unexpectedly delightful evening.

When it was over, they lay silently side by side for a while. It was only then that she wanted to see his face. She had a curiosity about what a thoroughly satisfied man looked like in peaceful repose. It was just too dark in the bedroom for her to see anything except his profile.

"Thank you . . . that was nice," she said quietly.

He didn't answer her. He didn't move. He just lay there looking up at the ceiling.

"Are you all right?" she asked in a concerned voice.

She could see him smile as he turned his face toward hers. "All right?" He laughed softly. "I think I died and went to heaven."

She laughed with him, kissing his cheeks and forehead and finally his mouth. He wrapped his arm around her, pulling her body close to him once more. They fell asleep.

When Buckley opened her eyes, she saw Seymour silhouetted near the window. He was trying to find his clothes in the darkness.

"What are you doing?" she asked sleepily.

"Getting dressed."

"Why?"

"I have to go home," he whispered, pulling on his pants.

"Go home? What time is it?" she said, sitting up in bed.

Seymour was struggling with his shirt, having already stuffed his tie into his pants pocket. "Shh . . .

I told you . . . I have to go home.''

Buckley turned on the little lamp beside the bed, glancing at the clock.

''Why are you whispering?'' she asked in some astonishment. ''And . . . why are you going home at two-thirty in the morning?'' She yawned. Then a new thought occurred to her as she studied his silent struggle. ''Seymour, did you lie to me?''

''No—I never lied to you,'' he whispered frantically.

''But you told me you weren't married.''

''I'm not married!'' Seymour said in exasperation, still wrestling with his shirt sleeves.

''Please stop whispering!''

''Okay,'' he replied in a normal voice.

''Seymour''—Buckley eyed him suspiciously—''if you're not married, why are you going home in the middle of the night?''

''My mother will worry,'' he mumbled.

''What!'' Buckley burst into laughter. ''Your *mother* will worry? I don't believe you just said that!''

Seymour remained totally disheveled despite his recent efforts. He was blinking rapidly, trying to adjust his eyes and his psyche to the light.

''I told you, I live with my mother. And my mother worries about me!'' he said more defensively. ''Will you please stop laughing? It's very rude.''

''I'm sorry.'' She tried to be serious. ''What can I do to help? I know! Why don't I call your mother and say I invited you for a sleepover . . . that you're all right and that she shouldn't worry?'' Buckley teased, reaching for the phone.

''Don't you dare!'' Seymour replied with a resounding note of real panic in his voice. ''Put down the phone and listen to me,'' he said, trying to be authoritative again. ''I'll be gone the rest of the week. I've promised to take Mother to visit her sister . . . we'll be back after the holiday. Buckley, *please* . . . think about our conversation at the restaurant. It's very important.''

''Okay. What holiday?'' she asked, taken by surprise.

''Passover. Comes every year,'' he replied.

''Oh, of course,'' she answered without knowing a single thing about it.

Seymour was now dressed. He walked slowly to the bed and leaned over to kiss Buckley good-bye.

''You promise? You'll help me find T.J.'s father? We'll really track down Josh Marks?''

''I promise, Buckley. Monday. We'll start first thing in the morning.''

''Don't go,'' she pleaded. ''Please? Stay with me?''

''I'm sorry, I can't. Good night, Buckley.'' He kissed her. ''For God's sake, take care of yourself. See you next week.''

''Drive safely!'' she called out after him.

Chapter 12

One of the things Vivian enjoyed most about her new life was the opportunity to sleep until noon if she wanted without having to justify her laziness to anyone.

She had always been a night person, never understood what other people found interesting about springing out of bed at the barbaric hour of six or seven o'clock in the morning. Since her husband died, she'd altered her personal schedule to suit her preference. The first meal she ate during the day was what most people called lunch.

This particular morning Vivian was up and dressed in time to hear the service doorbell ringing at twelve-thirty. She couldn't remember ordering anything specific for delivery today but didn't give it much thought as she left her dressing room, prepared for an interesting spring round of shopping, followed by dinner and the ballet with Tony Marshall, the ambitious young man from the company's advertising agency who flattered her to advance his career but was attractive and useful. By using a few well-placed hints about Buckley's rebellious, insolent behavior, Vivian had managed to turn Tony into her willing surrogate.

As she entered the dining room, she saw Estelle place a curiously small bouquet of ragged spring flowers in an ugly plastic container on the table by her single place mat next to a pot of English breakfast tea.

"Estelle?" Vivian demanded with immediate pique.

"Yes, ma'am?"

"What the hell is that?" Vivian pointed at the bedraggled bouquet.

"Flowers for you, Mrs. Simpson," Estelle replied evenly.

"You call those horrible weeds . . . *flowers?*"

"The deliveryman said, 'Flowers for Vivian Simpson.' "

"That will be all, Estelle," Vivian snapped, feeling sure the woman was being rude but too curious about the strange event to make any more of a scene so early in the day. Later she'd chastise Estelle severely for something irrelevant to punish her for her rudeness.

"Yes, ma'am," the woman said as she disappeared back into the safety of the kitchen.

Vivian poured some tea into her daintily flowered Limoges cup and settled back to enjoy her breakfast. She absently picked an envelope out of the flowers, noticing that it was larger than the usual florists' cards and did not have either her name or her address on it.

As she finished tearing open the sealed envelope,

she realized the enclosure was not just a note card but appeared to be a letter. She pulled out the folded piece of plain white paper and opened it flat. Her first reaction was astonishment. This looked like a child's kindergarten project. All the individual letters forming words were cut from magazines, their sizes and shapes irregular, the spacing almost random, without punctuation.

It took her a full minute to begin deciphering the message. She found herself spelling out words as though putting pieces of a jigsaw puzzle together to discover the picture they created. Slowly a terrible crawling sensation filled her body. The fragments of meaning crept through her consciousness like maggots wriggling out of rotting garbage in the summer heat. The impact of this deadly kindergarten message attacked her nervous system before it hit her brain.

"Je-sus . . . Mother . . . Christ!" she whispered, her eyes transfixed on the sheet of paper lying in front of her, interrupting the otherwise-immaculate dining-room table. The brightly colored misshapen letters broke into a thousand prismatic fragments, dancing crazily in her mind. They affected her as little else had been capable of doing since she was a young farm girl. Her blood pulsed so fast her heart seemed out of control. She came very close to fainting.

Vivian reached for the soothing warmth of her tea. She had to hold the delicate porcelain cup with both hands. Even so, she spilled a few drops of tea on her spotless place mat.

Fighting to regain control, she reread the letter sitting untouched in front of her.

* * *

Dead Buck in Meadow No Accident Your Secret Safe If These Flowers And $10 Thousand On Grave at 4 Today.

The Hunter

Vivian neatly folded her napkin, leaving the breakfast Estelle prepared for her completely untouched. She left the dining room and found her private telephone book, thumbing quickly through it for the number she needed.

"United Grocery Company," the switchboard girl answered.

"Mr. Damian, please."

"I'm sorry, ma'am, Mr. Damian passed away four months ago. Would you like to speak to someone else?"

"What?" Vivian asked, stunned.

"Mr. Damian died four months ago. Could someone else help you?"

"Died?" Vivian whispered in disbelief.

"Yes, ma'am," the nasal female voice repeated.

"Thank you," Vivian said, and hung up.

Damian dead four months. Damian had been her only contact. He said it was all guaranteed. He told her the organization took care of everything . . . anonymity . . . everything. Now he was gone, and she didn't know any of the others, not even their names. Damian was her last contact from the past.

It was almost one o'clock in the afternoon. Vivian had only three hours left before the dreaded appointment.

She would have to decide quickly. What was the best course to take? She stood quietly. Thinking.

Blackmail was unexpected. She hadn't calculated it as a risk. Ten thousand dollars was nothing compared to the millions awaiting Vivian once the estate was settled, but it would make a considerable dent in the insurance money she was getting by on these days.

However, she would never willingly surrender everything she'd worked for all these years. She felt entitled to Buck Simpson's money and was determined to get it.

The decision was made. She'd just have to outsmart him, whoever he was. She had never met a man she couldn't manipulate. If she could find a way to identify him, she could handle him. Then the $10,000 would be a relatively small price to pay.

Vivian walked slowly into the library where Buck Simpson's gun collection was mounted in a glass case. She took the key out of a desk drawer and opened the case. Carefully she chose a .38-caliber revolver for which she knew there was still ammunition here in the apartment. It would fit easily in her purse, and she was sure she'd remember how to use it.

She returned to the dining room, grabbed the flowers and emptied the water out of the plastic vase into her bathroom sink. She shoved the entire arrangement into a department store shopping bag retrieved from the back of her closet. Getting to the bank was no problem, but driving out to the cemetery would take more than an hour, if she didn't get lost. Vivian realized she'd never been back after the funeral. She quickly decided she'd need a map.

"I'll be back late this afternoon," she called out to Estelle as she hurriedly left the apartment.

Vivian tried to appear calm during the interminable time she waited for the parking attendant to bring her silver Mercedes up from the building's underground garage.

She explained to the bank manager that she needed the cash for some gold coins she'd been wanting to buy when the price dropped, and he obliged her without hesitation. Buck Simpson's personal life insurance policy had long ago been paid, and there was no doubt her combined accounts held a great deal more than the required $10,000 she withdrew today.

On the way out of town she chose a busy gas station to get a county map. As the attendant cleaned her windshield, Vivian traced her route to the cemetery. The shopping bag on the seat next to her was leaking, causing a small dark spot on the leather upholstery.

She looked at the clock on her dashboard. It was already two o'clock. It was as though the world were moving at two different speeds. Time on the clock was flying, while her personal experience of these hours was in slow motion. She observed herself performing each task in this predetermined sequence of events. Surely this was not the independent Vivian of just a few hours ago. Hadn't she made up her mind never to do another human being's bidding? Wasn't she free from demands and encumbrances for the first time in memory? How, then, had this ragged, dripping clump of reluctant springtime flowers changed her entire existence without warning?

Vast expanses of unbroken countryside held neither joy nor comfort for this woman. The profusion of trees, the rippling hillsides, mile upon mile of nature's bounty brought back only the terrible memories of her farm girlhood.

The clock on the dashboard indicated it was past

three o'clock. Vivian checked the map furtively. She was only about five miles from the cemetery. She realized that the last time she had traveled this route her attention must have come into sharper focus during the end of the journey because now the sights she sped past definitely looked familiar.

The first sign announcing her approach to the cemetery appeared discreetly at the side of the road. Only one more mile left. She rolled down her window about two inches and breathed deeply of the stinging fresh air.

The enormous ornate iron cemetery gates sprang like a mirage immediately to her left. She stepped on the brakes, slowed her car enough to make the turn and swung into the wide driveway.

A guard stepped out of the small gatehouse to assist her. She slowed her car to a stop, rolled the window down further and stared blankly into the elderly man's face, temporarily forgetting what she'd intended to say.

"May I help you?"

"Could you direct me to the Simpson family plot?"

"Take this road around to your right. Follow the yellow markers over the first hill, and then take a left. It's about a hundred yards north of parking area three."

"Thank you."

Vivian had only a vague idea what he'd said. The words came through to her in a totally disconnected fashion almost as though he'd been talking to her underwater. Her primary concentration was focused on searching the grounds for some evidence of her blackmailer, the man who called himself the Hunter.

She remembered the part about "turn right" and

proceeded slowly from there, hoping she might recognize the correct way once she began retracing the path of the funeral procession.

Parking lot three was a distinct memory. She parked her car at the far end, some distance from the other two vehicles. Vivian could see the entire cemetery grounds from this knoll, and there wasn't another person in sight.

She opened her purse and lightly touched the loaded gun and withdrew a folded wad of bills from her wallet. Methodically she counted each $50 and $100 bill, making sure the amount was exactly correct. She concentrated on one task at a time, never daring think beyond until it was finished to her satisfaction. With a deft movement she removed the disfigured bunch of flowers and their unsightly container from the shopping bag on the seat beside her. Then she rolled the money into a smooth cylinder and inserted it in the middle of the plastic vase. Vivian held the container away from her at arm's length, studying it as an artist might, before opening the car door and heading for the Simpson family plot.

It was a short distance up the knoll, which was surrounded by the only large trees in the cemetery. This must be the original part, she thought as she stepped gingerly around the older grave markers, which were beginning to sink into the pale green earth, some listing to one side or another, giving the area a snaggletoothed appearance.

Several steps farther brought her to the family plot entrance. It was surrounded by a low iron fence with a little gate in the middle of one side. Her husband was buried with all the other members of his family: his first wife, his father and mother, his uncles and aunts and one sister. She shivered involuntarily, realizing there was also a space for her. One day she was destined to be lying next to her husband again in death.

"I'm not free after all, Buck Simpson," Vivian murmured as she hesitated at the little ornamental gate, clutching the ugly plastic vase.

Vivian had to force herself to open the wrought-iron gate and enter the grave site. Her watch read 3:53. Awkwardly she bent over Simpson's grave, setting the flowers next to the headstone. As she was standing upright again, she saw that the vase was about to fall over and she grabbed for the container just in time to keep the contents from spilling on the ground. This time she leaned the bouquet firmly against the cold marble for support. Then she backed away slowly until she felt the iron fence brush against her legs. It was exactly four o'clock.

Again Vivian looked around the cemetery park grounds for any sign of another person's presence. She waited, her hand placed casually on top of her open purse only an inch away from the gun.

It was beginning to get cold as the sun slipped behind the ancient trees, casting long shadows. She decided to walk back to her car to wait for the Hunter to pick up his bounty and then follow him. It was too cold to stand on the hill any longer.

As Vivian's foot touched the asphalt of the parking lot, it suddenly dawned on her. How could the Hunter be so sure she was the one who ordered Buck Simpson's murder? Damian had personally handled her husband's assassin; Vivian had only paid Damian the money. She never saw the killer, never knew his name. Only Damian knew both of them. Damian was dead.

Vivian spun around to face the hilltop family grave. Suddenly she ran back to get the money, the flowers. No one knew she had done it. How could they prove it? Damian was dead.

The flowers were gone. Gone. The flowers were gone! There was no other human being in sight. The flowers had vanished, and she was the solitary visitor.

"Jesus . . . Mother . . . Christ!" Vivian gasped, ashen as a ghost herself. Her eyes searched frantically for any clue to the person who was blackmailing her and had vanished without a sound. She was completely alone in the hilltop silence. Around the other side of the hill and beyond her vision, a blue sedan sped through the deserted cemetery and left through a seldom-used truck exit.

Tears of rage flooded her face. Her mistake was so monumental, so catastrophic it could never be obliterated. She would have to live with it forever. A black wave of panic enshrouded her, cutting off her oxygen, paralyzing her body.

How could she have been so stupid? Why hadn't she figured it out sooner? No one would ever have known. She could have gotten away with murdering Buck Simpson.

This moment marked the beginning of another life for Vivian. She'd left the protected sanctuary of wealthy widowhood forever. She now had to find and kill the blackmailer. There was no other choice.

His greed would force him to return. Vivian knew that the Hunter's appetite for easy money would never be satisfied with only one payment.

She would wait. The next time was still a clean slate. He wouldn't elude her twice.

Her panic began to subside; her pulse returned to

normal. She got back in her silver Mercedes and pulled out of the parking lot.

At the opposite end of parking area three in an unmarked police car John Needham sat slouched behind his newspaper. He had observed Vivian's entire afternoon from a discreet distance. At the moment none of it fitted her personality, but Needham's work had trained him to be patient.

Chapter 13

People at the airport car rental place smiled amiably but were not very helpful. They'd given Buckley a map, keys to a bright yellow subcompact and several different opinions on the best route to Josh Marks's address on Beachtree Road. The conversation was not reassuring. California is an amazing place, she thought. So many contradictions are taken for granted.

In Pennsylvania the weather was still cold, there were no leaves on the trees, only crocus buds braved the frost to signal springtime. Here in California everything was emerald green from the winter rains, and wild yellow mustard flowers dotted the hillsides. The sky was a pale, clear blue with one or two small white clouds toward the horizon.

Buckley immediately noticed the difference between these western roads and the ones she was used to driving. The highways were clean and beautifully maintained, but whoever was responsible for road signs thought either all drivers carried binoculars or everybody in California knew where he was going. What should have taken her an hour took two and a half hours.

After stops at three gas stations to ask for directions, Buckley finally located Beachtree Road and swerved the little car off the highway. She was filled with a sense of victory as she drove down the narrow, winding street.

Beachtree Road was an exclusive artists' colony that ran for a mile and a half along a spectacular stretch of ocean, dotted with low sand dunes, pieces of gnarled driftwood and tufts of beach grass. It was a private community. The houses had been built over a period of many years, representing changes in architectural taste as time moved by. A house that looked like a miniature Mediterranean villa stood alongside an angular redwood modern. Scattered among the more expensive houses were modest, older beach cottages.

Buckley didn't see any people on the entire road, only a few parked cars. Strange, she thought, it's like a beautiful ghost town. Maybe this was a totally lunatic plan after all.

It had taken days of diligent sleuthing to locate Josh Marks. T.J. could only remember seeing a faded photograph of his father near the ocean and hearing one brief reference Vivian made several years ago to "the California beach bum."

Using Uncle Zack's office phone, Seymour and Buckley had called information for every beach town in California, hoping that Josh Marks was still alive and not quite successful enough to have an unlisted phone number.

Seymour's patience and painstaking efforts eventually paid off. They located a J. Marks Photography in a small central coast beach city. For days Seymour and Buckley took turns calling the phone number hourly, staying up half the night in an attempt to catch Josh at home.

In exasperation Seymour called information again, telling the operator that he was an out-of-state attorney who needed to contact Mr. Marks on an estate matter and required his correct street address.

Miraculously Josh called back the day after they sent him an urgent telegram. Buckley was ecstatic. At last one piece of success. Her happiness vanished when Josh refused to see her or discuss anything with them over the phone. He was not interested in being involved in T.J.'s problems.

Three days later Buckley was on a plane to California. She was determined not to give up when their first real hope had finally appeared. Now she was just two houses away from his address, and she was scared. She had to convince Josh Marks he could solve the problem without a major sacrifice to himself or his independent life-style.

Please, God, help me, she prayed silently, looking up at the clear blue beach sky. Buckley took a deep breath and parked the rented car in front of a weathered cottage numbered 2024 Beachtree Road.

Earlier that day Josh decided to try running off the anxiety he'd felt since waking up this morning. Running on the beach usually made him feel better about himself. The sound of waves temporarily obliterated all thoughts of conflict. The physical effort involved assuaged his anxiety. From years of experience Josh knew the anxiety would come back as soon as he returned to the house, but he was grateful for even a few hours of peace.

The unwelcome call several days ago from that girl Buckley Simpson had unnerved him. It was probably the cause of his anxiety attack this morning. He tried never to think of his son, T.J., or of his brief marriage to Vivian, which had been an unmitigated disaster.

When they'd first met, Josh found Vivian irresistibly beautiful. She had a quality of mystery about her, seductively elusive. By the time their destructive relationship was over Vivian had regularly served his balls to him for breakfast, lunch and dinner like a basket of hard-boiled eggs.

What began as youthful infatuation ended with Josh's knowing in his gut that Vivian was the ultimate cold-blooded bitch. When she told him she was getting a divorce and taking their son away from him Josh willingly accepted. As far as he was concerned, she could take even T.J. if she would just get out of his life and leave him alone.

After that Josh moved to Mexico for a while, worked the beach cities and tourist traps alternately as gigolo or free-lance photographer, trying to forget everything but the present moment. Slowly the pain of his mistakes began to subside. He moved to Europe and then to South America for several more years.

Eventually he found out that Vivian had remarried, and for the past five years neither she nor T.J. had haunted him. At last he was able to pick up some of the pieces from his Mexican and European contacts, return to his favorite California beach and slowly begin rebuilding his career.

Lately life hadn't been so bad. At fifty-two, Josh

was just old enough to attract those mindless young girls still searching for the ultimate father image. It didn't bother him at all that most of them were perfectly satisfied with the provision of a little sex, a little dope, a few Sunday brunches and not much else. Amazing what most people settled for in gratifying their needs. Well, Josh mused, it wasn't up to him to be their father adviser, just their father image.

When the telegram from Buckley arrived, he knew he should have returned it "addressee unknown." Maybe he just couldn't stand not being harassed for two days in a row. God knows, that seemed to be his lot in life. To make matters worse, the last few years spent in therapy two days a week had succeeded only in making him more dependent on the everlasting struggle.

His anxiety attacks recurred predictably anytime the idea of becoming successful *and* happy at the same time dared occur to him.

Josh had never remarried. Just the thought of committing himself again to a long-term relationship sent him into cold shock. He had brief affairs and casual friendships but never anything he couldn't walk away from easily.

The ocean breeze felt good against his bare skin. His lean, muscular legs carried him easily the last half mile back to his house, though he'd been running on the beach several hours.

As he reached the last sand dune before turning toward the path leading up to the cottage, Josh noticed a young woman standing on the patio. He had no idea how long she had been watching his progress up the beach. She didn't seem to have been there just a moment before, but since he hadn't paid particular attention, he couldn't be sure.

He slowed to a walk, clearing his lungs. The girl on his patio didn't move. Josh saw that she wasn't dressed like any of the young women around here. Her appearance was more tailored, less casual. He walked steadily but did not hurry. He wanted to use these few minutes to assess her, try to figure out what sort of person she might be.

Although she had a rather tight-assed look about her, as Josh got closer he was surprised to notice the girl was prettier than his first impression. Maybe if she took her hair out of that knot on top of her head and put her makeup on more skillfully, she'd be very interesting.

Get ahold of yourself, you wonky old man, Josh said to himself, and smiled pleasantly as he approached her.

"Looking for someone?"

"Yes," she replied very seriously. "Josh Marks. Do you know where I can find him?"

"Sure, I'm Josh Marks."

"You're Josh Marks?" Buckley Simpson blurted out, unable to mask her surprise.

Josh laughed easily, feigning wounded pride. "I don't usually have that effect on women."

"I didn't mean to be insulting, Mr. Marks. I'm Buckley Simpson. We spoke briefly on the phone."

The easy smile Josh bestowed on attractive strangers faded instantly. "Why don't we go inside? It's getting cold out here."

He led the way into the beach house through sliding glass doors that opened onto the patio. The piercing, intense way the young woman looked at him made him feel underdressed. When he finished running, he usually felt exhilarated but now the ocean breeze was chilling against his still-damp skin.

Buckley was embarrassed to have gotten off to such an inauspicious beginning with this man who was so important to her cause. She'd meant to appear more mature, more self-possessed. She had expected a man who looked appropriately fifty years old. What she found, to her overwhelming surprise, was a tanned and lean, obviously charming bachelor with only his salt-and-pepper hair betraying any signs of advancing age.

The living room of his house was eclectically furnished with an eye toward durability and comfort. Dominating the room was a modular couch, softly inviting. An antique oak trestle table and four mismatched chairs set in one corner defined the dining room. Near the front door was a small but efficient kitchen with a bar counter and several leather-covered barstools. Two brilliant modern paintings dominated the single expanse of wall. The rest of the house was down a hallway lined floor to ceiling with samples of Josh Marks's photographic work.

Josh took an open bottle of California white wine out of the kitchen refrigerator. He put the wine bottle and two glasses on the counter. "Can I offer you a drink?" He smiled pleasantly.

"Yes, thanks."

How easy he is, Buckley thought. So different from what she had imagined. He was more like a person her own age, with more experience. As she studied him, she saw the almost uncanny resemblance between Josh and T.J. They had the same features, the identical physical build; even the teasing twinkle in Josh's eyes was similar.

"Help yourself," Josh said, indicating the wine

and bowl of strange-looking snack crackers he'd taken out of a package with Oriental lettering on it. "I have to shower and change, or I'll be very unpleasant company. Won't take but a few minutes."

With that, Josh picked up the wineglass he had filled and disappeared down the hallway. Buckley was left alone in the room. First she heard the sound of soft music, then the steady stream of shower water. She walked over to the bar, filled the remaining glass with wine and lifted herself onto the barstool's leather seat. She swiveled herself around to face the sliding glass doors on the opposite side of the living room.

The low sand dunes rose slightly just beyond the patio. Slender sea grasses swayed in the light afternoon breeze. She looked out past the dunes to the Pacific Ocean, flat, blue and enormous, stretching into eternal horizon as far as she could see. In the distance there was a lone sailboat. She could hear the strident cries of the sea gulls as they swooped back and forth across the water.

It wasn't too hard to understand Josh Marks's reluctance to become involved with T.J.'s crisis once you saw his present life. He was insulated from the push and pull of the world as long as he lived here on this enchanted beach. Why should he give that up for remote concepts such as family or justice?

The sound of shower water stopped abruptly. Buckley took a sip of the cool white wine, turning her head toward the hallway. How am I going to get through all that charming worldly exterior? she wondered.

She stared out toward the giant blue-green ocean, feeling very small and alone. What do I say to make him care? I've come almost two thousand miles. Yet here I sit, casually sipping white wine and enjoying the spectacular view.

Suddenly, with all the stealth of a cat, Josh Marks was standing beside her. She was startled into fully focused attention. For one brief moment, in silence, the two people looked directly into each other's faces. Each was intent on deciphering every detail, assessing the scope of the confrontation about to occur.

"Didn't mean to startle you," Josh opened, still pleasantly. He was now dressed in light slacks and a wool sweater with a heavy gold chain around his neck. As he refilled his glass, Buckley could not stand the debonair atmosphere any longer.

"Josh, I've come a very long way and gone to a lot of trouble to find you. Please, can we talk about T.J.?" Buckley's voice was a little shaky; her hands were damp with nervous perspiration.

Josh felt extremely uncomfortable under the thrust of her directness. He felt her eyes searching him, all her senses trained on him. Although reasonably he knew he was not under attack, that was how it felt. He instinctively moved away from her, walking across the living room to the couch.

"Sure," he said without sounding very convincing. "Sure, we can talk about T.J."

Buckley sensed that Josh's turning his back on her was symbolic of the way this whole conversation was going to end if she couldn't do something to change his mind. She slipped off the barstool and headed after him.

"Josh, I know that you haven't seen T.J. or been in touch with him for a long time. But *please*, just listen to me for a few minutes. Just give me a chance to explain what's happened." Her voice was urgent without being hostile. Her eyes were riveted on him, trying to pick up some clue from his expression.

Josh sat on the couch, motioned for her to sit near him and leaned back, waiting. "Okay . . . I'm listening."

Buckley sat down, took a deep breath and began. She detailed what exactly had happened, beginning at the point of her father's death, including the will, ending with Cooper's stealing Mr. Williams's car from boarding school and T.J.'s arrest.

"T.J. had absolutely nothing to do with it. Mr. Havenhurst probably paid Williams some money under the table, Williams agreed not to press any charges against Cooper and the entire event would have been forgotten if it weren't for Vivian."

Josh stared out at the beach and beyond to the vast Pacific Ocean. He twirled his wineglass around in his hand absentmindedly. A slight frown crossed his forehead from time to time, but he showed no other emotion.

Buckley leaned forward, gaining momentum as she continued talking. "The only reason T.J. is sitting in the juvenile detention facility right now is that they don't have anywhere else to place him! Vivian won't have anything to do with him. Mr. Williams will not let him back into the school because she told him not to. The juvenile authorities can't find a foster home for a teenage boy almost sixteen years old, and all the group placement openings are filled. I offered to take him the first day, but they won't permit that either because I'm under twenty-one, and they say I'm not considered a responsible adult. Josh, you're the only hope we have left! You're his real father. They would listen to you. You could be his legal guardian. They'd release T.J. to you; they've already told me they would. All you have to do is say you'll be responsible for T.J. until he's eighteen. That's just another two years. You won't be alone. I'll help, Seymour will, too, and there'll be my trust fund from the estate. *Please*, Josh?"

"It's not that simple," Josh said, staring out at the ocean.

"It *is* that simple, Josh! It is just that simple, believe me." Buckley's voice sounded calm and assured, but inside she was shaking.

"You're so bloody naïve I can't believe it." Josh suddenly exploded. "Your sheltered, righteous upbringing really shows, Buckley. You know as much about how the real world works as a six-year-old, you know that? You think all you have to do is be right . . . to work hard and the world will reward you. Well, let me give you a rude goddamn awakening, young lady. There isn't anything about the fucking world that works the way you think it does. Not one goddamn thing . . . understand?"

Buckley stared at him, feeling the tears fill her eyes as she sat there silently, frightened by his sudden anger.

"Jesus. Where have you been all these years? Protected by your daddy's money, sheltered by the mighty corporate umbrella, coddled by society's image of wealth and power. Kid gloves . . . that's how you've been handled all your life. Well, honey, here it is . . . welcome to the *real* world! Here's exactly how it is. If I lifted one finger to help T.J., within twenty-four hours Vivian would have my ass for chopped liver!"

Josh walked quickly to the bar and filled his empty

wineglass. He took a long drink, trying to calm himself. In a slightly softer but no less vehement tone he continued talking.

"You really don't know anything about Vivian, do you?"

Buckley opened her mouth to answer, but Josh held up his hand to halt her saying anything.

"Vivian not caring what happens to T.J., as you put it, is only the beginning. What Vivian really wants is to *destroy* T.J."

"Why, Josh? That's what I don't understand. He's her son. How could she hate him so much?"

Josh took a deep breath, partly to give himself time to find the right words and partly to calm himself. "Vivian never wanted T.J. from the beginning. If I hadn't stopped her at the last minute, she would have had an abortion. We were not getting along well at the time. As I look back on it now, maybe I did the wrong thing. Maybe T.J. shouldn't have been born. But then, years ago, I was still a young man. I was in love with Vivian. I wanted a family. Maybe I had some romantic notion that if Vivian had a baby . . ." His voice trailed off into silence as he stood quietly, deeply involved in his own bitter memory of another, faraway time in his life.

Buckley nodded her head sadly and sighed. "But that was a long time ago. Why is she trying to destroy him now?"

Josh looked at the girl as though she were a poor student in a college lecture class asking a stupid question. Very slowly, as if talking to someone who didn't understand English very well, he continued. "Buckley, *now* is just a continuation of the way she's always felt about T.J. Only now, since the death of your father, T.J. is of no further use to Vivian. She *never* wanted the boy, never loved him. Now that your father is dead, there's no mileage she can get out of him. He's useless to her. To Vivian, everything must serve a purpose or she discards it. People are no different to her from material possessions." Josh smiled, making a macabre joke. "Come to think of it, people are probably of less value because she can't sell them or trade them in for a new model!"

"I still don't understand."

"Very simple. Vivian will never allow T.J. to get that hundred thousand dollars. Believe me, she'll find a way to get rid of him."

Buckley was trying to follow him, but he saw her confusion, he saw the tears in her eyes.

"Let me explain Vivian a little better to you." Josh walked back to the couch and sat very close to Buckley, speaking almost in a whisper as though he were still afraid someone would overhear his words.

"For over twenty years, before Vivian married your father, she was employed by a man named Benjamin . . . you don't need to know his last name. Benjamin ran information, prostitutes and contraband all over the world. Among his clients were not only individual customers of enormous wealth but also government agencies, foreign generals . . . anyone who could pay the price but couldn't afford to have his identity linked with the transaction. Vivian started out as Benjamin's pawn, his private prostitute, his little gift to the clientele. She graduated to being his favorite courier. It was Vivian who made the actual deliveries, Vivian who took the major risks and Vivian who was paid with something far better than money. Her reward was power."

Josh studied Buckley's innocent, shocked face. He was genuinely sorry that this unpleasant task of revelation had fallen to him. He wished he could turn back the clock for both of them, but he couldn't.

"I found out too late that I was just a momentary diversion in her life when Benjamin was in some sort of trouble. He arranged our marriage to protect Vivian. They just used me as a cover. Vivian never loved me. I doubt if she ever felt anything for me . . . except contempt." Josh continued slowly. "We were married only four years, just long enough to have T.J. and learn to hate each other. Oh, in the beginning it was different. I fell madly, insanely in love with her from the moment we met. She was the most exotic creature I'd ever seen. She was all my wildest dreams come true. Loving her was a consuming passion with me—the only real passion of my entire life, and it destroyed me." Josh smiled an ironic smile filled with remorse and hatred.

Buckley was speechless. She sat staring at Josh, mesmerized by the onslaught of this new information. Her mind labored to fit the pieces of this bizarre puzzle together, but it was overwhelming her.

"By the time she left I didn't care whether or not she took T.J. with her. I knew I was going mad. She was ripping my guts apart, devouring me and laughing as she saw her torture take effect day after day." Josh felt his morbid fear of Vivian return. He felt a deeply buried panic begin to grip him once again. He got up and opened the sliding glass door to the narrow patio. Dusk was just beginning, and with it the late-afternoon sky started to turn a brilliant orange.

It looked as though the sky were on fire. Buckley had never seen a western sunset play out its volcanic explosion of color before.

Josh continued, picking up a previous train of

thought. "I guess you also don't know that Benjamin introduced Vivian to your father. I was in Europe at the time and saw a picture of them on Benjamin's yacht. I know that Vivian just used your dad as a retirement program when she got too old to be effective in Benjamin's business."

"Oh, my God!" Buckley whispered, feeling a wave of nausea coming over her. She fought against the sickly, faint sensations. Unsteadily she walked out the open door to the patio. Josh pulled up a chair for her, seeing the color had drained from her face. Buckley sank down into the deck chair, breathing deeply of the damp, cool air. Josh pulled a second chair close to her, sat in it and looked sympathetically at the distraught young woman.

"I know. Ever since I made the fatal mistake of finding out the truth about Vivian, I've lived with all those same shitty feelings."

Buckley smiled weakly. At least he wasn't yelling at her. Slowly she regained her composure. It was just in time for Josh to land another blow of unwanted, horrifying information to her already swimming brain.

"Buckley, after Vivian got bored destroying me personally and left with T.J., she still wasn't satisfied. She wasn't content until she destroyed my professional career too. Eleven years ago, through Benjamin, she managed to spread the rumor that I'd become an acid freak, sort of the Timothy Leary of commercial photographers. I didn't work for six years after the divorce. I became paranoid. I started running . . . to Mexico . . . to Europe and South America. Running away from Vivian became my whole distorted way of life. It got so bad that I didn't know specifically who was chasing me. All I knew was that I had to keep running."

Josh reached out and took Buckley's cold, clenched hand in his own. He smoothed her skin softly as though trying to provide some small measure of comfort in the midst of the excruciating pain both of them were feeling.

"Listen to me . . ." Josh said very quietly. He spoke so softly his words were barely audible above the crashing sound of the ocean waves.

"Listen very carefully to me, Buckley. Vivian is an evil woman. She is like the deadly black widow spider, poisonous, consuming . . . carnivorous. She is very sick, very cruel and absolutely lethal. She is not just immoral; she is without conscience as you and I know it. There is no way to reach her as a human being, no level on which to appeal to her. If she gets it into her head that *you* are standing in the way of her plans for getting rid of T.J., she will destroy you."

Buckley shuddered involuntarily. Like a blazing flash of lightning, the memory of that look on Vivian's face when Buckley overheard her on the phone with a strange man while her father was still alive flooded over her body like one of those cold ocean waves.

"There's nothing to stop her. Everyone who really knows her is deathly afraid of her. She's made it her business to collect gossip, scandal, secret information about anyone remotely connected with her world for years now. She's a veritable storehouse of classified information which she wouldn't hesitate for a minute to use if it suited her purpose. You just can't fight that; you're not equipped. She'll annihilate you."

It was as though Buckley had mysteriously stepped over the invisible edge of a barrier. She felt the terrible fear begin to subside.

"Josh, if I don't do everything I can to get T.J. out of Grasslands, Vivian won't have to destroy him because keeping him locked up will do that for her. I know T.J. He's like a young wild horse . . . it'll kill him. Please, Josh, you're his father, our last hope. Please . . . help us!"

Josh threw his wineglass against a large planter box at the edge of the patio. The glass shattered in a thousand little pieces. He grabbed Buckley by the shoulders and shook her until her teeth rattled.

"Goddammit! Didn't you hear one word I've said? What are you . . . a complete idiot? Don't you understand that helping T.J. would be like committing suicide? I'm too old, you dumb shit . . . I'm too old for moral crusades. All I want is for the whole fucking world to leave me alone. I don't bother anyone . . . no one messes with my life. I don't give a shit about having money or a famous name. I've learned not to care about love or family or anything! You're asking me to throw away the little I have left in this stinking world for a juvenile delinquent I don't even know. What do you offer in return? Nothing. Just a lot of empty words about responsibility. Well, do you know what I think about responsibility? I think it sucks!"

Buckley's voice was clear and steady. Her thoughts were now arranged with absolute clarity. "Josh, you can yell at me all you want, and it won't change anything. T.J. *is* your son. That is one thing you cannot run away from; it's a simple fact. I can understand what you did years ago. You had to survive. You first had to preserve yourself. But if you don't help T.J. now, it won't be Vivian that you'll have to worry about. You can't hide the truth from God, Josh. Even you can't run away and hide from eternity."

She stopped only long enough to take a deep breath and continue, as though reading his mind. "Oh, I know you think I'm a fool. Maybe I am, too. Maybe I should just take the easy way out. Maybe I should just say it's too damn tough and go back to my sheltered way of life, as you call it. But I can't do that. It's too late for me. I made T.J. a promise, and somehow . . . I don't know how . . . but I'll find a way to keep it." She paused again, this time to synthesize her thoughts. "T.J. is innocent. He doesn't deserve to be punished for the rest of his life because two crazy people brought him into the world by accident. He shouldn't have to *die* because he was a 'mistake' and nobody loves him. I will never participate in a human sacrifice to the black widow. We are not yet barbarians!"

Josh walked away from her, his eyes searching the sand dune and the horizon for an omen that never appeared. Buckley followed him quickly. "How could you care more about T.J.'s life before he was born than you care about him now? You saved him then. Please, Josh, for God's sake, don't turn your back on him now!" Buckley never took her eyes off Josh.

"I'm sorry . . . I really am sorry. You shouldn't have come here," was his answer. For the first time in memory Josh felt stinging tears filling his eyes. His heart was beating so fast he wondered if he was going to have an attack right here on the patio. Why? Why had he answered that telegram? Everything he'd salvaged from these past years, the pathetic scraps of his jinxed life, was now flying apart. What the hell was he going to do? No matter which course he chose the only outcome was certain destruction. It was a black hole into which he was about to disappear.

"I can't help you," he said very quietly, unable to face her.

"You mean you won't." She stood, preparing to leave. Buckley pitied Josh for being such a coward. She felt miserable because she'd failed to convince him to help T.J., and she couldn't stand the sight of Josh another moment. She had to get out of this house. There was an air of jaded hopelessness about Josh that made her feel scared and stupid at the same time. His words made some sense, but they added up to monumental defeat for all of them, Buckley, T.J. and finally Josh himself.

Buckley wiped the tears from her cheeks with the back of her cold hand. Without so much as another word, she walked into the living room to get her purse. Josh followed her silently, knowing that she was going to leave, that he'd left her no other choice.

He went to the front door to open it carefully and slowly. It was almost dark outside. The late-afternoon sun had nearly disappeared below the horizon. Only a final burst of blazing color was visible, and it would be gone within just a few more minutes, returning the world to darkness once again.

Without looking directly at the girl, Josh asked, "What are you going to do now?"

Buckley walked to the door. "I'll go back to the airport and wait for the next plane. When I get home, I'll just have to find another way." There was an uncomfortable silence between them.

"What . . . are you going to tell T.J.?" Josh asked reluctantly.

"I honestly don't know, Josh," Buckley answered.

She turned and walked toward the street. Traffic noises and the desolate, irritating cries of the sea gulls filled her ears. She wished she'd never told T.J. she'd try to find Josh Marks. It would have been better for all of them to be able to hold on to that last spark of hope. As she heard the gravel on the walkway crunching under her footsteps, she wished with all her heart that she'd never set eyes on Josh. But there was no going back to that innocence again. Another door had just slammed shut.

Chapter 14

Vivian looked at her watch nervously, realizing she was nearly late for their appointment. She knew from years of personal experience that one of the things Benjamin disliked most was being kept waiting.

Honking the car horn to show her annoyance with the cautious driver directly ahead of her brought no result. A bumper-to-bumper stream of cars inched forward at its own halting speed. The museum parking lot was only one more block, but the clock on the car's dashboard was running faster than the traffic. She honked again, desperately trying to move the immovable, speed up the hopeless congestion.

Almost thirty years ago, when Vivian was just eighteen years old, right off the farm, the first person of consequence she met in the city was Benjamin.

"What do you do?" he asked Vivian casually over blaring 1950's rock-and-roll music at the disc jockey's promotion party.

"Whatever's necessary," she snapped back at him.

Vivian had learned quickly that the fastest route to big money was through her own body. "And you?" she said, mildly curious.

"The same," he replied with a sly grin. Benjamin studied the thin girl who looked like a cheap porno-magazine model. There was something about her that intrigued him. She had an instinctive sense of style under that garish amateur exterior.

At twenty-nine, Benjamin was almost a millionaire. He had started out running a classy prostitution ring for businessmen who required a bit of discretion while satisfying their baser needs and had branched out into a full-service operation supplying drugs, male or female prostitutes, private parties and a special international courier service complete with his own chartered planes plus an occasional yacht or two when needed.

"Where are you from?" He continued the casual probe.

"What's it to you?" Vivian answered as she started to walk away from the nosy bastard.

"Hey . . ." Benjamin laughed softly, gently taking her arm and turning her back toward him. "Cut the defensive crap . . . I'm on your side."

Benjamin had been looking for an unusual young woman he could train to suit his more particular clients. It wasn't enough just to hire her; he needed to own someone without strong emotional ties, someone who wouldn't be missed if she disappeared for months at a time. He also needed a woman with no previous police record, no morals, no religious convictions. He had a hunch this little tart Vivian he'd just bumped into at tonight's overcrowded party was the perfect candidate.

"How about dinner?" He smiled pleasantly.

"How much?" Vivian asked too professionally.

Benjamin laughed. His tanned handsome face, dark eyes and expensively tailored clothes made him easily the most attractive man in the room. He had an offhanded sureness about him that came from being both street-smart and very rich.

"I don't pay, sweetheart," was his cocky answer.

"I don't put out for free, buster," Vivian said sarcastically.

The smile left Benjamin's face. His eyes were cold as ice. "Fifty."

Vivian looked back at him without flinching. "A hundred."

"Sold." He turned on his heel and walked out of the room.

She put her drink down on the nearest table and followed him, grabbing her coat from the long rack near the exit.

His apartment was only a short taxi ride from the party. She was completely unprepared for the elegance that greeted her as she entered the two-story penthouse he called home. His Oriental houseboy, Mr. Chin, took her coat, bowed and ushered her into the huge living room. Vivian had never seen anything like this place. She felt gawkish, inept and every bit the street whore she'd recently become.

The sound of a champagne cork popping somewhere behind her startled Vivian. Mr. Chin poured two glasses, handed the first to Benjamin and the second to her. As if by magic the little man then vanished. Benjamin stood by the terrace door, smiling. His good humor had apparently returned.

"What do you do for a hundred dollars? Must be something special, huh?"

Vivian felt another sting of incompetence. Handsome as the stranger was who stood mocking her now, she felt no physical attraction to him. She did her work with the same detachment she'd trained herself to have when she killed rabbits back on the farm. Vivian knew this john was challenging her, daring her to give him his money's worth.

"Where do you want to find out?" she answered provocatively, taking a long sip of the strong, bubbling champagne.

Benjamin laughed again. "Not bad for an amateur. I think you're going to do just fine, honey."

He led the way through a dimly lit hallway to his bedroom. The huge bed was covered with a fur spread. All four walls and the ceiling were mirrored, music was playing and another bottle of champagne was being chilled in a big silver ice bucket.

So this is it, Vivian thought, slowly beginning to undress for him as he walked around her studying all angles as though buying an animal at public auction. This is the prince's lair, she mused to herself as she stepped out of her thin, clinging dress, allowing it to fall easily on the floor.

Benjamin stood silently in front of her, still fully dressed. She stripped naked and took one step toward the fur-covered bed. He held her arm. "Vivian, undress me," he commanded quietly.

She did as he asked, feeling first the muscles in his body as she slid his clothes away and then the warmth of his tan skin as his nakedness appeared.

They moved onto the soft fur bedspread. He never uttered a sound, never came inside her, never evidenced emotion of any kind. She lay exhausted and covered with sweat. In a moment she turned over to find him studying her dispassionately again.

"You're a freak, you know that?" she mumbled with mixed curiosity and anger. She'd worked hard and now had the creepy feeling he wasn't going to pay her.

"Baby, you don't know what freak is." Benjamin laughed that deep, condescending laugh of his that made people feel idiotic. "If you're going to work for me, you've got a hell of a lot to learn."

Vivian raised herself up on one elbow, staring at Benjamin. She thought back to how she'd hated her father, how he'd taught her to despise all men after him. She didn't feel hatred for Benjamin, but then she didn't allow herself the dangerous luxury of many feelings at all these days. His proposition was a hell of a lot better than being out on the streets by herself, and it was better than being hungry. "Okay . . . I'll learn."

In a month she was ready for her first weekend extravaganza. Benjamin bought her an entire wardrobe of expensive clothes, had her hair and makeup redesigned at an elegant beauty salon, and together they drove to the country in his Rolls-Royce.

"My clients are usually invited with their wives," Benjamin explained as they drove through the heavily wooded countryside toward the ocean. "This house belongs to the chairman of a large insurance and banking conglomerate," he continued. "You are being introduced as my fiancée, and on the surface everything will look like a perfectly proper corporate weekend retreat." There would be golf and tennis, shopping tours for the wives and a scenic cruise. Vivian was to keep her mouth shut, tell everyone that she was a fashion model and follow his instructions to the letter.

"Now you're going to get a taste of *real* freak city!" he said as they turned into a long treelined gravel driveway leading directly to the weekend manor house.

Vivian and Benjamin were the first to arrive. A uniformed maid greeted them at the enormous carved wooden entrance, showing them into the two-story foyer while the houseman collected their luggage.

It was like a journey into a foreign land. The enormous house was built like a Gothic cathedral. Stone floors echoed each footstep, and in the main rooms there were fireplaces large enough for a man to stand inside. The beamed ceilings were painted with intricate designs, and tapestries hung from several walls. Every room on the ground floor had leaded glass windows which looked out onto the formal gardens and to the ocean beyond. The house sat perched on a bluff, merging, as it descended, into enormous boulders upon which a thundering dark ocean unmercifully pounded, sending giant plumes of white sea spray into the air.

Vivian had never seen the ocean before. It scared the hell out of her. She immediately had visions of being thrown off this cliff and pummeled to shreds by the violent crashing waves. It was a monstrous power beyond human control.

During the course of that weekend Vivian presided over a luncheon orgy attended only by the male guests who were supposedly playing golf while their wives were taken on a carefully escorted sight-seeing tour.

By the time the women came back from the day's touring their husbands were showered, dressed for dinner, and the entire household had returned to its proper order. Not a hint remained of the afternoon's erotic escapade.

Dinner was the epitome of formality, complete with carefully fabricated golf scores and boring chatter about the beautiful weather. Vivian, dressed in a black sequined gown, sat quietly next to Benjamin, smiling contentedly. She took pleasure in noting a flash of well-concealed envy as several of the older wives took a fleeting glance at the sparkling diamond necklace and earrings she wore tonight. They were Benjamin's gift to her just before dinner. Vivian wore her diamonds like a young queen. Although neither love nor happiness was a concept in Vivian's psychological vocabulary, she was thoroughly satisfied with her new life.

For the next ten years Vivian and Benjamin worked together with almost legendary success. He demanded total obedience to his orders, and she expected an elegant life-style in return. Neither had reason to be disappointed.

Since they never lived together and Vivian was forbidden to inquire into Benjamin's personal life, she didn't realize that he had gotten himself into serious trouble until it was too late.

When he came to pick her up one Saturday night as usual, Benjamin was nervous and surly. She noticed his foul mood but didn't comment on it. When she returned from her bedroom, wearing a new full-length mink coat, Benjamin stopped her. His face was deadly serious; his eyes had that cold, remote look she'd seen the first night they met.

"Vivian, the job's over for a while. You'll be taken care of, don't worry. I've made some arrangements for you that will seem perfectly natural while I'm gone."

"Gone?" she asked, sensing this was not one of his routine business trips.

"Just listen to me and keep your damn mouth shut!" he said viciously. "I want you to get away from here for a while. You're too spoiled to go back to being a common street whore, and if you stay in town by yourself, they'll kill you just to piss me off." Benjamin did not bother to explain who "they" were. "I'm introducing you to a photographer, Josh Marks, tonight at the party. You're going to act like it's love at first sight. Then you're going to marry him . . . immediately."

"Married!" Vivian burst into laughter. "Married!" She continued laughing. "I'm never going to get married, Benjamin . . . so you can just forget it."

Benjamin grabbed her arm, his fingers biting into her skin, purposely hurting her. Without warning he hit her across the face and threw Vivian onto the floor. He had a terrible look on his face as he stood towering over her.

"You'll do exactly as I tell you and we'll be together again as soon as this is over. Otherwise, there's an appointment for you at the morgue!"

She was terrified. For a split second she wasn't sure whether he was going to kick her, stomp on her face or maybe even kill her himself right this moment. Many other men, her father included, had been quick to slap her around, but never Benjamin.

"Get yourself together. We're leaving."

One week later Josh Marks asked Vivian to marry him. Benjamin gave them a small private wedding, after which he disappeared.

When Vivian discovered that she and Josh were going to live in an artistic California beach community, she was morose. Josh was too weak for

Vivian, too naïve to suit her taste.

Josh fell hopelessly in love with a gorgeous woman who was impossible to domesticate. She refused to cook, had an aversion to supermarkets, possessed no artistic talents and declined all attempts to learn new skills.

The next year was merely a game with Vivian. She acted out of boredom, returning to the tactics of her girlhood. When Josh did something that would normally please her, she reacted to him with anger and ridicule. She methodically emasculated him, destroying his self-confidence.

Then, to Vivian's great annoyance, she discovered she was pregnant. Josh went totally berserk when he overheard her planning an abortion. He threatened to sue the doctor and beat her black and blue if she went through with it. Against her better judgment Vivian endured her pregnancy and bore him a son. Since she had no maternal instincts, she hired a housekeeper and kept as far away from daily care of the child as possible.

Their son, T.J., was only three years old when Vivian heard from Benjamin again. Within twenty-four hours of Benjamin's call Vivian and T.J. were packed and gone forever from Josh's life. Vivian decided to take the boy along not out of any maternal feelings but because she had the instincts of a scavenger plundering the battlefield. She was determined not to leave anything of value behind. When T.J. was a little older, she told him that Josh had abandoned them and forbade his name to be mentioned again.

Vivian pulled her car into the museum parking lot. Hurriedly she pulled her fur coat out of the back seat, threw it around herself, locked the car and walked as quickly as she could without noticeably running toward the side entrance. It was getting dark. The museum would be closing in another half hour.

Vivian and Benjamin were to meet in the Renaissance Room on the second floor. Although it had been a number of years since her last visit, she knew this small museum by heart. The stone steps were familiar, as were the heavy carved columns and the damp winter smell that prevailed through all seasons. As her feet flew up the steps, she heard the hollow echo surging ahead of her. He would hear her footsteps, too, knowing the sound of them from long ago.

How many different places they had met over the years. Europe, Mexico, the Caribbean. They had met in castles, on the seawall of a tiny island in the Mediterranean, on a yacht off the coast of Yucatán, on the steps of a pyramid in the jungle, at a corner table in the dining room of a hotel in Paris, in a dozen museums, including this one. In her memory were private landing strips on tops of mountains, tiny airports hidden in cornfields. There were passport checkpoints from Venezuela to Hong Kong. Though she no longer worked for him, twenty years of association, as she traveled the world as his special courier under the guise of a lady of leisure with a sense of adventure, were hard to forget.

Almost seven years ago, on his instructions, she'd flown to Paris, taken the overnight train to the south of France and arrived aboard the yacht he'd arranged to have waiting near Cannes.

She looked back on those sparkling Mediterranean days with a certain fondness. In the prime of her beauty Vivian had subtly beguiled the stranger on board, the man Benjamin introduced as Buck Simpson, an American millionaire. She didn't need instructions after all these years. She made their romance seem naturally spontaneous, evolving out of languid, sun-filled days and the excitement of Monte Carlo gaming tables. She withheld herself just long enough to make Buck Simpson secure in his assumption that she was not ensnaring him, not a pawn of coincidence, not insurance on his business deal with Benjamin. Once convinced, Buck Simpson allowed himself to be seduced by her succulent laughter, her impossibly beautiful body and the perfect elusiveness of her international past.

Simpson fell in love with her, shedding the years of his self-imposed bachelorhood in less than a week. As soon as the loan from Benjamin's contacts was confirmed, Simpson asked Vivian to marry him. He returned to the United States with his loan money and a promise that she would soon follow. Benjamin threw a going-away party for Vivian on the yacht that lasted three days.

Vivian turned the corner into the museum's Renaissance Room. Benjamin was standing with his back to her, studying a sumptuous Rubens painting. As usual he was immaculately dressed. His nearly white hair, his tan face, the perfect cut of his clothes and the casual touch of his raincoat combined to create the picture of a cultured, handsome middle-aged man.

When Vivian entered the room, it was as though he sensed her presence, in the same way carnivorous animals and their prey know one another's exact location at all times.

Although he had taught Vivian well over the years,

she was still his student, not his peer. She was very good in her own way, some would say she was masterful in her own right, that it had become instinctive for her, but she knew there would always be that slight difference. It was enough to maintain his superiority.

She smiled casually as she walked toward the Rubens painting and Benjamin. "It's been a long time."

Benjamin was deeply annoyed. Vivian knew she was almost ten minutes late.

"Lack of discipline creates boring people, don't you think?" Benjamin smiled that deadly, cold smile.

Vivian swallowed the stern rebuke without displaying any emotion. Her eyes turned upward to the enormous painting hanging directly in front of her.

"What do you want?" Benjamin said as though speaking to the painting.

"To work for you again." Vivian spoke with urgency.

"You mean, you need help," Benjamin replied, watching her carefully.

"Yes." She nodded, knowing she'd been caught.

"Are you going to tell me the problem, or are we playing a game of twenty questions?"

Vivian was on treacherous footing with Benjamin. He was a man of few words, without mercy or compassion. Power and profit were his only concerns; nothing else affected him.

"Benjamin, I'm being blackmailed," she said very quietly, knowing better than to lie.

He raised his eyebrows in a rare display of curiosity. His cold, dark eyes penetrating her face searched for whatever shreds of elusive truth it might contain.

"For what?" he asked as casually as if he'd been inquiring about the time of day.

"Murder," she whispered, her eyes imploring his understanding and help.

With speed and accuracy that startled even Vivian, Benjamin took her arm and propelled her to an adjacent room in the museum which was deserted. He gripped her arm so tightly she knew it would be bruised when he released his hand. He silently shoved her into a small alcove, well out of sight of the guard's desk. With his free hand he grabbed her by the collar of her dress, twisting the fabric until he nearly choked her.

"You're a dumb cunt!" he whispered viciously, his cold eyes blazing with open fury. "Murder?" he repeated. "You dare show your stupid face around me and ask for help after being involved in *murder*?" He shook her violently until her head bobbed back and forth, the blood vessels standing out in purplish blue lines.

He leaned his body into hers, forcing Vivian back against the stone wall. "Who did you murder, asshole?"

Vivian gasped for air as he released his chokehold on her throat just enough to allow her to answer him.

"Simpson . . . but I didn't do it . . . I took out a contract with Damian . . . but he's dead now . . . I don't know how the killer found me."

Benjamin tightened his grip, wanting to kill her on the spot, his face crimson with rage. "I'm going to say it only once. Don't you ever come near me again . . . do you hear me? Never. As far as I'm concerned, you don't exist, I never heard of you. I can't believe after all those years you'd be so stupid. I'm a legitimate businessman now, Vivian, and you're not going to get me into this with you! Too bad I didn't just leave you in the gutter where you belong!"

"Benjamin . . . please . . . you knew Damian. Just help me find out the names of his hit men. I'll handle the rest."

"Too late for that," he answered sarcastically. He let go of her so abruptly Vivian fell back against the wall. On her neck were the reddish marks left by his fingers. She swallowed several times, trying to get her breathing regulated once again.

Benjamin turned his back on her and walked quickly out of the deserted museum. He had already formulated his own plan. This very evening he would send his valet, Mr. Chin, to get the name of Damian's hit man. For the next few months Benjamin was going to make it seem as though he had vanished. Vivian had made a fatal error in coming to him.

Benjamin looked back over their long years of association with nothing but regret. His only protégée had turned out to be a dismal failure. His once-beautiful Vivian was now nothing more than a trained attack dog that had dangerously turned on her master, never to be trusted again. She was a killer bitch that had to be destroyed.

Alone, with only the sounds of the museum closing around her, Vivian straightened her clothes, picked up the contents of her purse that had spilled onto the cold marble floor during her struggle with Benjamin and then left by a side exit.

Seething with fury, she knew the only thing she

could do now was wait to be contacted by the Hunter again. This time she wouldn't be so stupid. She'd find a way to meet him, to identify him, to kill him. After all, she still had money from the insurance, and she was sure to get control of her stock sooner or later.

Chapter 15

When Buckley returned to her office Monday morning, she was exhausted from her California trip, late by half an hour and in a bad mood. On her desk were two phone messages and a mountain of work. She hung up her raincoat, put her bag and umbrella in the corner beside a stack of reference books and picked up the messages.

The first message was from Seymour. It had only his name, phone number at work and the word "Urgent." The second said the Mr. Henry wanted to see her in his office immediately. Together the two messages created an ominous feeling, a nervousness that seemed to envelop Buckley. Should she call Seymour first or go straight to Mr. Henry's office? The decision was made for her when the phone rang.

"Buckley Simpson," she answered the call, trying to sound calm.

"Buckley!" Seymour's voice sounded frantic. "I've been trying to reach you since yesterday!"

"The plane was delayed. I didn't get home until

past midnight," Buckley replied, knowing she sounded as weary as she felt.

"Buckley, sit down. We've run into some real trouble. T.J. has disappeared."

"What!" Buckley nearly shouted into the phone. She realized immediately that the door to her office was still open and slammed it shut. Almost whispering now, Buckley asked, "What do you mean, *disappeared?*"

"He's not at Grasslands. I went up there yesterday. Mr. Watkins called after you left for California, said T.J. was extremely depressed, wouldn't eat, and I decided to visit. By the time I got there T.J. was no longer at the facility. No one would tell me where he'd gone, and neither Tanner nor Watkins was anywhere around."

Buckley sank into her chair. She felt the last bit of courage draining out of her. Josh Marks's words came back as though someone switched on a tape recorder in her brain: "What Vivian really wants is to *destroy* T.J." The nightmare was coming true. T.J. was slipping away.

"Hello?" Seymour's voice sounded confused.

"I'm still here," Buckley said flatly.

There was dreadful silence. Dammit, she thought, biting her tongue to keep from saying more than that out loud.

"Seymour, listen. Please keep trying to reach Watkins. I just can't do it here at work. I'll meet you at the seafood restaurant about six. We'll try to figure it out. And . . . for God's sake, if you reach anybody . . . *don't* say anything about Josh. He's terrified of Vivian and won't help. I'm not sure yet, but I think I'll just have to tell T.J. I couldn't locate him . . . *if* we can find T.J.!"

"Buckley, are you all right?" Seymour's voice was filled with concern.

"No. As a matter of fact, I'm not all right at all."

"I'm sorry. I'll do what I can. See you at six." Seymour's last words were quiet, compassionate.

She hung up the phone and sat thinking for a moment. I don't know what the hell I'm doing anymore, she thought. It's like I'm trapped in this terrible dream.

The phone rang again. It was Mr. Henry's secretary.

"Mr. Henry wants to see you immediately," the woman announced rudely, and hung up.

The only other time Buckley had been formally summoned by her boss was to receive a raise. She wondered where Tony was, realizing that she hadn't seen him in almost a week. She didn't even know if he was in town. Strange that she hadn't thought about him even once in the past ten days.

Buckley looked at her watch. It was almost eleven o'clock. Walking down the long corridor, Buckley tried to organize her mind and put it back on a professional track.

As she approached the reception area, without saying anything directly to Buckley, the secretary rang Mr. Henry.

"Go right in," the secretary said disapprovingly.

Buckley opened the office door just as Mr. Henry looked up from a rather large report sitting before him.

"Come in, Buckley, and please close the door," Mr. Henry said in an even voice.

Buckley shut the door and sat in the chair directly opposite him. He took off his glasses and leaned back slightly.

"I'll come right to the point, Buckley. Your work has slipped . . . badly. We'd gotten a few complaints before, but I attributed them to the fact that you were new. I thought it would be just a matter of time, experience and further training. But recently the complaints have begun again."

"Complaints? I don't understand," Buckley said with complete candor.

Mr. Henry looked uncomfortable. He turned his face toward the large window near his desk, looking out at a beautiful view of the river. "Buckley, your dad single-handedly set me up in business. He lent me the money to start this agency, then gave me his company account. He was my first client. For a while he was my *only* client." Mr. Henry's voice trailed off as he watched one of the long coal barges slowly crawling across the river surface far below his office window.

It was with some effort that he continued. "When he died, I lost an irreplaceable friend. He was a great man, a man of vision and strength. I feel a responsibility to him even now. Having you work here was the most natural thing in the world for me. But I can't jeopardize my entire agency over a moral obligation. I hope you understand."

As she listened to him speak, it was slowly beginning to dawn on Buckley that this meeting was more serious than she'd anticipated.

"I know you've had some personal problems in the last few weeks, Buckley, but I'm afraid I didn't realize how seriously they affected your ability to do your job. Friday I was informed by Tony Marshall that an entire commercial package was unusable. He told me it was your project, and the results are inexcusable." Mr. Henry paused to take a deep breath.

"Tony said the company's marketing department is so angry . . . they threatened to remove the entire account if you weren't replaced."

Buckley was so stunned she didn't think to ask for the specifics of what had gone wrong.

"What about putting me on one of the other accounts?" she asked, hoping to hear a positive reply. "One mistake, if it really is my mistake, under normal circumstances isn't enough to get fired from the agency." She was sure Mr. Henry knew how emotional Tony could be and how unreasonable clients are when anything goes wrong. He was not in the habit of firing good people just because a client temporarily went crazy. He transferred his people to another account on the theory that once they were out of sight, business could continue.

Mr. Henry turned his back to Buckley, staring down at the coal barge slowly inching along the dark river surface. He alternately clenched and flexed his hands nervously. For him to hedge and beat around the bush was unlike him entirely, considering that not a month went by in this agency without at least one crisis.

"I've thought of that, of course," Mr. Henry continued speaking. "Unfortunately the other accounts are fully staffed, and business is slow right now." Finally, he turned to face her. "The last thing in this world I want to do is let you go. You're like family to me, Buckley. I detest being put in this position, believe me, but I can't risk losing that account or penalizing the rest of the staff. The best suggestion I can offer is to ask you to take a few months' leave of absence. Maybe it'll all blow over by then, and if it does, I'll guarantee your job back. Meanwhile, you'd be free to look elsewhere—take a vacation—

whatever you want. I'll even advance you a month's pay if you need it."

Through the fog of her own thoughts Buckley heard Mr. Henry say, "In memory of your father, I'm truly sorry."

It was all over. Buckley stood stiffly. Mr. Henry could no longer look her straight in the face.

She extended her hand. "I'm sorry, too, Mr. Henry." She felt an enormous sadness.

As she walked down the long corridor leading back to her own small and windowless office, Buckley wondered if this was the reason Tony had disappeared so completely. He was the consummate player of corporate politics, always careful to align himself with the winning side, avoiding trouble like the plague. She realized he'd probably known she was being fired days before she found out.

She closed the door to her office cubicle behind her and sat silently at her desk. Why would Tony Marshall do this to her? Why would he go behind her back when just a few weeks ago they had been so close? Where would she find another job as good as this one? How would she explain her sudden departure? Whom could she ask for a recommendation? She couldn't even cry. All she felt was humiliation. After a moment she noticed that a large stack of new work had been removed from her office during the time she'd been in with Mr. Henry. "Boy, it doesn't take long . . . does it?" she said aloud.

It was pouring rain outside. The torrential spring downpour was trying its best to wash the whole world clean. Even though it was almost dark, Seymour could see the first hints of tiny leaves on the trees that lined the riverfront boulevard. He arrived at the small seafood restaurant before Buckley, glad to sit quietly, sipping his drink.

About ten minutes later Buckley arrived, soaking wet. Seymour was surprised to see that despite her physical discomfort, Buckley appeared to be in rather good spirits.

In fact, Buckley was operating on sheer nerves. She was forced into a corner, face-to-face with decisions she never knew she'd be called upon to make. It was a crucial turning point in her life. She had spent the afternoon alone in her office, going over every detail, making a rough outline of the sequence of events, unsuccessfully trying to match them up with the new information that had besieged her.

"Seymour"—she opened their conversation—"do you think there's something wrong with me? I mean, am I missing a major chromosome that makes everyone else smarter than I am?"

He smiled at her intentionally dramatic analogy, so typical of Buckley when she wanted you to agree with the conclusion she'd already reached. "No. I don't think there's anything catastrophically defective."

Leaning forward, she zeroed in on his evasive answer. "Then you do think there's something wrong with me? It's just not a terminal condition, is that what you mean?"

Seymour couldn't help laughing at her serious face. She seemed so little right now, so determined to understand the confusion confronting her young life.

"I do not intend this as humorous, Seymour. This isn't funny."

"You're right." He brushed some lingering raindrops from her forehead and wiped his hand on the napkin beside his drink. Seymour dreaded the information he had to give her, wishing there were some way to ease into it but knowing full well there wasn't.

The waiter appeared, and Buckley ordered a full bottle of wine. Seymour raised his eyebrows quizzically. By way of answer, Buckley made a small, all-encompassing gesture with her hand.

"I'm celebrating. Mr. Henry fired me this morning." She swallowed hard, determined not to show one bit of self-pity.

"What?" Seymour was visibly shocked. "Why?"

"I'll tell you later. But first . . ." She reached into her bag and pulled out a yellow legal pad with several pages of handwritten notes. "Seymour, we have to look at this entire situation differently."

"Okay." He nodded, relieved to hear that she was thinking positively. Why, he wondered, was every minute with her making his task more difficult? He now realized he should have told her about T.J. right away. But it was too late. She was off on a tangent all her own.

The waiter reappeared, opened the wine bottle and poured her a small glass. Buckley tasted it expertly and nodded her assent for him to fill it up. As soon as he was out of hearing range, she continued.

"There's a pattern to all these events, and I've been trying to figure out what it is." She turned the note pad around so Seymour could read. "Can you see?"

"Sure. You have nice handwriting."

"No . . . Seymour!" she said with exasperation. "I mean can you see the pattern . . . can you understand what's really going on?"

"I can read what you've got here. I'm not sure I fully understand what it all means."

"Maybe we're both missing the same chromosome," she replied, trying to smile. Buckley drank her first glass of wine and poured a second. At this point she didn't care if tomorrow held a hangover.

"Okay, seriously." Seymour began deciphering her notes. "What I see is that Vivian has cards equaling a royal flush in this poker game and we're sitting with two of a kind."

"That's just what I mean!" Buckley nodded encouragement. "Somehow we've got to take an entirely new approach. Ever hear about the half-full versus the half-empty glass?" She pointed to her own wine. Buckley took a few sips and asked, "Now what is it . . . half-full or half-empty?"

Seymour shook his head. "Are you all right?"

"No . . . of course I'm not. Half the time I feel like I'm totally losing it . . . going crazy. Do you think I'd be acting this way if I were a normal, well-adjusted person?"

"Buckley, this may not be the greatest timing for what I have to tell you, but . . . I finally got Watkins this afternoon. After a lot of sidestepping, he told me that T.J. was transferred to the county psychiatric ward for observation. They assured me he's all right now, Buckley, but I'm afraid T.J. tried to commit suicide."

The color drained out of Buckley's face. Quietly she folded both hands on the table in front of her, looking squarely at Seymour. "What Josh told me to watch out for is coming true! Seymour, he told me that Vivian will somehow destroy T.J. My God . . . Seymour . . . we've got to do something quickly. Suicide. *That's* what she's counting on . . . of course! This is all beginning to make a hideous kind of sense."

Seymour looked across the table at Buckley,

reached over and took her hand. He felt her shaking. The strain she was under showed clearly now in her tired eyes and pale skin. With all his heart he wished he could give her the solution. He wanted to take her in his arms, provide her with some small measure of warmth and comfort.

Buckley leaned her elbows on the table and cupped her chin in the palms of her hands. "You know what our problem is? We're not devious enough."

"Really?" Seymour glanced at her.

"Really. It's all beginning to fit a pattern, even T.J.'s trying to kill himself. You know, I didn't realize it at first when Mr. Henry fired me, even afterward, when Tony Marshall was nowhere in sight; but I've been thinking about it all day, and I'd be willing to bet a hundred dollars that Vivian is the one who engineered my losing the job and is somehow involved in T.J.'s suicide attempt. The problem is my mind doesn't work like hers, and I can't figure out how she does it."

"Buckley," Seymour began gently, "I want you to be very careful. If Vivian really is as evil and sick as Josh says . . . you should stay out of her way. It's not going to help T.J. to put your own life in jeopardy."

"I know that. Believe me, the trip to California taught me a lot. But what am I going to do? How can I live with myself if I give up now?"

"What you're really talking about are moral values, Buckley. Unfortunately they're very often incompatible with reality. You have to realize that in this case they may be standing in the way of your own common sense and self-preservation."

Buckley nodded thoughtfully, finished her wine and filled the glass again. She wasn't hungry, and her mind was racing a mile a minute.

"You're right. Shit. Why can't I be more cynical and devious? Josh was right. It's hell being so damn stupid about the way things really work. The worst part is that the more I find out, the more I hate it! This world is really a crappy place, y'know that?" She slurred the last few words. The wine was having its effect on her empty stomach and keyed-up nerves.

"Come on, Buckley . . . this isn't like you."

"But I'm not like me anymore! That's what I've been trying to tell you! I can't be like me because it's not enough. Look, for the past two months I've begged and pleaded and yelled and screamed and cried . . . I've cried a lot . . . and where has it gotten us? Nowhere! So all that stuff is out. We have to find another way. Please . . . Seymour . . . don't tell me to forget it . . . I need you to help me."

Seymour rubbed the back of his neck as though fighting off a tension headache. Now he was wishing he was more like his Uncle Zack, who always seemed to think of workable solutions to insurmountable problems.

"The way I see it . . . Vivian has all the cards. So maybe there's a way to work a compromise instead of thumping heads with her all the time."

"What kind of compromise?" Buckley asked, showing the first flicker of interest.

"Well, if what she really wants is the money T.J.'s supposed to get, why not offer it to her now in return for T.J.'s freedom? Get her to sign him over to you or me, or to Alphonse, and pay her off. When the will comes out of probate, you can then get Alphonse to release some of your stock, sell it carefully and give Vivian the cash."

Buckley looked at him as though he'd just sentenced her to eternal purgatory.

"I don't know if I'm strong enough to do that," Buckley said honestly.

"Why? Because you're afraid, because it's morally wrong or because you hate her?"

"All of the above," she said very quietly, feeling her blood run cold at the thought.

"I understand, believe me I do."

Buckley pondered the idea silently for several minutes. Then she folded her napkin and set it on her empty place mat. "Okay," she said, getting up. "Wish me luck." Buckley smiled a thin, scared smile and kissed Seymour lightly on the cheek. "Think good thoughts," she whispered, and hurried out into the night.

Chapter 16

Vivian's living room was heavily perfumed with fresh flowers this evening. On the lovely French antique table, between two formal side chairs grouped comfortably near the couch, a brilliant display of apple blossoms and narcissus complemented all the other colors in the room.

Tony Marshall tried to appear at ease with Vivian. He was expert at intimidation in his own environment, used to getting his own way with the inhabitants of his working world. But Vivian Simpson was a decidedly different experience. Something happened to Tony when he was around people who possessed genuine affluence and power. He couldn't help feeling inferior to them in a way that rendered him inept despite the charming exterior he was always careful to maintain.

Vivian set her silver liqueur glass back on the bar and turned to face the strikingly handsome man who had been her paid escort for another evening. Nothing would please her more right now than to see his elegantly proportioned body lying naked on the pale satin sheets of her large bed. She envisioned the tanned skin and gently rippling muscles his clothing now covered. She felt a surge of pleasure, knowing it was only a matter of a few more minutes, a brief and discreet exchange between them, before she felt the warmth of his body against her own. She amused herself with the idea of collecting a male harem for her enjoyment. She could see them in her mind, ensconced in various boudoirs, their naked bodies languishing until she sought her pleasure from them.

Vivian vaguely heard a phone ringing in the distance. The housekeeper popped her head around the dining-room door.

"For you, madame," Estelle said quietly.

"Thank you, Estelle." Vivian turned to Tony. "Excuse me."

"Who is it?" Vivian asked as soon as she closed the kitchen door.

"Ms. Simpson," Estelle said demurely.

"Who *is* it, I said!" Vivian demanded, annoyed with the woman's stupidity.

"Ms. Simpson."

"Godammit, woman! When I ask you a simple question, I expect an answer." Vivian was furious. Estelle was mocking her in some obscure way.

"I'm sorry, madame, I've been trying to tell you . . . it's Miss Buckley Simpson."

"Buckley?" Vivian repeated. "On the phone?"

"No, in the lobby," Estelle said pointedly.

"The lobby!" Vivian didn't like being caught by surprise. "Tell them no one is to be allowed upstairs. Tell them I'm not home."

"Yes, madame," the short housekeeper dutifully

replied, and softly padded her way back to the house phone.

Downstairs, in the spacious and elegant condominium lobby, Buckley stood impatiently waiting for Otto, the night desk man, to return. As she tapped her fingers in exasperation she couldn't help noticing details of her surroundings. It hasn't changed that much since Dad and I lived here, she thought. A few plants have been replaced, maybe some of the carpet, but that's about all that is different.

Buckley hadn't been in this building since just a few weeks after the funeral, but she'd lived happily in the apartment upstairs for almost ten years. It seemed very strange having to stop at Otto's desk tonight, announcing the fact that she was here to visit the apartment that used to be her home.

Poor Otto was very uncomfortable with the strictly enforced building rules when it came to Buckley. She had been his favorite of all the children he'd come to know during his years of employment in this building.

When he returned, Otto's fingers fidgeted with bits of paper on the desk, and his eyes never left the countertop. "I'm terribly sorry, Miss Buckley . . . Mrs. Simpson is not presently at home."

Not thinking twice, Buckley replied as she walked toward the elevators, "That's okay, Otto . . . I'll just wait for her. Estelle can let me in."

Distraught, Otto ran after her. "Miss Buckley . . . please . . . I can't let you upstairs without proper authorization!"

Buckley turned to face the panting Otto.

"Authorization! But, Otto, that's absurd! I used to live here."

"Miss Buckley . . . *please!* I have my orders," he pleaded. "Things has changed," he mumbled softly.

"Okay, Otto. Okay, I don't want to get you in any trouble."

Greatly relieved, Otto bowed apologetically and returned to his position behind the desk. "Thank you, Miss Buckley," he said gratefully.

She left through the revolving front door, the same way she'd entered. But years of being a kid in this building had taught Buckley every delivery access the building possessed. She knew the trash chutes as well as she did the service elevators. Through a series of complicated passageways, starting from the back sub-basement, Buckley made her way up the fifteen flights to the apartment where Vivian now lived.

Maybe it was all the wine she'd consumed earlier in the evening that made this seem like a last great childhood adventure. Farthest of all from her mind at the moment was what she was going to say once she actually confronted Vivian face-to-face. It was the adventure itself that involved her concentration, as she tried to remember which unmarked door led to a passageway and which to a storage room. Buckley couldn't see herself, but she was smiling. Her face had shed the extreme tension of these past weeks. Temporarily, at least, she appeared confident and even happy.

With a definite sense of triumph Buckley emerged somewhat breathlessly on the fifteenth floor. At the very end of a long, elegant corridor was the front entrance to Vivian's apartment. Just around the corner and out of her immediate vision was the service door. Buckley recalled that she still had her old keys to the apartment. She was quite sure Vivian would have had the locks on the front door changed, but she wondered curiously if the service entrance had also been redone.

Vivian lay silently on the mauve satin sheets, her eyes closed. She felt moderately disappointed in Tony. Though his athletic physique promised glimmering brilliance, he was rapidly becoming ordinary.

"I'm afraid I have to be going. It was a wonderful evening, Vivian." His mellow voice broke through the quiet. She opened her eyes to find him fully dressed, standing beside her bed.

She smiled at him, knowing full well she would discard him. Without saying anything, Vivian slipped on her robe, tied it at the waist and paused just long enough to allow his kiss to land on her mouth one last time.

At that exact moment Buckley Simpson opened Vivian's bedroom door. With the sight of Tony kissing the woman she'd been following through the maze of recently acquired information, some of the pieces of the puzzle Buckley had struggled to put together suddenly fell into place.

"I knew it!" Buckley said with surprising calm.

Vivian was visibly startled. The last person she expected to see staring back at her in this private moment of conquest was Buckley Simpson.

"Hello, Vivian. Hello, Tony."

Tony Marshall knew there was no way to camouflage the fact that he and Vivian had just been in bed together. There was no place for him to hide, no graceful way of making himself invisible. Ordinarily he would have felt no guilt in the presence of two women he was sleeping with simultaneously. But this was no ordinary confrontation between jealous women. He'd played his cards to the hilt in this little poker game, and he'd just come up a big loser. Neither Vivian nor Buckley cared about the fact that they'd both been to bed with him, and Tony knew it. He'd fallen for Vivian's con game and made himself an eager pawn for her to trade. The embarrassment made his face flush uncomfortably.

"You're blushing. I didn't know men suffered from that affliction," Buckley said with a touch of amusement.

"I was just leaving." Tony tried to extricate himself as rapidly as possible.

Buckley unexpectedly blocked the door. "I'll bet you were," she said. "By the way, do you have any idea how idiotic you're going to look when Mr. Henry finds out you lied to him?"

"It's all done now, Buckley," Tony said quietly. He picked up his jacket.

Buckley stepped aside, watching him leave with a lingering sensation of bitterness. He'd been the first real love affair of her life. To see him so thoroughly humiliated was not a victory.

Quickly regaining her composure, Vivian walked into the adjacent living room. "I'm surprised at you, Buckley, sneaking around like this. All you had to do was let me know you wanted to see me. You didn't have to resort to this kind of underhanded breaking and entering."

"I didn't," Buckley replied quickly. "I simply used my keys."

Vivian made a mental note to fire Estelle. The housekeeper had been given specific orders to tell the locksmith to change both doors.

"It's time you and I had a talk about T.J."

Buckley continued. "I have a business transaction for you to consider."

"It's very late, Buckley, and I'm really not interested," Vivian replied in her most convincingly bored voice.

"Look, Vivian, I didn't come here to waste time. I know what you're planning to do, and it won't work."

Vivian's face flushed with anger. "If you don't get out of here this instant, I'll call the police!"

"No, you won't." Buckley smiled calmly.

The older woman stopped, realizing that Buckley was no longer the adolescent girl Vivian recalled. Deciding to call her bluff, Vivian started walking toward the telephone.

"You dial that number, and I'll expose everything I know about you."

"I have no idea what you're talking about."

"How about you and Benjamin . . . for openers?" Buckley said steadily. "There's more about Josh and T.J., but I didn't come here to recite a whole dirty laundry list."

"Well then, why don't you get on with what you did come here to discuss?" Vivian asked, mentally circling her prey. It occurred to her immediately that Buckley hadn't mentioned Buck Simpson's death. At this point, not including her father had to mean Buckley didn't know anything about Vivian's involvement.

"I told you. I have a proposition for you. A business deal."

"Really?" Vivian's eyes blazed with disdain.

"You and I have a mutual interest," Buckley started, beginning to shake inwardly at the thought of what she was about to say. "I have something you want, and you have something I want."

"Is that right?"

"What I'm offering is a trade. You sign the release papers for T.J., and I'll pay you a million dollars in cash as soon as the will comes out of probate."

Vivian laughed right in Buckley's face. "Where did I ever get the impression that you might have inherited some of your father's intelligence?" She continued viciously. "T.J. has become a juvenile delinquent, a sociopath, a danger to himself and society. I'm only doing my duty. As his mother I think I should know what's best."

"That's a lie, and you know it." Buckley broke her restraint and yelled.

Vivian slapped Buckley across the face. For a split second Buckley wished she could strangle Vivian on the spot. She wouldn't have felt one shred of guilt or remorse.

Buckley stepped back a pace, just out of Vivian's reach. She didn't dare allow herself the danger of getting too close. "You think you're so goddamned clever. You think you're the only one who can play this game. But when I get through telling the press and the board of directors everything I know, there won't be anything left to this pretty life-style you've set up for yourself, you worthless bitch!"

Buckley walked away from Vivian, toward the front door. There she stopped momentarily. "You'd better think about it, Vivian. If you don't decide to take the money and let me know in five days, I'll do exactly what I said. You don't want to lose all this, do you? After all, you're too old now to go back to prostitution on the streets!" She let the front door slam shut.

Chapter 17

Vivian wasted little time putting into motion a plan which was designed to checkmate Buckley. Several days later she was in a creaking red and white city cab bouncing over potholes which unpleasantly jarred both driver and passenger.

"Goddamn politicians!" The bearded cabby grumbled. "See that?" He pointed at another gaping hole, swerving to miss hitting it with his right front wheel. "Graft—that's what it is. They could fix these damn streets if they wanted to. God knows they bleed us dry with all their taxes. Getting so an honest man can't make a living anymore. Graft, inflation—stupid I call it. They're all crooks if you ask me. Let me tell you, a bunch of promises don't make much of a meal!"

"This will be fine. You can let me off here," Vivian said firmly.

"Okay, lady," the cabdriver replied, pulling sharply over to the curb. "That's four eighty-five," he said, flipping the meter handle.

Vivian adjusted her dark glasses, then took six bills from her wallet. "Keep the change," she said, opening the cab door quickly.

"Thanks!" she heard him say just before she slammed the door shut.

She hesitated for a moment on the deserted sidewalk, waiting until the cab was well on its way before she walked toward the rent-a-car office.

"What a weird dame," the cabby muttered. He'd picked Vivian up outside a coffee shop and dropped her off on a downtown street corner. Maybe she's meeting some guy and doesn't want her husband to trace her, he thought as he drove down the empty street and out of sight. Everything about her—the dark glasses, the scarf over her hair, the nondescript clothes—marked her as a woman who didn't want to be easily recognized.

Vivian walked quickly. She rented the car with an alternate driver's license she'd kept updated from the old days when she had multiple identifications, and she spoke to the girl at the counter in a phony southern accent. She had planned the transaction to be smooth and efficient. She was enjoying herself as she reverted back to the tactics she'd learned so well during her years with Benjamin.

She checked the city map, then headed the compact car toward the expressway going out of town. Traffic moved steadily as she passed through a suburban section and farther out toward an area of junkyards, industrial buildings and truck terminals. After glancing alternately at the map and then at the signs, she finally turned off the expressway and descended into a rundown neighborhood of narrow, winding streets.

Vivian swung the car down a dirt alley between two gray buildings. At the end of the alley was an ancient dilapidated garage and auto repair shop.

She parked the car and got out slowly, looking for any sign of workers.

Inside the garage it was rather dark except for two large work lights hanging from the ceiling by long thick black cords. Vivian could see the legs and torso of one mechanic sticking out from underneath a car up on jacks. "Joe?" she called out in the same southern accent she'd used in the rental office.

From a dingy room toward the back of the garage an older man stuck his head around the corner. "Yeah?" he said in reply.

Vivian adjusted her dark glasses again and walked toward him. When she got within ten feet, she could smell the rancid odor of week-old sweat and see the beard stubble on Joe's grease-stained face. "Ugly son of a bitch," she mumbled entirely to herself.

"Joe, I'm the one who called this morning . . ." she began slowly.

"Yeah? What about?" Joe questioned her suspiciously, carefully assessing this strange woman who approached him.

"Why don't we go somewhere we can talk privately?" Vivian answered.

"Hey, Skeeter, take a lunch break," Joe yelled at the young mechanic, who scrambled out from under the car.

"Okay, Joe . . . see ya in a bit," the kid said, wiping his hands on a greasy rag.

When the assistant mechanic was out of earshot, Vivian pulled a piece of paper from her pocket. "You still do contract house work, Joe?" she asked casually.

"Who wants to know?" he asked in a noncommittal, surly tone.

"A friend of Benjamin's," was her reply.

Joe looked mildly surprised. "Thought he was out of the business the last few years."

"He is. I'm not," Vivian answered steadily.

Joe sighed, rubbing his greasy hands together. "Yeah . . . I still do that work now and again. God-damn inflation's gonna bury all of us."

"Fine," Vivian said, extending the piece of paper toward him. "This is the address. It's an apartment. Second floor. One occupant who keeps irregular hours but is usually gone most weekdays."

Joe took the paper scrap, studied it a minute and looked back at her. "Good neighborhood . . . that'll cost you."

"How much?" Vivian inquired, taking out her wallet.

"Depends on what has to be done."

"I want the place ransacked, vandalized. It's got to be very effective and look like a real burglary. I want your men to make it seem like a cult job, you know . . . slogans and blood. You've got to guarantee it within forty-eight hours."

"Twenty-five hundred," he said flatly.

Surprise registered on Vivian's face for the first time. "*That's* inflation, with a little highway robbery thrown in for good measure!" she replied sarcastically.

Angry and somewhat defensive, Joe started to back away from her. "Hey, lady, I didn't ask for your lousy business! You want a job done . . . you pay for it."

Vivian smiled calmly. "I didn't say I wouldn't. Just remarking on the high cost of doing business these days."

She took a small folded stack of money from her wallet and counted out twelve well-used $100 bills.

"Half now," she said, handing Joe the cash.

The scraggly man's eyes glistened as he snatched the money and stuffed it into his pants pocket. "What about the occupant?" he asked.

"If your boys want to have a little fun, that's okay, too. But tell them to finish what they start. No loose ends, no possibility of someone testifying," Vivian replied. Joe couldn't see her eyes behind the dark glasses, but they were sparkling with excitement.

"Okay," he said, and unceremoniously disappeared into the darkened back room.

Vivian walked back to her car with an unmistakable look of pleasure on her face. At least that was one problem settled.

Too bad the Hunter wasn't so simple. He had just mailed her instructions to meet him in Trinidad the day after tomorrow with another payment of $50,000. He was getting greedy; she had to keep him quiet until after the estate was settled and she took possession of her share of the $19 million.

As she drove back to town with the radio blaring, Vivian found herself obsessively thinking about this invisible man who was blackmailing her. She wondered if he was following her regularly, how much he'd learned about her past. She tried to imagine his face, what he might look like when they finally met. Facing danger again filled her with excitement. It was what she'd missed during the placid, boring years of her retirement marriage. The thrill of the hunt was with her again.

Chapter 18

"There are no handles on these doors," Buckley said to the burly male nurse who guided her into the open ward room of the county psychiatric hospital.

"All the better to keep them locked up." The snaggletoothed man grinned weirdly. "All in a day's work around here," he said with a stultifying seriousness.

Her eyes searched the ward room, trying to pick out some sight of T.J. The hospital was located in an ancient stone building with iron bars on all the windows. The interior was painted a military shade of green, giving an eerie drabness and uniformity to the faces of the boys who milled about.

There were various mismatched, bedraggled couches in the center of the room and a small television set blaring forth an afternoon game show. The sounds of a rock radio station competed fiercely with the television program and the boys' conversation to create a hollow din in the large room.

Buckley's entrance with the male attendant was

heralded with whistles and catcalls from inmates nearest the main doorway. The oversized man smiled his craggy, lopsided grin as he turned the medieval key in the ward's door, locking all of them inside the room together. Buckley felt the stares of a dozen hungry male teenage eyes scanning her body and then her face. Without having to be warned, she knew better than to expect any protection from the ward attendant. This private world she was entering had different rules from any she'd ever known.

It was with a sense of relief that she finally picked out T.J. in the midst of a crowd. She saw him at almost the same time as he turned his attention toward the commotion near the ward entrance.

His face was a jolt to Buckley. T.J. had deep circles under his eyes. He was much thinner than the last time she'd seen him in the juvenile detention facility. He no longer looked like family. How strange it was to see so radical a change in someone you knew so well, someone you'd grown up with in the same house.

"T.J.?" Buckley called softly as she walked toward him.

He was seated sideways on the frayed arm of a couch, hunched forward like an old man in pain. A momentary spark of recognition came into his thin face, then faded away almost as quickly. He tried unsuccessfully to smile.

"Hi there, sis," T.J. said, half greeting her, half making the offhanded introduction between her and the three other boys seated near him.

Buckley started to move closer to him, to hug him. This was the first time she'd seen him without a glass partition or bars between them since he'd been arrested nearly two months ago. Suddenly she realized his wrists were bandaged.

T.J. stopped her before she was able to put her arms around him. He held her firmly.

"These are my buddies. Zoltan, Conch and," he said, indicating an olive-skinned boy no more than eleven years old, "the Whirlybird!" T.J. broke into laughter along with the other three. "Guys, this is my sister, Buckley."

As she looked from one face to another, she recognized a common sallowness in each skin color. Zoltan was a tall black boy with muscular shoulders and long legs. He acted as though he were the leader of this particular group, as indeed he was. He had a nasty scar on the side of his face, but he was otherwise a handsome young man. Conch had bright red curly hair standing straight up from his head, making him look permanently electrified. He had a broken front tooth and a tattoo on his forearm. His eyes were unpleasantly narrow, too closely set and somewhat glazed. He looked a bit slow, not exactly retarded, just slower to respond than the rest. The youngest boy, the one T.J. called the Whirlybird, was on a wavelength all his own, a study in constant motion, playing with imaginary objects, dancing to music only he was able to hear.

"Brought you some stuff," Buckley said as cheerfully as she could. Momentarily everyone stopped doing his own thing, even the Whirlybird. Their attention was riveted on whatever Buckley was about to produce. She could almost see their mouths salivating as she pulled assorted candy bars and chewing gum out of her bag. She wasn't sure whether T.J. should get all the loot to divide up as he chose or if she should give a portion to each of the other boys herself. She watched T.J. to try to get some clue. He held out both hands framed by their pathetic bandages. Buckley put as much as he could hold into his cupped hands; then she divided up the rest among Zoltan, Conch, and the Whirlybird. Almost in unison they ripped open the candy wrappers and stuffed the small bars into their mouths, throwing the wrappers carelessly aside.

"I need to talk to you, T.J.," Buckley said quietly, not wanting to offend his group.

Zoltan stood, motioned to the other two and, with his mouth stuffed, mumbled, "You're okay, sister."

The three of them aimlessly wandered off together, leaving T.J. and Buckley alone in that part of the large ward room.

"What are they here for?" Buckley asked, trying to keep a casual tone of voice to cover her nervousness.

T.J. barely looked up from the torn candy wrappers. "Zoltan ran a car theft gang; Conch raped a teacher."

"And . . . the Whirlybird?"

"Killed his mother's boyfriend," T.J. answered with his mouth full. "The guy used to beat up him and his mom. One day ol' Whirlybird stuck it to him, and they've had him locked up here ever since."

"What?" Buckley's face unmistakably registered her fright at being locked up with such dangerous young men.

"It's okay . . . don't worry . . . they're good guys. They won't hurt you—they're my friends."

"T.J.," Buckley whispered, "I thought this was the nonviolent ward!"

"It is." He smiled weirdly. "You should see the real loons."

Buckley sat gingerly on the couch without bothering to take off her coat. T.J. shoved several packs of gum into his pockets but continued eating the candy.

"You're going to make yourself sick!" Buckley whispered, feebly trying to joke and show her concern at the same time.

"I'm already *sick*," T.J. snapped back. "Or did you think I was here on vacation?"

"T.J., stop it!" Buckley said seriously. "You are *not* sick. You have to pull yourself together. How can I help get you out of here if you think like that?"

"Doesn't make much difference anymore what I think. Who the fuck cares if I think or don't think?" T.J. said without looking at her.

"I care . . . Seymour cares . . . Mr. Watkins cares . . . Dr. Tanner cares . . . a lot of people—"

T.J. interrupted angrily. "Don't talk to me about Dr. Tanner! That asshole is the reason I'm in this funny farm. He probably gets a kickback for every juvenile delinquent he sends to the loony bin." T.J. looked directly at her for the first time. "You want to know who's *really* crazy? I'll tell you who's crazy . . . Dr. Tanner's crazy. You want to know something else? That sweet bitch of a mother . . . Vivian . . . that cunt told Dr. Tanner she was afraid of what I'd do to her if they let me out! She actually told him she was afraid for her safety . . . that I had this 'murderous' temper, see . . . that I was violent and all that kind of crap. Me . . . violent! Good old chickenshit, candy-ass, pasty-fall guy, T.J.—*violent!*" he'd raised his voice progressively so that the last few words were loud enough to get immediate attention from the burly male attendant Buckley had met on the way into this ward. The attendant shot T.J. a look of warning, which T.J. acknowledged immediately with a defensive, apologetic gesture.

"Dr. Tanner never told me anything about this," Buckley said softly, trying to calm T.J. without confronting him directly. "Dr. Tanner told me that you'd become terribly depressed, that you tried to kill yourself," she said, referring to his bandaged wrists. "That's why he recommended the transfer," Buckley recounted.

"I know Dr. Tanner and Vivian are together in all this, so don't try to con me into believing any different!"

Buckley felt the instant pain of a headache spring out of nowhere. This place was beginning to make her feel ill.

"Buckley," T.J. whispered, bending close to her. "This place is terrible . . . I can't stay here. I'm scared I'm gonna die here, Buckley. You know what they do to you?"

Buckley silently shook her head no.

"If you get out of line, they shoot you full of Thorazine. They keep you so doped out of your skull you don't think about anything for days and days. They don't want anybody getting rowdy while they're in here . . . makes too much work for them. Know what, Buckley? Thorazine sucks!" He finished talking and sat quietly staring at the last empty candy wrapper.

"I'm really sorry, T.J. I'll talk to Dr. Tanner. I'll—"

He interrupted again, his depression turning to anger. "Don't you dare talk to that fart! Listen, Buckley, they don't give a shit if you get well. All they care about is keeping everybody quiet . . . so don't you cause me any trouble on the county wards of paradise lost!"

"You're on Thorazine, too?" Buckley asked with horror.

T.J. laughed quietly. It was a mean, cynical sound. "Hell, yes. Everyone is. This place is just one big legal fix!"

Buckley felt the pain throbbing from her eyes and forehead to the back of her neck.

"You thought the holding tank was bad? This place is a real joke!" T.J. fought back his tears, turning his head away. "Buckley?" he whispered.

"What, T.J.?"

"Don't let me die here . . . okay?"

"Oh, for God's sake, don't talk like that! Don't even think like that . . . please, T.J. I know it doesn't seem to be . . ." She never got to finish her sentence because T.J. broke in once again.

"What happened to my father?" he asked out of nowhere.

Buckley hesitated for a moment, debating how to answer. "I wasn't able to find him. We had the right address and all, but . . . he'd gone away . . . South America, someone said." Quickly she added, "I'm sure he would be here if he knew."

T.J. glanced at her over his shoulder, his bloodshot, hollow eyes trying to search out the truth. "You're lying," he said in a very cold and distant tone of voice.

"I'm not!" Buckley responded quickly, trying not to sound defensive or trapped.

"You're lying, Buckley. I never thought you'd do that to me." His eyes filled with tears. "The whole world is a lying sack of shit." He turned away from her again. "Why don't you just get out of here? Just leave me the hell alone."

T.J. got up and left Buckley sitting by herself on the couch. She opened her mouth to call to him but decided against making any kind of scene with so many people milling around the ward room. Wearily, with her headache pounding fiercely, she got up and walked slowly toward the exit.

The same male attendant who had admitted her now blocked the passageway, dangling his ring of enormous keys. "Have a nice visit?" he asked mockingly.

"Fine. Thank you," Buckley replied without looking at him.

"See you again next week?" the hulking man asked in an all-too-direct way. "I'm on duty every afternoon but Friday."

Buckley tried to appear completely dense to what he was saying. "How nice," was all she said while obviously waiting for him to let her out, showing no interest in the man personally.

He turned the key, swung the big door open, and she left without uttering another word.

Despite a blinding migraine headache, Buckley went immediately to Dr. Tanner's office. Her timing was perfect. The young psychiatrist had just finished his last appointment for the day.

"Dr. Tanner?" She knocked on the open door. "Buckley Simpson, T.J.'s sister. I'd like to talk to you."

"Come in, Buckley." He motioned for her to sit in the chair next to his desk.

"I've just been upstairs with T.J." She paused, trying to see past his professionally blank expression. "Why do you have him on Thorazine?"

Dr. Tanner put all his papers in a neat stack and moved them to one side, clearing his desk. He then directed his full attention to the distraught young woman across from him.

"T.J. is currently assigned to a juvenile nonviolent ward for evaluation. As you know, he tried to commit suicide. The medication is an insurance policy, for his own good."

Buckley's headache throbbed. "Dr. Tanner, this hospital is destroying my brother. Even though he has been cleared of any charges, he can't get out of here because now he's a victim of circumstances."

"I can't deny that some of what you're saying is true, unfortunately. But we have his mother's written consent for this evaluation."

"Dr. Tanner, before I accuse you of unforgivable collusion as well as malpractice, there are a few things I think you ought to know. First, Vivian Simpson wants the publicly administered juvenile justice system to destroy her son. Second, the woman you're so quick to believe spent twenty years as a prostitute and smuggler before she married my father. Third, she is a pathological liar."

"T.J. never told me any of this," Dr. Tanner replied in a noncommittal tone of voice.

"How could he? Most of this information T.J. doesn't know, thank God," Buckley said, trying to compose herself. "But even if he'd told you . . . would you have believed him? Would you have taken his word against Vivian's?"

The psychiatrist sat thoughtfully in silence, mentally reviewing T.J.'s file and the options available. He knew the judge in this case already seemed convinced that Vivian Simpson's version of this situation was accurate.

"Weren't you trying to locate T.J.'s father?" Dr. Tanner asked, changing the subject.

"Yes. But I'm afraid he won't take custody of T.J. Please don't tell him that," she added quickly. "I already told T.J. we couldn't find his father, and I don't think he could take anything more right now."

"Then there's a real problem because T.J. has to have somewhere to go, and Mr. Watkins says there simply are no available foster homes or group placement openings. Your best bet is to talk directly to the judge. In good conscience, I simply cannot release a fifteen-year-old to nothing more than a life on the streets!"

Buckley became extremely impatient and agitated. "Dr. Tanner, what the hell is going on here? The judge won't set a hearing date, even though I checked on those regulations myself and found out he should. Is that your definition of good conscience? Mr. Watkins seemed to be a decent man but went on a week's fishing vacation without assigning T.J.'s case to anyone else while he was gone. Is that the way this system is supposed to work? The hospital on your recommendation is shooting T.J. full of Thorazine to keep him quiet, and no one seems to give a damn that a totally innocent human being is being destroyed! Now, where in the hell is the justice of that?"

"There isn't any," Dr. Tanner said slowly. "But the system also has to deal with serious offenders, addicts, gang members."

"Dr. Tanner, I must remind you once again. T.J. Simpson no longer has any such charges against him. Everyone now admits that. But he's now at the mercy of a system that's slowly killing him because no one considers him a person anymore. He's become a case, a rule, a number, a regulation, part of a process and a real problem. Furthermore, T.J. is convinced that you have taken sides with his mother. Have you, Dr. Tanner?''

''No, I haven't, I assure you. My interests are with T.J., but it's been very difficult for any of us to help him.''

It was hard for young Dr. Tanner not to begin feeling angry and become defensive. His fundamentally humanitarian values were tested to their limit during his few days a week at this institution. His caseload was staggering; the positive results were few. He had seriously considered terminating his service contract when it came up for renegotiation. The time had come to face the fact that he, too, was becoming burned out. In order to preserve his own professional integrity, he had to resign.

''I'd offer to pay for your help directly, Dr. Tanner, but I'm afraid I'd be accused of trying to bribe a county employee. If you'll just not work against us, you can count on me to support any cause you choose . . . your own clinic, if that's what you want, I promise.''

''That won't be necessary,'' he answered curtly.

Dr. Tanner ran his hands through his damp, curly hair. She was right. He'd made a professional error. He'd fallen into the trap of too much work and too little time. T.J. should never have been referred to this facility. He should have been sent to a private hospital. The other boys here were not first offenders. They had been in and out of correctional facilities most of their lives. They formed an elaborate underground society, and T.J. had been a sitting duck for the gang that ran this place right under the noses of the orderlies and guards. ''I'll see what I can do. But remember, the judge still has to render a decision."

"Thank you for your time, Dr. Tanner." Buckley stood, realizing it was already dark outside. She checked her watch and knew she wouldn't get home until almost nine o'clock tonight. She was tired and hungry.

The rest of the week Buckley was like a woman driven by a force outside herself. With tireless energy she began tracking down every piece of information she could find on Judge Harding, who was presiding over T.J.'s case.

First she went to the newspaper files. She spent hours poring through microfilm, taking notes. She discovered that Judge Harding was running for higher office in the upcoming statewide elections. It didn't take long for her to locate his campaign headquarters in the downtown area.

Seymour's uncle Zack had extensive political connections in the state government and through them located a list of the judge's campaign contributors. Buckley's suspicion was confirmed. Both Mr. Havenhurst and Vivian Simpson were prominent on the long list of influential citizens supporting Judge Harding. Uncle Zack also found out that the judge played golf every Saturday morning at the same country club where several of Zack's closest friends were members. At Buckley's urgent request, Zack got her Judge Harding's tee-off time for the coming weekend.

It was barely light as Buckley drove into the country club parking lot. Zack's description of the grounds enabled her to find the path to the locker room and pro shop without difficulty. Although the day promised to be warm, there was a definite chill to the early-morning air, a slight mist hanging over the emerald green fairways. Buckley pulled her sweater tightly around her and buttoned it securely against the cold breeze.

From a recent newspaper photograph Buckley recognized Judge Harding's face immediately. She was surprised to see that nothing about his golf clothes indicated the somber prestige of judgeship. He wore bright plaid pants, an electric blue pullover shirt, multicolored golf shoes with yellow socks, and he topped off this garish rainbow with a red hat. He needed to lose about fifteen pounds around the middle and had slightly bowed legs. Under different circumstances Buckley would have simply dismissed the ungainly little man as a laughable figure. But today she walked directly toward him and introduced herself.

"Yes . . . Buckley Simpson . . ." Judge Harding replied with a smile. "Your name does sound familiar."

"It should," Buckley said. "I've been calling you about an appointment for nearly three weeks!"

"Well, I try to give all you hotshot reporters ample time," the judge said jokingly, "but my schedule at court has been pretty full lately."

"I'm not a reporter, Judge Harding," Buckley told him, closing the distance between them. "I called to talk to you about T. J. Simpson, whose case has been delayed in your court several times now."

Judge Harding's professional campaign smile disappeared. He picked up his golf bag and started for the nearest electric cart. Buckley followed quickly, determined not to let him slip through her fingers.

"Judge Harding," she said firmly, "we are going to talk about this whether you like it or not."

"Get in," he said, pointing to the empty seat on the passenger side of the fringe-roofed vehicle.

Buckley jumped into the cart and sat down just in time to keep the judge from driving off without her.

When they were out of earshot of the other golfers, Buckley turned toward Judge Harding. "I know that this election is very important to you. I also know that both Mr. Havenhurst and T.J.'s mother have been major contributors. How do you think it would sound to the voting public if they found out that you were holding an innocent boy to protect your political future?"

The normally florid color in Judge Harding's chubby face drained away, leaving an ashen pallor which was accentuated by the cold early-morning sunlight. He kept his eyes on the treelined path, guiding the electric cart farther away from eaves-dropping ears.

"What do you want me to do?" he asked in a hoarse voice.

"Only what you should have done in the very beginning."

"It's no longer that simple."

"Compared to what?" she asked pointedly.

He shot her a look of extreme irritation, but she also noticed the fear glinting at the corners of his eyes. She saw the tiny beads of nervous perspiration on his forehead just beneath the brim of his hat. Buckley waited patiently for his answer.

He stopped the cart in a deserted area of the golf course in a small grove of ornamental trees. "Young woman, you're way out of line. I run my court as well as any other judge on the juvenile court bench.

There are some cases that are more complicated than others. T. J. Simpson's is one of those cases. Sometimes there aren't any easy answers."

"I don't care about your personal problems, Judge Harding. I don't give a damn if you win this election or not. All I care about is getting my stepbrother out of your detention center and off your psychiatric ward. I am no longer above using everything in my power to do that! If you refuse to release him, then I'm going to the press with the facts of this case, and your political future will go right down the toilet. I'm fed up with delays and excuses."

"You don't know what you're getting into. I'm afraid you're either hopelessly unrealistic or downright stupid."

"Your insults won't change anything," Buckley flashed back at him. "It's your reputation on the line, Judge Harding, not mine. There's very little left that can be taken away from me. I'm fully aware that this is a rather dangerous game, but I don't have much to lose."

"Get out," he demanded unceremoniously.

"Okay." Buckley smiled. "See you at the press conference!"

Judge Harding's face clouded with anger. He drove off in the golf cart without another word.

It was a long walk back to the clubhouse and parking lot. Buckley felt strange, trudging along the path by herself, attracting the curious stares of golfers as she passed. However, as the sun warmed the spring air, the walk was pleasant.

There was a newfound sense of satisfaction in this confrontation with Judge Harding. She didn't know if she'd actually accomplished anything by it, but it made her feel less frustrated. She was fed up with the endless delays and feeble excuses. She was determined to help T.J., whether or not he continued to believe in her. Sadly she realized that in her haste she'd also told Judge Harding a sobering truth about her current existence.

The string of events seemed to have begun with her father's death and ended with T.J.'s attempted suicide. In between she'd broken off her love affair with Tony and lost her job. The one person she thought she could count on, Alphonse, had disappointed her the most. Seymour was all that currently stood between her and being totally alone. The strangest part of it all was the subtle way in which it had all come about. One day everything was fine, life was progressing smoothly, and the next day it had slipped over the edge into chaos. Suddenly staring her in the face were tragedy, loss, sorrow, tears. An endless string of trouble.

Where had her laughter gone? She couldn't remember really laughing in a long time. Yet there used to be whole months when she'd felt happy, fulfilled and creative.

She got into her car and drove aimlessly and alone for the remainder of the day, stopping at a quaint country village inn during the late afternoon for something to eat.

Chapter 19

As Buckley wearily turned the key in her apartment door that night, all she could think of was taking a hot bath and going to bed. She failed to notice that her key didn't turn the dead bolt; it only unlatched the lock.

Before she had gone three feet inside, her hand yet unable to reach the light switch, Buckley tripped over an unseen object. She never had time to orient her eyes to the darkness. She found herself sprawled on the floor.

Slowly her eyes began adjusting to the darkness. With only the assistance of light from the hallway Buckley made her way to the wall switch and flipped on the living-room lights.

"Oh . . . my . . . God!" she gasped in horror. The sight that greeted her was sickening. Buckley's apartment had been broken into, upholstered furniture slashed, tables overturned, lamps smashed, windows broken. The curtains had been pulled off the walls, ashes from the fireplace scattered in a grayish black smear. Everything in the place had been wantonly destroyed without hope of repair.

Like a woman in a nightmare, Buckley wandered from living room to kitchen. Nothing had been spared. Her dishes and glasses were broken. Food was smeared on the countertops, the refrigerator door left open after its entire contents had been emptied onto the floor. In the bathroom her cosmetics and nail polish were strewn across the floor; water had been left running in the bathtub, causing a small flood. She turned the water off and opened the drain while staring at the overflowing tub, then proceeded to her bedroom.

This little haven of personal safety was perhaps the most horrible sight of all. Buckley's bed was stripped, the mattress slashed. On the wall above her nightstand someone had painted the word "DIE" in huge letters with bright red paint which looked like blood dripping down the white wall.

On the floor lay her little cat . . . dead. Someone had slit her throat. She lay in the small pool of blood.

Buckley screamed, dropped to her knees beside the cat that had been her faithful companion and gently touched the matted fur.

"I was wrong . . . there was more that could be taken away," Buckley whispered.

She felt as though she'd stepped off firm ground into an abyss. She was falling through the darkness with nothing to stop her descent. Fear and pain tore at her. She buried her head in her hands and cried until no more tears came.

When her sobbing ceased, she lifted her head to look around her once more. Her first impulse was to grab her purse and run out of there, never to return again. It terrified her to think that she might have opened the apartment door when this vandalism was still in progress. Anyone capable of such destruction would surely have killed her, too. If she had returned a few minutes earlier, she might have been murdered. She might also be lying dead. She found a small hand towel and carefully wrapped it around her poor little cat. "Sorry," she whispered. "I'm so sorry."

Buckley knew she had to leave the apartment. But her car was nearly out of gas, and it was almost ten o'clock at night. Buckley felt sick to her stomach, scared to death. She got up from the floor of her bedroom and walked to the kitchen. She felt like the lone survivor of a disaster. Buckley brushed away some debris on the counter, picked up the receiver on the wall phone and dialed Seymour's number. There was no answer. She hung up and dialed another number.

"Alphonse?" Her voice sounded far away and unsteady. "It's Buckley. Please help me . . . could you come to my apartment right away? Something terrible has happened." She listened to him for a minute. Her eyes had a glazed look. Leaning on the kitchen counter for support, she continued. "My apartment has been vandalized. No, I'm not hurt, but they killed my cat. I just can't stay here." She listened again, nodding her head as though Alphonse could see her through the telephone. "Yes, please. I wouldn't be so scared with you and Carolyn. And could you call John Needham? Do you have his number?" She waited a moment. "He told me to call if I ever needed help. Thank you." She hung up.

Buckley walked back into her living room. She turned a small table upright, straightened a pillow on the couch, but she knew these were completely futile gestures.

She sank into the nearest chair, desperately wishing she could have her previous way of life back again. Insignificant as it may have been, the safe routine of her old job, a boyfriend and a regular income seemed like heaven on earth right now.

"I can't believe all this is really happening to me," Buckley muttered out loud. Her words wandered around the disheveled room, finding no ears except her own upon which to land. In the hollow emptiness, there was a rancid scent of fear. She heard her own terror pounding on her brain. She was standing on the edge of space again, looking out into eternal darkness. One wrong move, and the darkness would engulf her forever. She couldn't remember feeling anything like this before. She had never known what it was like to be terrified of living and yet scared of dying at the same time.

She wondered fleetingly if God had deserted her entirely. She closed her eyes for a moment, half in a prayer for mercy and deliverance, half in sheer exhaustion. Buckley fell sound asleep.

A strange sound filtered through her subconscious. Her eyes flew wide open. An involuntary scream escaped. She jumped to her feet in self-defense, grabbing wildly for some sort of weapon.

Directly in front of her stood a large man. He stared at her, making no move. Buckley screamed again, crying out for help but uttering only garbled sounds. She tried to run past the man, to escape this intruder.

Alphonse held her firmly, not intending to hurt Buckley, only to stop her. "It's all right. I'm not going to harm you, Buckley. It's me . . . Alphonse."

Buckley blinked her eyes in disbelief. The voice sounded vaguely familiar, but her brain was so filled with turmoil and confusion that it took a minute for thc man's identity to register.

"Alphonse!" she finally gasped, allowing her rigid body to relax slightly. Her hands, which had been raised into fists of self-defense, unclenched and fell limply beside her body. She felt her knees go weak as though she were going to faint. Alphonse helped her back into the chair. Buckley started to cry again. Fear and relief were so mixed up now that she was no longer able to distinguish between them as the source of her renewed tears.

"Buckley, I'm so glad you called me," Alphonse said quietly. "You're right . . . you can't stay here. It's too dangerous for you now." He sat near her on the arm of the shredded couch. "I'm sure it's Vivian," Alphonse added in a hoarse, choked voice. "I couldn't tell you before, but she threatened me when I refused to help her get rid of T.J. I'm not proud of the choices I've made lately. I lost my nerve, tried to play it safe. But that's over now. I owe you a tremendous apology for violating my oath to your father." His voice trailed off into silence as he stared at the wanton destruction surrounding the two of them.

"I underestimated Vivian, never thought she'd go this far. But she's gone crazy." Alphonse took Buckley's face in his big hand and tilted her head up slightly, gently forcing her to look at him directly. "She's been after all of us, and you're next. I know you are. Please try to trust me, Buckley. I swear, I'll do everything I can to help you."

In a voice that sounded very unsure and childlike, Buckley asked, "Alphonse, you wouldn't lie to me, would you?"

Tears welled up in the older man's eyes. "No, I'm telling you the truth. On the memory of your father and our friendship of a lifetime, Buckley . . . I'm not lying."

Alphonse took her hand in his as though renewing the bond between them and his obligation to fulfill the promises of long ago.

"The night before your father died, he told me

that he intended to change his will as soon as we returned to the city. Although he did not specify the reasons, I got the impression he was going to divorce Vivian."

"Divorce?" Buckley repeated the word that would have changed her life.

"That's right. If he'd lived another week, your father would have changed his will to protect both you and T.J. Then he would have filed for divorce from Vivian. I found some notes in his desk at the office indicating he'd already made an appointment with his attorney and outlined his intentions regarding the estate. They were dated the day we left on the hunting trip."

Buckley's heart ached for all of them, most of all for her dead father. How terrible it must have been for him to come to that decision and never to have shared it, not even with his best friend, Alphonse.

"Do you think Vivian knew?" Buckley asked, not quite daring to hear the answer. She was on the verge of drawing the most horrendous conclusion. Her brain balked at fitting these last few gruesome facts together, yet she could not stop now.

"Yes. Now I'm sure she did."

John Needham suddenly appeared at the living-room door, startling Alphonse and Buckley.

"Didn't mean to alarm you, Buckley," John Needham said.

"Alphonse, you remember John Needham." Buckley introduced the two men, not realizing they'd recently seen each other.

Neither Buckley nor Alphonse could have known the depths of the homicide detective's personal interest in this case. Twenty years ago, when Needham was hardly more than a rookie, he'd been assigned to the vice squad doing undercover work. His memory of Vivian Simpson emerged from those nights. The two had met only once before, but her beautiful arrogance and casual disregard had impressed him. Had they met under different circumstances, Needham might have admired the elegance with which she'd paid off the vice squad. She had convinced the young Needham not to arrest her if she turned informer. After he agreed, Vivian had quickly vanished, having had no intention of honoring her part of the bargain. Needham had shared the sizable bribe with two other officers. None of them figured on Vivian's turning their names in to department headquarters. His two buddies were suspended from the force. Needham's job was saved only because his commanding officer owed him a considerable favor. John Needham figured he had an old score to settle with Vivian one day.

"As you can see," Buckley said, indicating her vandalized apartment, "I need some help. Thank you for coming. Ever since I started trying to help T.J., terrible things have happened—"

"You think this is related to T.J.?" Needham asked.

"I'm sure of it. Everything else has been."

"By the way, I ran a check on the car you reported, the blue sedan. Did you ever see it again?"

"No," Buckley replied. "What did you find out?"

"It's registered to a man who worked as one of those exotic dancers, a male stripper in a club down by the county line. We got an anonymous tip on him right after that. Rumor has it he was a real sharpshooter back in Nam and hired out as a hit man from time to time, following his army discharge. It was enough for a search warrant. The curious coincidence is that we found out from his friends that he suddenly came into a rather large sum of money and, when we searched his apartment, learned that he owns a Mannlicher SSG sniper rifle which was purchased eight years ago when he returned to the States. He's reportedly an avid hunter. Goes up north every deer season."

"Oh . . . my God!" Buckley's face turned ashen. How could she ever forget the name of the terrible gun that killed her father?

"I had a tracer put on this man, but not soon enough. First name's Sam. Last name's usually an alias. He left the country over a week ago. Ballistics is checking out the rifle."

"Are you by any chance saying . . . my father's death . . . wasn't an accident?" Buckley asked, feeling a terrible pain lumping itself in her chest like a fiery knot.

"It's beginning to seem that way," Needham said, "but there's only circumstantial evidence so far."

"My God . . ." Buckley said, the pain burning its way through her heart. She'd considered many strange and inexplicable reasons for his death, but murder was never one of them.

"Do either of you happen to know where Mrs. Simpson is?" Needham inquired.

"She left on a brief vacation several days ago. The Caribbean, I think. I know she keeps a place in St. Croix," Alphonse volunteered.

"Mr. Needham," Buckley began very slowly, "Alphonse just told me that my father was going to divorce Vivian and change his will, but he died before he was able to carry out his plans.

"You said my father's death might not be an accident." Buckley forced herself through the next few words. "By that, did you mean to insinuate that Vivian may have hired the man you call Sam to kill my father?"

"It is possible," Needham answered directly.

Buckley closed her eyes against the terrible stinging tears, biting her lower lip to retain some control. Alphonse gathered her in his arms, trying to soothe away the pain.

"My God," Alphonse murmured.

"What do I do now?" Buckley asked, feeling anger and desperation welling up inside her. "Can I press charges against her? Can you arrest her?"

"There's nothing you can do at the moment, Buckley." Needham answered her quickly. "We need more than these thin shreds of purely circumstantial evidence. Vivian Simpson is a clever woman. It would be a bad mistake to tip our hand too soon. If she finds out that she's under suspicion, we'd simply be giving her the time she needs to cover her tracks and build a good defense. In any case, even if there is more real proof, I don't want you to hope for too much. Under the best conditions it's very tough to get a conviction these days, and even so, she probably wouldn't get more than half a dozen years in jail."

"What?" Buckley was near explosion. "You mean to tell me that she can kill my father and the most she's going to have to pay for that crime is a few years in jail?"

Needham simply nodded his head in affirmation. "She wasn't the one who pulled the trigger. But even if she were, and we could prove that at her trial, chances are she'd still get life imprisonment, not the death sentence."

"Something is terribly wrong," Buckley said, shaking badly. "That's a perversion. . . . I'm sick to death of everything's being turned upside down. What is the matter with our laws? How can you sit by and let this happen? If Vivian killed my father, she should receive equal punishment. What the hell is so special about her that she deserves to live when my father is dead? He never did anything to hurt her!" she shouted, tears of outrage streaming down her face. "It's wrong!"

"I know it's wrong," Needham answered quietly. "Believe me, I know." He took out his little notebook and wrote in its quickly. "Buckley, you shouldn't stay here for a while. My advice is to remain out of sight somewhere safe. Don't tell anyone where you are, and give me a call in a couple of days. I should have more information by then."

Buckley looked at Alphonse, who kept his arm around her protectively. "She's going to stay with me and my family. We'll take good care of her."

"Thank you, Alphonse," Buckley said, seeing they shared the same terrible understanding.

"Get whatever you need to take with you tonight and let's go home. Carolyn is waiting for us."

"Alphonse—my cat."

"Just get your things. I'll take care of her. We'll bury her in the garden. Don't worry, dear, there's nothing more you can do."

Chapter 20

Heads turned ever so slightly as the beautifully dressed woman approached the airport lounge area alone. Her clothes were custom-designed; the jewelry she wore was expensive but not gaudy. Although Vivian showed no outward sign of acknowledgment, she was secretly delighted at the interest generated by her late arrival for this flight.

Before any stranger had an opportunity to approach her, the announcement was made to board the plane. Vivian noted an unaccustomed nervousness in herself with a touch of displeasure. She realized the clever assurance with which she had previously conducted all her business was missing. While she was sure that her carefully constructed plan to bring only half the blackmail money demanded by the Hunter would work, Vivian wished Benjamin were available to back her up as in the past.

She picked up her burgundy leather briefcase, and lightly flicking the fabric of her skirt smooth, she took the first few steps toward the boarding door.

As she fastened her seat belt, Vivian knew this was not an auspicious beginning. Her first business trip after all these years, bizarre as it might have been, should have gotten off to a better start. The second message from the Hunter had determined the time and place of their next exchange. Vivian would not allow herself to bungle the opportunity this time. She actually looked forward to his challenge, to trapping him in his own game. His sprawling childish note inviting her sarcastically to join him for a weekend in the tropical paradise of Trinidad and Tobago also demanded $50,000 for his prolonged silence. This would be the last hand of the game. Once her initial terror of exposure subsided, Vivian rather enjoyed the macabre unfolding of events.

Almost unconsciously she ran her fingers over the smooth surface of the burgundy leather case beneath her seat. It gave her great pleasure to feel the soft texture because she knew its enticing contents would attract and ensnare the man she was to meet. The pretty stewardess took her drink order and disappeared farther down the aisle.

Wind-whipped rain lashed across the runway as the crowded 727 aircraft landed with a succession of bumps and skidded to an unnerving stop. It had been a long ride. The airline scheduled intermittent stops at every major island in the entire Caribbean chain. First there was steaming Puerto Rico, then came the emerald waters of St. Croix, next it was St. Lucia, then Barbados and finally Port of Spain, Trinidad. The farther south they traveled, the more lilting and foreign the sounds of conversation became. Conservative business clothes now mingled equally with turbans and flowing island prints. Dark faces trimmed with gold hoop earrings bobbed up and down along the aisles. A baby cried endlessly. The plane was now jammed full.

Vivian stretched wearily and prepared to disembark with the human procession descending the 727 aircraft, which sat nearly a hundred yards from the tin-roofed terminal building. Rain and a strong tropical wind buffeted Vivian as she stepped outside onto the swaying steep stairs. Light from inside the terminal shimmered in the darkness. There were no attendants to shield them with umbrellas. Vivian's hair and clothes were dripping as she entered the fluorescent brilliance of the large room.

She was pushed and shoved along with several hundred others from different airlines, all funneled into two lines. First they passed through the health inspection check, had their certificates stamped and then were separated into six long lines awaiting passport clearance. Wind howled through the cavernous hangar structure.

The long lines of exhausted passengers inched forward at a maddeningly slow speed. Vivian noticed that every official had an identification badge with something written in green bold-faced type above his name and photograph, but she was not yet close enough to decipher what the notice said. She also noted that there was an unusual number of armed guards in the terminal building.

Suddenly a voice broke through. "Passport, please," the island accent requested. Vivian found herself face-to-face with an Indian woman who wore a red caste mark on her forehead and was dressed in a quasi-military uniform. In an automatic gesture

Vivian handed the woman her open passport, officially stamped health certificate and signed declaration statement. In the moment it took for the customs official to check her documents, Vivian read the badge clipped to the woman's uniform pocket. Along with her name and snapshot were the words "State of Emergency" in bold green print.

"Reason for journey?" the woman inquired.

"Vacation," Vivian answered.

As her passport was being stamped for emigration, Vivian looked more carefully at the guards. At closer range she realized these were army men dressed in battle fatigues, carrying automatic rifles.

The customs official handed Vivian back her passport, inquiring, "How long are you staying?"

"About a week," Vivian said quickly.

She tucked the passport securely in her purse and hurried toward the airport exit, hoping there would be no problem finding a taxi into the city. It was still pouring rain.

As Vivian walked quickly down the long covered ramp, a lanky young native approached her, speaking in a heavy island accent. All she could understand was the word "taxi." In the darkness she could see a group of five or more black men congregated near the ramp exit. She didn't see any cabs.

"How much?" Vivian asked hesitantly, scanning the darkness for a sign of more reputable public transportation.

"Twenty dollar T.T.," the man replied, grinning widely. The huddled group of men near them broke into action as other passengers began departing the terminal. In a language Vivian barely understood, the men started hustling the tired travelers for cab fares into the city.

"I don't have any local money," Vivian answered. "Only American dollars."

"Okay," the highly suspect driver replied, reaching for her suitcase. "Twelve dollar American."

"Ten," Vivian snapped, remembering vaguely that there should be an exchange rate of two to one.

"Okay, lady," the man answered.

It was only as he started farther out into the nighttime blackness that Vivian realized he'd already gotten her suitcase and she had no alternative but to follow him.

There were no lights in the parking lot. The black man disappeared almost immediately into the rain-soaked void. Only the lighter portions of his print shirt were visible. It was like following some strange fractured beacon. The wind quickly obliterated any sound of his footsteps. Vivian followed in the direction she had seen him vanish.

It was with distinct relief that she located both the driver and ancient black car just as he was putting her suitcase into the front seat. Her first impression of Trinidad was of the pitch-darkness of night, the blue-black of his skin, the grayish black of this dilapidated car. Instead of the lush brilliance of a tropical paradise, Vivian experienced the somber, ominous feeling of a church funeral.

It was with real trepidation that she entered the taxi. She wasn't even sure it was a taxi. There was no meter, no sign on top, no special license in evidence. As the rumbling heap started through the parking lot, she seriously wondered if she was being kidnapped.

The car careened through the open countryside at a terrifying speed. Vivian could see almost nothing through the steaming windows except a few roadside trees and vast emptiness. All of a sudden the solitary taxi burst into a main intersection with people and traffic and the sound of steel drums. It was a miracle the driver didn't hit several pedestrians as he crazily threaded his way through the human throng. Vivian peered out the window at makeshift shacks with their tin roofing and outdoor faucets. They tumbled one on top of the other, rambling along the side streets and up the hillside slopes. In some places there was barely the width of a single vehicle between the helter-skelter rows of houses.

The taxi skidded around a corner and headed up a long mountain road. This is it, Vivian thought. She was positive the man had kidnapped her for a voodoo ritual, a cannibal feast or some equally dreadful island magic.

Suddenly the taxi swerved again. Vivian knew they were going to be plunged to their deaths over the steep cliff. She grabbed onto the door handle, fully prepared to open it and jump if necessary.

She peered through the front windshield and saw the main entrance to a large hotel built on the hillside looming straight ahead of them. With an enormous sigh of relief she realized this nightmarish ride was nearly over. The car had barely come to a halt before she had her door open and quickly exited the black deathtrap with its lunatic helmsman.

Vivian suspiciously surveyed the hotel, expecting the worst. However, everything visible about it looked like a perfectly normal luxury hotel on any island catering to a tourist trade. There were lush tropical plants, beautiful perfumed flowers, brilliant even in the night's darkness, and a polite porter in uniform to take her suitcase.

The walkway into the hotel was made of wide teak-wood planks, polished and luminescent. The spectacular lobby was designed to replicate a jungle village but soared three stories high. She could hear the sound of steel drums coming from the main dining room, which was turned into a nightclub later in the evening.

Her room was perfectly ordinary but adequate. She had a small balcony overlooking the tennis courts and a garden. It wasn't luxury, but then she was planning to be there only a couple of days.

Vivian was mystified that there was no message from the Hunter awaiting her arrival. To add further insult, she hadn't met one attractive man on the entire journey. Vivian looked in the bathroom mirror, wondering uncomfortably if she'd lost her attractiveness. Slowly a weariness descended upon her. Perhaps subtle changes had taken place that she'd failed to notice.

She turned on the hot water in the basin to wash her hands. It was a small comfort to feel the grime of travel melt away under the soapsuds. She thought about taking a cool shower but decided to listen to the music in the nightclub and have a few drinks instead.

On her way through the lobby Vivian impulsively detoured to the nearest telephone and asked the Indian operator for a long-distance line to the States. She needed to call someone familiar just to reassure herself. She thought of Tony.

"Very sorry, madam," the operator's lilting accent came back. "All outside lines are temporarily out of order."

Vivian was stunned. "Out of order? You mean I can't get a long-distance call through?"

"Very sorry. No calls at all tonight," the operator continued with unctuous politeness. "Please try again tomorrow."

Vivian stared at the telephone as she replaced the receiver. There was no possible contact with the world beyond this hotel. She felt a shiver go down her spine as she heard a violent surge of steel drum music coming from the nightclub.

At the bar she ordered an enormous tropical drink with the complimentary ticket the check-in clerk had given her upon arrival. "That's the least this place can do," she said to the bartender, who smiled and shrugged his shoulders.

"Happens. Since independence, nothing work . . . *all* the time!" He laughed. "You get used to it. Few things cannot wait until tomorrow. Enjoy yourself."

Vivian sat looking out the window at the city lights far below. She was beginning to be sleepy. It had been an arduous all-day journey.

The drink was some exotic concoction of fruit juices, rum and something else that was difficult to distinguish. It tasted terrible. She decided to leave it on the table and go to bed. "Never expect something for nothing," she muttered. As she was leaving the crowded bar, Vivian caught a brief glimpse of the cocaine dealers in a dark corner exchanging their wares. One of the men smiled at her and subtly invited her over to their table. Vivian smiled back and accepted.

For two days Vivian waited to be contacted by the Hunter. She lay in the sun, swam in the hotel pool, ate her meals alone and waited for the phone to ring or someone to show up in person. The cocaine dealers were her only brief amusement.

The third morning dawned steaming hot and overcast. Vivian opened the door to her balcony, hoping to get some relief from the claustrophobic heat. Outside, the air hung heavy with an impending storm. Giant black thunderclouds loomed overhead, filling the morning sky with darkness. Directly below her balcony two native men were working with large curved machetes, cutting down the overgrowth of jungle vines that threatened to cover the entire garden. Vivian was startled by a strange sound. She looked down. An enormous black beetle was scurrying directly toward her bare feet. Vivian ran for the safety of her room, slamming the balcony door behind her.

There were very few things in this world capable of frightening Vivian. A giant black centipede creature that crawled out of the jungle was one! She felt her heart pounding fast. Her skin was covered with tiny bumps as she shivered even in the sweltering tropical heat.

"I've got to get out of this stinking place," she said aloud.

Quickly she walked over to the phone by her bed, dialed and listened for the operator.

"I'd like to call the airlines," she said abruptly.

"Sorry, madam. The hotel phone lines for outside calls are temporarily out of service."

"That's what I was told three days ago! Yesterday you said it would be fixed this morning," Vivian snapped back.

"Perhaps it will," the operator replied politely but without sounding as though there were much real cause for optimism.

"If there's no phone service, *how* do I change my plane reservations?"

"Please, take taxi to airline ticket office in the city."

"Thank you." Vivian abruptly hung up.

Without waiting for breakfast, Vivian dressed and hurried to the lobby. She took the first available taxi.

In the morning's broken sunshine she saw the island beyond her hotel for the first time. As her taxi descended the long hill into the city, she saw the spacious polo grounds coming into view first. They were completely deserted. The former Queen's Hotel on the park was crumbling into ruins. What had once been the epitome of English Victorian colonial elegance was now a shabby government building about to collapse. Several drunken derelicts and a few stray mongrel dogs wandering through the weeds were all that populated the remains of the Princess Court across the street.

The taxi turned a corner into the main street. Building after building had been demolished, but the rubble had never been removed, so that gaping holes remained, resembling a city recently bombed. The narrow sidewalks were jammed with people. A small herd of goats shared the roadway with vehicles trying to inch their way through a hopeless traffic jam.

After fifteen minutes and a journey of only six blocks the cab finally made its way into an industrial section near the commercial docks. Several oil tankers lay at anchor in the harbor. The humid air stank of petroleum fumes and dead fish. Every factory and office building was surrounded by ten-foot chain link fences with rolls of fresh barbed wire strung across the top. Even the entrances were guarded by fully armed soldiers.

Suddenly the events at the airport came back to her. "State of Emergency," she remembered seeing on the official badges. My God, she thought, this whole place must be in a revolution. Vivian asked the driver if he would wait for her as they pulled in front of the airline office. The man looked surprised but shrugged his shoulders and nodded his head.

Inside, the ticket office was complete turmoil. There were ten other people trying to change their reservations, but no one seemed to be in charge of the customers. Everything here was done by hand. Pieces of paper were all that took flight as the antique ceiling fans blew capriciously.

Finally, Vivian caught the attention of one harassed young man.

"No flights to the United States today," he said hurriedly. "All flights booked tomorrow."

Vivian was desperate. "Is there a waiting list?" she asked urgently.

"Waiting list longer than reservation list," the man said with an air of resignation.

"Well, what about one of the other islands? Barbados, St. Croix?" She tried to sound hopeful.

"All flights to other islands originate here in Trinidad, terminate in Puerto Rico with connections to U.S., except Tobago. You like to go to Tobago?" He smiled hopefully.

Jesus Christ, Vivian thought angrily. What the hell good does Tobago do me? Then I'd really be screwed. Trinidad's sister island of Tobago is even farther from the civilized world than this hellhole.

"No," she answered, trying to remain calm. "Tobago won't do. I want a flight to the United States."

The man shook his head negatively. "All we have

is one opening on this afternoon's flight to Venezuela or a seat on the plane to Switzerland tomorrow morning."

For a moment Vivian seriously considered taking one of the two available choices. Anything would be better than where she found herself: stuck in a smoldering tropical revolution.

"No. Just put me on the waiting list, and make me reservations on the first flight you have."

The man looked through a stack of handwritten reservation pages. Vivian's heart sank as he thumbed past one day after another.

"Nothing else. Sorry."

"Where to?" the driver asked over the sound of the clicking meter as Vivian reentered the taxi.

"Back to the hotel," Vivian answered, and leaned back despondently in her seat. She didn't want to smell the stench of sweating humanity or hear the din of goats and crying babies. She was frightened by the soldiers with their rifles and bayonets.

She was also dripping wet. Nervous sweat mixed with the humidity that permeated everything. Her clothes were soaked, sticking to her body, itching her skin.

Once inside her hotel room, Vivian paced angrily back and forth like a caged animal, her mind racing for a solution. Suddenly she heard a strange sound and felt a hand on her shoulder. Vivian screamed. The man's hand clamped quickly across her mouth, instantly muffling the sound of her scream.

Her eyes wide with terror, Vivian was slowly turned to face the intruder. He was about thirty years old, moderately good-looking, dressed in an expensive dark suit. She saw a strange glint in his brown eyes, a narrow smile on his dry lips.

She didn't try to struggle with him, instinctively guessing it would be dangerous. This was a man on the brink of violence. She would have to be very calm, very cooperative. Vivian knew he could hurt her.

"Let me introduce myself," the man said with mock politeness. "My name is Sam. I am the Hunter."

Vivian's eyes swept his face, noting every detail for future reference and identification. It was not difficult for her to see that he was crazy.

Sam loosened his grip on her mouth and released her from his grasp slowly while watching her for any quick move.

"I believe we have some business to transact," Sam continued. "There is a matter of fifty thousand dollars to collect." He waited for her reply.

"Yes. It's in the briefcase," Vivian responded without moving a muscle, without pointing to the location.

Unexpectedly Sam reached out his hand approaching her face. Vivian flinched involuntarily, thinking he was about to slap her. Instead, Sam gently ran his fingers across her chin and down her throat. "You have a very beautiful face." His eyes were fixed obsessively, visually caressing her softly curved mouth.

Chills went down Vivian's backbone, reverberating outward to her arms and legs. She saw no way out of this except to cooperate and try not to show any outward signs of the terror she felt.

Sam's strong fingers clutched firmly around her throat. His face and nasty sour breath closed in upon her until his tanned skin almost touched her. Inwardly she recoiled, but physically she remained remarkably still.

"You'd like to get rid of the Hunter and the problems he's caused, wouldn't you? You'd like to stop worrying if he was going to mess up your pretty life."

Vivian made only the slightest movement of her head, indicating her answer was yes.

His deranged eyes hungrily devoured her face; his incredibly strong fingers tightened around her throat. If Sam were to carry out the orders he'd received from Benjamin, he would have to kill the woman right now. He shouldn't risk her finding some way to escape. But he wanted to count the money first. He didn't like being cheated and had no reason to trust this beautifully venomous creature.

Sam released Vivian, shoving her backward onto the bed. Slowly he moved toward her, his features twisted by excitement and greed. "Lay still!" he said hoarsely. "Don't struggle or I'll kill you!"

Her throat aching and throbbing, Vivian lay very quietly with her eyes closed. She tried to make her mind a blank, her body numb. Whatever came next was going to be something she had no desire to remember. She heard the man's footsteps and his breathing.

Sam opened the briefcase and began counting out the money. As he finished, his face flushed with rage. "This is only half what you were ordered to bring!"

He grabbed her shoulders, shaking her violently, slapping her across the face. "You stinking whore! Where's the rest?"

"I'll get it for you. I promise. You didn't give me enough time!"

"Now you have just five days for the rest of the

money to be at your apartment." He threw Vivian across the bed in disgust.

As she heard the hotel-room door slam shut behind him, Vivian slowly opened her eyes, carefully checking to make sure this wasn't another trick. He was gone. She was still alive. There was no solace in either one of those revelations.

In a fit of violent temper Vivian reached out, ripped the cursed hotel telephone wire out of the wall and threw the useless instrument across the room. She drenched herself in hot water, scrubbing her body with soap, and followed that with an ice-cold shower, but it did no good. The minute she dried off, she started perspiring profusely again until the sweat was running in rivulets down her bare skin. A small blue bruise began spreading under her right eye where Sam had hit her.

She took a couple of tranquilizers and began packing her suitcase. Her hands shook the entire time she stuffed expensive clothes haphazardly into the bag. Slamming the lid shut, she called for a porter.

It was dusk as she paid her bill and checked out of the hotel. The ride to the airport through the hopeless rush-hour traffic was endless. She chewed up and swallowed several more tranquilizers, feeling the pieces stick bitterly in her throat.

Beside the road water buffalo were tethered in the fields awaiting the next day's work. Deep jungle green mingled with the bright colors of the natives' clothes as they walked to their shanty houses. An oppressive dampness filled the air.

Once at the airport Vivian walked unsteadily past the armed guard in the terminal, carrying her own luggage. She presented herself at the crowded ticket counter, determined to stay right in this spot until an airplane carried her out of here. A Pakistani woman stood at the counter, processing passengers and writing names on several lists.

"When is the next plane to the United States?" Vivian asked weakly.

"There is one in an hour, but it is full. All I can do is put you on a waiting list. May I have your ticket?" the woman asked politely. Vivian pulled out her ticket and several $100 bills, putting them on the counter with the ticket folder covering the American money. Deftly the woman slid the ticket off the counter, allowing the money to disappear into her free hand.

Vivian's eyes met directly with the eyes of the Pakistani woman. Neither of them said a word. The woman nodded her head almost imperceptibly and left for a moment.

Vivian held her breath. Either she was going to buy a seat on that plane or the woman was reporting her to the soldiers, in which case Vivian might well find herself thrown in prison. The woman returned with a boarding pass and Vivian's ticket. There was no hint of expression on her face or in her coal black eyes.

"There was one cancellation. You are scheduled to depart on Flight One-nineteen, Gate Six," she said, handing Vivian both the ticket and her precious boarding pass.

"Thank you . . . very much," Vivian murmured gratefully. She proceeded directly to Gate 6, where she was body-searched three times by the army soldiers. With 200 other sweating travelers, Vivian boarded the hulking jetliner in the sultry darkness.

Chapter 21

Buckley felt tired but resolute as she drove to the indoor firing range from Alphonse's house. Once inside, she went quickly to the heavy glass display case, which, although smudged by the sweaty palms of a dozen hands within the past few hours, still glistened. Deep inside, deceptively silent, lay an impressive array of handguns. At the far end of the case were the sinister-looking automatics, black and steel gray and rectangular. Next to them the revolvers started down the line, arranged first by caliber, then by brand name.

There were two men behind the counter, both wearing holsters. They could have been father and son, but neither spoke with that special familiarity. The older man had a thick beard. He walked with a slight limp but was visibly athletic despite his age. His partner, Alan, younger by about twenty years, was clean-shaven and heavyset. He spoke with a country twang. His eyes constantly scanned the large room as though electronically attached to the closed-circuit camera overhead. It was unusually quiet.

Buckley was the only woman in the place. Newly arrived, she waited her turn, feeling the curious eyes trained on her, assessing her. As she stared through the glass at the shiny revolvers, she had the weird sensation that her father was standing beside her, as though he'd come back to help her when no one else would.

An invisible touch moved her hand toward one of the smaller revolvers in the middle of the case. An inaudible voice told her to choose the modified Ruger, the little one that would fit her hand perfectly. Today, instead of tears filling her eyes when she thought about her dead father, a strength from him flowed through her exhausted body. She breathed deeply and straightened her back.

"Have you decided, miss?"

"Let me see that one." Buckley pointed. "The Ruger."

Alan looked mildly surprised. "That's a three-fifty-seven Magnum. You sure you can handle it?"

"I'm sure," Buckley said quietly, not at all certain she was right. It had been many, many years since she'd even touched a gun. Her father had taught her to shoot a rifle when she was just eleven years old, but he had let her near his revolver collection only twice. Part of her early training had been simply learning a profound respect for the power of the weapon itself. She'd had to learn every part, how to care for the guns and how to clean them. Only then would he teach her how to shoot them.

He unlocked the display case and removed the gun-metal gray Ruger with the black grip, modified and rounded specifically to fit a smaller hand. The chamber was open, exposing empty cylinders where the bullets would go. He handed her the heavy little Ruger, watching her carefully to see whether or not to trust her on the range.

Every move Buckley made was exactly right. She could almost hear her father's voice coaching her through the motions of handling this deadly weapon. Her hands were steady; her movements, sure and calm. She looked like an expert.

"You with the police academy?" Alan grinned as though discovering her secret identity.

"No," Buckley answered in a monotone, her mind totally engrossed in the coldness of the gun, the feel of the handle grip. She deftly seated the gun in the cupped palm of her left hand, positioning her right hand around the grip with her index finger outstretched next to the trigger.

"I'm only giving you a target load, just so you know," Alan said, dumping a plastic bag of rather large bullets on the counter with a thud. From a shelf behind him, Alan pulled a set of ear protectors and goggles. He plopped them on the counter beside the bullets. "Take station six," he said, handing her five bull's-eye targets. "Fifty feet is the end of the range, twenty-five at the first white line."

Buckley nodded, put on the ear protectors and goggles, stuck her two fingers through the opening created by the dislodged chamber so as to carry the gun safely into the range, picked up the targets and package of bullets. She pulled open the first heavy door leading to the range, and let it close behind her before she opened the second door, which admitted her to the range itself.

She went to booth six, and put her gun and bullets down on a small counter. Carefully she clipped the target onto a pulley and then pushed a button which mechanically conveyed the target out to the white line, twenty-five feet away. She opened the plastic bag, allowing the bullets to sprawl over the counter. Very slowly and deliberately Buckley began loading the .357 Magnum revolver, turning the chamber evenly as each slot was filled. With a snap she closed the chamber and checked to make sure it caught in place. She took a deep breath and spread her feet apart for balance. Her eyes never left the gun she held in both hands. Keeping her arms straight and both eyes open, she slowly moved the gun into position in front of her. Her right index finger eased around the trigger. She squeezed the trigger toward her, hardly daring to breathe.

The sound of a tremendous explosion ripped through the firing range. A red tongue of firepower burst from the opening of the Ruger's barrel, and a bullet tore cleanly through the edge of the target bull's-eye. Buckley was momentarily thrust backward but never lost either her grip or her stance. For the first time fear surged through her body, and her hands started sweating so profusely she had to lay the gun down very carefully and wipe her palms on her sweater. She stepped up to the counter again, took another deep breath, picked up her gun and commenced firing until all six bullets were gone and the Ruger was empty.

At the time she was shooting, her mind was totally concentrated on the target and her gun. When the smoke cleared and she brought the target back to the booth, she saw all six bullet holes within the black area, two right in the middle of the bull's-eye. The smell of gunpowder filled her nostrils. A feeling of triumph encompassed her. She hardly noticed that the other customers had left the range.

Alan stood behind Buckley, frankly admiring the target round she had just finished. "Not bad!" he shouted. "How'd you like to move up a step?" He was holding three life-size targets depicting a man's body in an aggressive stance with a gun in one hand.

"What's that for?" Buckley asked, pointing at the large figure.

"I'll show you," Alan answered, moving in front of the booth to clip the three identical human targets onto pulleys at the twenty-five-foot line. "Leave your weapon and come out here," Alan yelled at her.

Buckley cautiously followed the heavyset man, reluctant to be in front of the protective booths, even though she knew only the two of them were on the range floor.

"You walk slowly, evenly, holding the gun close to your body. When you see the target move and hear me yell a number at you . . . one, two or three . . . you stop, turn, stretch your arms straight out from your body and fire two rounds immediately, then bring the gun back to a ready position close to your gut, like this." Alan demonstrated without having a gun.

"Okay," Buckley replied. She reloaded and started walking at the far end of the three targets, holding her weapon exactly as he showed her.

"Two!" Alan called out as the number two human target moved suddenly closer to Buckley.

She whirled forward, pointed her gun and unloaded two shots into the target's midsection. It was scary as hell, but there was no going back. Alan worked the targets, moving them rapidly to simulate several men attacking her. Buckley's senses were reeling from the noise, the excitement and the smell of gunpowder filling her nostrils. In less than a minute her six bullets had been fired and the noise stopped.

"Great," Alan yelled, patting her on the shoulder. "You're a damn good shot, you know that?"

Buckley smiled weakly. She thought: No one is ever going to make me feel as terrified as I was the other night. There is a point at which it all has to stop. You can't live every day scared to death of what's going to happen next. I may be all alone, but I'm not defenseless now. If I'm the only one capable of protecting myself, then by God, I will.

You can't really imagine the terror of your house being broken into. You don't know how you'll react until the time actually comes. But once it does, you erase whatever preconceptions you may have had, and you're never the same person again.

You are angry at the violation of your privacy and safety. To face imminent death at the whim of a stranger changes you forever.

All her life Buckley had thought of guns only in connection with her father and the sport of hunting. The other night changed her attitude forever. The other night changed more than her opinion about guns. It made no sense to her that innocent people could be killed and no one made to pay for killing them. How could anyone say that the death sentence for a convicted murderer was not justice? Didn't criminals give thousands of innocent people the death sentence every year? Everyone's screaming about the soaring crime rate, and yet there are no punishments as awful as the crimes committed. She thought about Vivian's getting off with only a few years in jail for the cold-blooded murder of her father. She could almost see that condescending smile on the woman's face. It drove Buckley crazy. She wanted to scream, It's wrong! Doesn't anybody understand . . . it's wrong! No wonder we have a whole society going berserk. They know they're going to get away with it. The courts and jails and prisons overflow, but nothing changes.

Buckley looked down at the gun clutched in her own hand. At that exact instant she desperately wished she had the guts to kill Vivian.

So this is how it happens, Buckley thought in horror. This is how personal vengeance replaces the system of justice. The one thing in the world she longed for was retribution, knowing full well that the chance of its coming through the normal legal channels was about zero. The one thing that would calm the storm of anguish she felt over her father's untimely death was seeing Vivian die for what she'd done. But that evidently might not happen.

On top of the months she'd spent trying to help free T.J., Buckley's realization of the staggering inequity of the justice system was now beyond her ability to comprehend. How could the laws of her country deal so harshly with the innocent and so liberally with criminals?

This new information about herself had a strange effect on Buckley. Instead of the frenetic anger she'd previously experienced with T.J.'s incarceration, she now felt possessed by a calm, cold fury. She was obsessed by the idea of equal justice.

Buckley was ashen but composed. Her hands stopped sweating. She felt the terror subside, and her body ceased to shiver as she loaded another round into the .357 Magnum Ruger and took one more try at the moving targets. Tomorrow she would find a way to buy a gun exactly like this one.

Chapter 22

Vivian had spent a restless night. Since her return from Trinidad she'd been constantly irritable. The attack of acute anxiety she'd suffered had not entirely subsided. Each day required increasing doses of her tranquilizers.

This morning she awoke feeling sluggish and discontent. It was exactly five days since her disastrous encounter with Sam. Another $25,000 was due him this afternoon.

Vivian sighed deeply, turning on her side to check the bedside clock. It was ten-thirty in the morning. She'd have to make her bank withdrawal before driving upstate to the juvenile court proceedings. Nothing was turning out according to her plans. She had been assured two weeks ago by Judge Harding that T.J. had no chance of release. However, upon her return she'd been notified by an entirely different judge to appear in court today. Something had gone wrong, and Vivian felt uneasy. She'd called Judge Harding's office, only to be told that because of sudden illness, the judge had transferred all his current cases.

The situation with Sam was even worse. She'd lost control. For the first time in twenty years Vivian felt afraid. It was a predicament from which she could find no convenient escape.

After she bathed, Vivian stood silently looking at herself in the large bathroom mirror. She picked up a bottle of makeup and began gently dabbing the neutral color over the bruised area around her right eye. Although skillful at camouflaging the signs of middle age, Vivian knew she might not be able to conceal this bruise completely. It reminded her unpleasantly of several similarly brutal encounters she'd had many years ago as a street prostitute, before meeting Benjamin, when she'd had to fend for herself. It caused a faint nausea in her stomach as she thought that perhaps after all these years she hadn't come so very far. What had all the struggle, the lying and careful planning really achieved? When it was over, wasn't she still enslaved? Wasn't she still being used without her consent, just as her own father had taken her against her will? Would her time of freedom, her moment of personal independence ever come?

It was getting late. Vivian would have to hurry if she expected to accomplish everything on her schedule.

By midmorning the humidity had reached ninety-eight percent. It was also unbearably hot. Great thunderclouds gathered in the west, filling the sky and threatening a downpour before noon.

Juvenile proceedings were held in the old court building, the one without central air conditioning. Despite the valiant effort of ancient ceiling fans, not a breath of air circulated inside.

Buckley's light summer cotton dress clung to her legs as she and Seymour walked down the long corridor. She had just been told about the new judge and hadn't expected to be summoned to his chambers at the last minute. Though Seymour tried to reassure her that nothing was wrong, she was still very nervous.

"What could he possibly want with me?" she asked Seymour barely above a whisper.

"I don't know. He's had only a few days to go over the entire case. Maybe it's just a simple clarification." Seymour sounded more calm and self-assured than he felt.

"About *what?*" Buckley insisted anxiously.

Seymour was about to answer when he spotted the door to the office. Simultaneously they stopped, staring at the number and the name on the door. Buckley desperately wished she were clairvoyant just for this one moment.

Seymour put his arm around her gently, but the look on his face was quite stern. "For once in your life, Buckley, please keep your mouth shut and let me handle this."

"Gladly," she agreed.

Seymour opened the door and held it ajar for her to enter. "Courage!" he whispered.

It was a welcome relief to see that the secretary, a woman about Buckley's age, was polite and friendly, a radical change from what Buckley had come to expect.

"Ms. Simpson?" the secretary inquired pleasantly before Seymour and Buckley had an opportunity to introduce themselves.

"Yes, I'm Buckley Simpson, and this is Seymour Feinberg, my attorney."

"Please come this way. Judge Foster is waiting for you."

Buckley shot Seymour a quizzical glance and took a deep breath, trying to steady her nerves and collect her thoughts.

For some inexplicable reason the judge's chambers were about fifteen degrees cooler than the outer office. The judge himself sat behind his baronial desk, composed and seemingly unaffected by the sultry temperature. As Buckley and Seymour entered, he stood and extended his hand in greeting.

"Ms. Simpson . . . Mr. Feinberg. I'm so glad you could make this appointment."

Buckley stared hard at the old judge. He had a clean, chiseled face and snow white hair. His light blue eyes seemed magnified behind the old-fashioned glasses he wore. His desk held a neat stack of papers and a single file folder, which was placed directly in front of him.

That file must be on T.J., Buckley thought as she studied its thickness. She couldn't help wondering what all those pages said about T.J., about her, about Vivian. On second thought, it was probably a good thing she couldn't read it, considering what a short fuse ignited her temper these days.

She sat in the chair indicated by the judge and folded her hands carefully in her lap, hoping they would stop shaking so badly. Seymour sat next to her, setting his briefcase on the carpet with a muffled thump.

"As you know," the judge continued, "I was assigned to this case unexpectedly. My predecessor, Judge Harding, was taken ill suddenly and forced to resign his responsibilities earlier than he'd anticipated. Because of highly unusual circumstances surrounding the entire matter, I decided to schedule a hearing immediately." His penetrating blue eyes studied Buckley. The slender, tired girl sitting nervously in front of him didn't fit his preconceived image of the relentless, angry crusader he'd found spicing the pages of the folder on his desk. She looked like a frightened child, undernourished and exhausted.

"Your Honor," Seymour interrupted, "I feel compelled to convey my serious objection to the manner in which this entire situation has been handled. Although my field is criminal law and not juvenile or family court, I must tell you that what has happened here is unconscionable. In the last five years I've defended my fair share of felony cases, and in each one the accused had a previous history of juvenile offenses. Most started like T.J. They came from broken or inadequate families and ran away from home constantly. Finally, they were arrested and served time in detention or correctional facilities. There was never the slightest doubt in my mind that the contacts they had with the authorities made their problems worse. The detention centers and correctional facilities were just training grounds for an entire life of antisocial behavior and usually adult prison. When I started practicing law, minors still shared jail cells with adult criminals and runaways were treated like juvenile delinquents. That's been changed. But despite those reforms, as a criminal lawyer I see a tragic cause-and-effect process at work. Judge Foster, we are manufacturing felons and murderers at an alarming rate in this country and everyone, including the courts, seems powerless to stop it. I cannot stress strongly enough that part of the problem, at least in view of my personal experience these past few months with Miss Simpson and T.J., is directly related to the juvenile justice system."

To Seymour's great astonishment, the elderly judge nodded his head in agreement. Behind the gold-rimmed glasses his clear eyes sparkled with intense dedication.

"Mr. Feinberg, I agree with you, and I'm sorry to say that it is a continuing source of great frustration. But there are some aspects that as a relative newcomer you may not have taken into account. At one extreme juvenile court must deal with accused murderers who are still minors. At the other we have children damaged by the epidemic of broken families. Far too many parents either don't understand their fundamental responsibility toward children or want schools and courts to take over for them. Most of the children we see in our courts are really the broken dreams of our entire society. They are the casualties of a battle between old mistakes and new value structures that haven't yet been built. Every day I see children who began life as innocent, unwanted victims of those broken dreams, and you're right . . . most of them receive no help and will inflict on others the violence or contempt for justice that they experienced. By the time they are in elementary school, they are in trouble. These kids are often slow to learn, fearful and unable to adjust. As they go through junior and senior high school, they become truants, alcoholics, pregnant teenagers, carriers of venereal disease, addicts, gang members, vandals, thieves and even murderers. What worries me most, as I decide the immediate fates of these young people, is the knowledge that they are also the parents of our next generation!"

"And by the time they get to me as adults, it's usually too late," Seymour interjected. "By then the entire process has failed."

"But we must not allow ourselves to get discouraged. Just because the problem seems temporarily insurmountable is reason enough to keep working hard to find solutions. Each of us has to give up the notion that someone else is responsible. Which brings me directly to the reason I asked to see both of you this morning."

The judge picked up the file folder which he opened to a specific place he'd previously marked. A slight frown crossed his forehead.

Buckley held her breath. Seymour's eloquence had moved her, and she felt the judge agreed with him. But what was the information in that cursed folder that caused the judge to frown? She racked her brain to guess what the man was going to say. God help us, she prayed silently. Please, God, don't let something go wrong at the last minute.

"Ms. Simpson, on behalf of the court I want to express my personal appreciation for the tenacity and unfailing loyalty you have shown toward your stepbrother during these past months. I'm sure it has been a hardship on you emotionally. It is unfortunate that the matter has taken so long. I'm sure you now understand the extreme difficulty the court faces in adjudicating the enormous numbers of juveniles under its jurisdiction."

"Yes, Your Honor," Buckley murmured, clenching her hands together so tightly her knuckles began to turn white.

"I want you to know that despite the considerable difficulties you have endured, some good has come of it. From today on, every juvenile under my jurisdiction is being assigned an advocate who will be personally responsible for protecting both the legal and civil rights of the minor. This court is determined to prevent the errors and inexcusable length of time it has taken to hear this case from ever occurring again."

Buckley looked to Seymour, who nodded his head approvingly.

"What about T.J.?" she asked.

"We are in receipt of Mr. and Mrs. Alphonse Mazzo's application for our foster parent program, which the court is willing to accept, whether or not Mrs. Simpson gives her consent."

"Thank you . . . very much," Buckley said in a choked voice, a thin smile of gratitude parting her lips.

The judge continued. "This court is deeply grateful to both of you. I wish there were more people who cared enough to challenge us when we're wrong. However, you may be sure that you've made a permanent difference here."

Seymour leaned closer to her, almost whispering. "That was a compliment, Buckley!

"Thank you . . . again," Buckley replied hastily. "Please forgive me, but I'm not feeling very well." She picked up her purse.

"I hope you feel well enough to be in court. We convene in half an hour," the judge said kindly.

Focused intently on the judge's face, Buckley replied, "Don't worry. Nothing on this earth could keep me away. I'll be there."

Seymour closed his briefcase, hearing Buckley's footsteps disappear. He stood. "Your Honor . . . please excuse her . . . she . . . well, she's been under terrible pressure."

"I understand completely, Mr. Feinberg."

"Thank you, Your Honor."

Seymour hurried out of the office. He was worried about Buckley. She was on the verge of collapse. He asked one of the matrons to check in the ladies' room for her. A few moments later the woman returned.

"She's going to be fine. If she rests quietly for a few moments, she'll be all right."

Seymour wandered back and forth near the women's room like an expectant father. The corridor outside the juvenile courtroom was beginning to fill with people. Conversations were muffled, hostile and anxious. Seymour wanted to walk outside for a moment but was afraid to leave for fear Buckley wouldn't be able to find him.

Finally, he saw her emerge from the rest room. Her face was pale, but she was walking steadily. Seymour took her arm, trying to smile in some encouragement.

"Let's go outside. You'll feel better without all these people around."

They walked as far as the exterior courthouse steps and stopped. Suddenly it started to rain. A flash of lightning streaked across the darkened sky. Thunder was not far behind. Mercifully the rain began to cool the scorching summer heat.

Buckley and Seymour stood quietly. She leaned against one of the columns for support. Slowly some normal color returned to her face. She looked out at the pouring rain, feeling somewhat comforted. This terrible ordeal would soon be over. Buckley chose not to burden Seymour any further, and she kept the new information Needham had told her about Vivian to herself.

Seymour gently brushed strands of hair away from

her face. He gathered her frail body in his arms, his heart aching for this delicate creature. He had fallen in love with her but wondered sadly if today marked the end of their brief and unequally involved relationship.

Buckley took this quiet moment to appreciate fully a new aspect of Seymour's character. He'd seemed to gain in strength and stature before her eyes as she'd watched him with the judge. Buckley realized she had been so wrapped up in her own struggle these past months she'd never bothered to discover what kind of man Seymour really was. She'd taken his friendship and compassion for granted. She'd never noticed what an intelligent and steadfast person he was, nor had she realized until this moment that she would miss him terribly if he left her life after today. In a peculiar way it was as if she were seeing him clearly for the first time.

As Seymour released her from his embrace, their eyes met, and he saw Buckley's look of frank curiosity. He could not tell what thoughts were behind the look. As though to lighten the intense wave of feeling that ran through him, Seymour reverted back to his earlier posture of good-natured humor.

"You know, Buckley, I'm very proud of you. If you ever change your mind about advertising as a career . . . let me tell you, with your perseverance and tenacity, you'd make a hell of a lawyer!"

Buckley smiled up at him. "Thanks. Coming from you, I take that as a compliment." They shared the soft laughter of a new communion with each other.

"It's time to go back," Seymour said gently after checking his watch.

"Seymour, I want you to know . . . what you've done for me is . . . beautiful. I'll never forget it," she said impulsively, and kissed him softly on the cheek, taking his hand in hers. Together they walked back inside.

The case of T. J. Simpson was next on the court's schedule. The courtroom had been cleared except for immediate family, attorneys and witnesses. There was no jury. A uniformed bailiff guarded the main entrance. Buckley identified herself. She and Seymour took their seats in the back of the large room next to Carolyn and Alphonse, who greeted them fondly.

It was strange for Buckley to see the woman she hated with such passion freely enter the courtroom without the slightest look of guilt or remorse.

She watched Vivian, who was wearing an immaculately tailored dark blue summer suit, wide-brimmed straw hat and dark glasses, sit crisply in the front row. Vivian behaved so demurely she could be waiting for the beginning of a Sunday concert instead of her son's court hearing. It would have been impossible for a stranger to believe this woman capable of systematic human destruction.

Empty rows of benches that looked like long wooden church pews separated Vivian from Buckley, Seymour, Carolyn and Alphonse. Except for the rustle of papers and the creaking of overhead fans, it was quiet.

Buckley was making such a herculean effort to control the waves of anxiety and excitement she was almost in a trance. She didn't identify the new voice she heard speaking quietly in the distance behind her. It was Seymour who clasped her arm, urging her to look.

To her astonishment Buckley saw Josh Marks enter the courtroom and walk steadily toward her.

She stood, hardly having time to comprehend the mirage she thought she saw.

"Josh?" she whispered as though waking from a dream. "Josh! Oh, my God . . . Josh, you're here!" Today she joyously greeted the man she had never wanted to see again. As she held out her arms to embrace him, Josh suddenly became the most welcome sight in the world.

"Seymour, Alphonse and Carolyn . . . this is Josh Marks, T.J.'s father!" Buckley introduced him, grasping his hand firmly as though to prevent such an unexpected gift of hope from disappearing.

The small group gathered around, shaking hands and repeating their own introductions.

Josh turned to Buckley. "If it's not too late, I've come to take T.J. home."

Buckley's eyes filled with tears of happiness. "It's not too late, Josh. Matter of fact, you're right on time."

"Seymour, could you present this letter to the judge with me? I'm not familiar with the correct procedure," Josh asked quietly.

Buckley watched as Seymour and Josh walked down toward the judicial bench to present this new development to the clerk of the court.

Carolyn took Buckley's hand and held it gently. Buckley relaxed a little, allowing herself to draw strength from Carolyn's gesture of compassion.

At the sound of voices Vivian turned in curiosity and was surprised to see her former husband standing tall and dignified in the center aisle.

Josh looked at her face, made direct contact with Vivian's eyes for the first time in eleven years. Immediately he recognized a strength in himself that had not existed when they were married. Silently he challenged Vivian to dare stand in his way. Josh had returned to claim his son, the boy he'd adored, the baby she had taken away from him. This time he was fully prepared to fight.

Across that cavern of time Josh studied the still-beautiful stranger he'd once loved. She was really the black widow spider, poisonous, capable of devouring her mate. The fear of her harbored deep inside Josh might never be completely purged, but in this moment he was resolute. Josh returned to take his seat next to Buckley. There was no reason to say a single word to Vivian.

"Josh," Buckley whispered, her eyes riveted on him, her mind brimming with unanswered questions, only one of which required asking, "what made you come back?"

As he turned his face toward her, thinking how to answer, Buckley realized the look of hopelessness had vanished from him.

"I needed to be free."

She frowned slightly. "But what you said to me about being left alone, about responsibility . . ."

He smiled gently. "If you must know everything . . . the truth is that Alphonse called me several times urging me to come back. Then, one day, I finally realized that running away and being free are incompatible pursuits."

Buckley stared at Josh, knowing he had just synthesized the final task that awaited her.

Silence was broken only b the thudding pound of the gavel. The judge was in place, and the hearing began.

Seymour immediately returned to the front of the court, requesting permission to approach the bench. He and the judge had a brief exchange which no one else could hear, and Seymour returned to his seat next to Buckley.

T.J. was ushered into court, looking frightened. He was led to a place at the side and sat down. Suddenly T.J.'s eyes widened with amazement. There could be no doubt he had seen his father. T.J. could not take his eyes off Josh, searching every detail about the man. He dared not hope and yet could not ignore the implications of his dream come true.

Buckley's heart was pounding fiercely. Seymour scribbled notes, pausing now and then to look at Buckley. Josh reached for her hand. They sat bound together in silent prayer.

T.J. related his version of the original incident so many months ago. In the enormous space of this courtroom the events seemed trifling, paltry, too insignificant to have been the catalyst for the battle of life or death that had ensued.

After T.J. left the witness stand, a procession of professional witnesses testified: the psychiatrist, Dr. Tanner, probation officer Watkins, and the arresting policeman. It was a hollow drone on the same sour note. No charges. No previous record. Unsatisfactory family environment. No recommendation for further sentencing.

It seemed to take forever. Josh kept his firm grip on Buckley's hand, and she drew patience from him like a living transfusion. At long last all testimony was over. Buckley strained to focus her attention rigidly on the judge. She leaned forward, listening carefully. She was finally beyond being nervous.

Buckley heard the judge order T.J. Simpson's file sealed with an adjudication of not guilty. The judge further ordered T.J. Simpson returned to his father's custody until he reached eighteen years of age.

The gavel pounded again. The file was closed. T.J. Simpson was free!

Buckley buried her face in her hands, sobbing with relief and joy. She wept openly, hugging first Seymour and then Josh as tears splashed on his shirt collar.

"He's free!" she sobbed. "T.J. is free!" She looked upward. "Thank you, God," she said quietly. Although she smiled and even laughed, she couldn't stop the tears streaming down her face as she stood.

T.J. stood awkwardly in the far aisle nearest the witness stand. A social worker handed him a small packet containing his few personal belongings. He wasn't quite sure after all these months if he dared believe that today he was really free. It was almost too good to be true. But T.J. would never forget what the judge had said. He was now free to go out into the world again, free to live his life once more, free from the terrible oppression of wards and jails and institutions. Most amazing of all, his father had come to get him. They would be together again. His father loved him after all.

Tears were still falling down Buckley's cheeks as she started running down the aisle toward T.J. At long last there were no bars or wire mesh or guards separating them. She threw her arms around T.J. They held onto each other for a long moment. Finally, she backed away, wiping her face dry, smiling at him.

"We won, T.J.," she said, shaking his shoulders gently. "We won!" She brushed away the last of her tears. "I don't know how the hell we did it, but we really won."

"Hello, son," Josh said quietly, suddenly overwhelmed by the years of buried emotion, of longing for his only child.

"Hi, Dad," T.J. said somewhat awkwardly in front of the crowd that was gathering around him. "I sure am glad to see you!" T.J. attempted a shy grin.

Josh could stand the separation no longer. He put his arms around his son in a bear hug as he'd done countless times those years long ago when T.J. was still a little boy.

"Dad," T.J. whispered hoarsely.

Seymour walked slowly toward them, reluctant to intrude. "Congratulations, T.J., Mr. Marks," Seymour said sincerely, extending his hand. T.J. shook Seymour's hand, not knowing how to deal with the emotions that suddenly flooded over him.

"Thank you for everything, Seymour. This family is eternally grateful to you," Josh replied.

Vivian stared at young T.J. without saying a word. Today was a humiliation, and she took the court's decision as a personal defeat. It was not losing her son that infuriated Vivian; it was the shame of feeling herself somehow on public trial, although she was never called by name, never asked to testify. Her hatred of her son was a feeling she would never conquer. She stood immediately after the case was closed, and without so much as a second glance or a word spoken, Vivian left the courtroom by a side exit. She had no desire to witness more of the family reunion.

Alphonse and his wife, Carolyn, waited patiently by the courtroom entrance. As the little group approached, Carolyn looked up at her husband and smiled.

"I'm proud of you, Al. It's not easy to do what your conscience tells you is the right thing."

Alphonse smiled back sheepishly. They both knew it was her conscience as much as his that had helped win this battle.

"We'd like to invite all of you to our house for the long-overdue family reunion," Alphonse said, looking at Josh.

"Great. We'd like that," Josh responded, keeping his arm around T.J.'s shoulder until they reached the exit.

Buckley caught a glimpse of Vivian leaving the courtroom. She realized the moment of their confrontation was right now; the opportunity might never happen again. Dread was suddenly replaced by a sense of urgency. Buckley tugged quickly at Seymour's arm and whispered, "Tell them I'll be along in just a few minutes. Tell them not to wait for me."

"Are you sure?"

"Don't worry," she assured him with a deceptive lightness. "I won't be long."

Buckley hurried through the courtroom's side exit where only minutes earlier she'd seen Vivian disappear. Her thoughts were suddenly crystal clear. Both Josh and T.J. were free. Now it was up to Buckley to untangle her own life from Vivian's destruction.

She saw Vivian standing beside her silver Mercedes in the parking lot and continued walking toward her, the exact words of their confrontation formulating themselves in her mind. Despite a gnawing sensation of tension in her stomach, Buckley felt a tremendous calm descend upon her.

"Vivian." She addressed the woman's back. "I know exactly how you tried to destroy both Josh and T.J. I also know you were responsible for my father's murder."

Slowly Vivian unlocked the car door, opened it and turned to face Buckley. The pallor of the older woman's face accentuated the harshness of her red lipstick.

"You're creating a scene. I don't like scenes, Buckley."

"I'm going to do more than that before this is all over," Buckley flashed back with venom. "My father was one of the finest men on this earth, and he never did a thing to hurt you in any way. But you are so insane and such a greedy bitch you couldn't wait . . . you killed him, Vivian, just as surely as if you pulled the trigger yourself. A trial's too good for you, Vivian, because you don't give a damn about laws and justice. My father didn't get any trial before you sentenced him to death, did he?" Buckley was shouting now. "So help me God, I'm going to see you pay for it! They ought to hang you in a public square, you street slut—"

Vivian got into her car and slammed the door. She started the engine, then lowered the window halfway.

"Fuck you, kid." Vivian's mouth twisted into a smile. "Prove it!"

Before Buckley had a chance to move one inch, Vivian gunned the Mercedes's engine and sped out of the parking lot.

Buckley's eyes were like two blazing fires. Her entire body shook in a convulsion of rage. Only one thought pounded in her brain, ran like a bolt of lightning along her nerves: I'm going to kill you, Vivian!

Chapter 23

John Needham got into his unmarked police car which was parked behind the precinct house. He rolled down the car window, leaning his head toward the two uniformed officers who followed him.

"You've got the address and apartment number?"

"Yes," the older policeman replied.

"See you there," Needham said without any sign of anticipation. Only minutes before, a Chinese man named Mr. Chin had called in the information that Sam and Vivian were meeting right now. This was exactly the break Needham had hoped to get. If he could apprehend both of them and some of the blackmail money he knew would be exchanged, there might be a chance of proving Vivian and Sam guilty. It was a long shot, but all he had.

Without activating either lights or siren, John Needham sped toward the luxury building in the Golden Triangle section of downtown.

It was late afternoon by the time Vivian returned

to her apartment house. A uniformed doorman held open the heavy front entrance door just long enough for Vivian to enter, closing it quickly behind her to prevent the stifling summer heat from permeating the luxury building's interior.

Despite the soaring temperature and pouring rain, Vivian returned to her building looking much the same as when she'd left, crisp and composed.

She hurried to the elevator, nodding coldly to the operator, who always insisted on chattering away about the latest building gossip.

Since she had fired her housekeeper, Vivian didn't ring the apartment doorbell but took out her keys and let herself into the empty house. She fixed herself a drink, her mind a frantic jumble of new plans. She had no time. Sam was due any minute. She had to kill him quickly. He was the only remaining source of evidence against her. Vivian took the same revolver she'd intended to use on Sam that first day and put it in her purse. She realized her hands were shaking violently and quickly swallowed the last of her drink.

In the background Vivian heard the service doorbell ringing. She set down her glass and walked to the service door.

"Okay . . . okay," she called out.

Before unlocking the door, Vivian looked out the peephole. What greeted her was the sight of an enormous flower arrangement.

She unbolted the service door and stepped aside to admit Sam, whose face was almost completely hidden behind the flowers.

"Put them over there on the table," Vivian said, not bothering to admire the fragrant, luxuriously expensive arrangement. She didn't have as much time for this transaction as she'd originally planned.

"If you've got the money," Sam said, setting the flowers down, "I have a real nice present for you, Vivian." He added, taking a square velvet jewelry box out of his pocket, "From Benjamin."

Vivian was reaching for her purse, which contained the loaded .38-caliber revolver, but she hesitated imperceptibly at the sound of Benjamin's name spoken so casually. At this last minute could Benjamin have finally decided to help her, as he always had in the past?

"The money's all here, Sam. Count it if you want," she said, opening her briefcase.

Sam figured she was telling the truth this time and never took his eyes off her as he opened the dark green velvet box and lifted out a single strand of luminescent pearls. Carefully he clasped the pearls around Vivian's long white neck.

She felt the cool softness of the pearls against her skin, remembering Benjamin's first gift to her had been an exquisite diamond necklace that had made other women jealous every time she wore it.

"You broke your promise, Vivian." Sam's grip on the pearls squeezed shut, pulling them taut. He knew the monofilament fishing line on which they were strung would not break. "Benjamin said to tell you—you two had a deal, remember?"

"Sam . . . don't!" she gasped, feeling the air supply in her throat closed off. "Please . . ." Vivian begged him, struggling to free herself from the choking pearls.

"Benjamin gave me no choice, darlin' lady," Sam muttered as his deft hands wrapped in pearls strangled her slowly. "He's a powerful dude. You understand, don't you?"

Vivian felt herself slipping into unconsciousness.

She tried to fight for her life, but Sam was too strong and his grip too tight. In what seemed like a moment of eternity Vivian knew she was going to die. How strange, she thought in the darkness that began to envelop her, how strange that my life began and ended in the sour stench of vulgar brutality. And all I ever wanted was to be beautiful. . . .

There was a muffled sound of footsteps in the hallway. Sam snapped his head around, focusing his attention on the sound of approaching danger. Vivian slumped to the floor. Sam looked frantically for an escape route, a place to hide.

Suddenly the kitchen door slammed. Sam looked disoriented, confused. He fumbled for his gun in the shoulder holster beneath his jacket, taking his eyes off the kitchen entrance for a split second as he did so.

John Needham and two uniformed police officers crouched at the apartment entrance, guns drawn.

"Freeze. Police. Drop your weapon and come out with your hands up!"

Sam fired twice, his bullets ripping through the kitchen door. He dropped to the floor, crawling on his belly as if he were back in the midst of jungle combat.

Vivian regained consciousness, her brain reeling from the sound of gunfire explosions all around her. She opened her eyes, realizing her purse was beside her on the floor. She slowly reached out and drew it to her.

Several more shots rang out. An officer took one shot, which grazed Sam's shoulder. He winced with pain but kept crawling like a human reptile. Another shot blasted away part of his neck. Blood spurted from the jugular vein as though Sam's throat had been cut. He fell to the floor motionless. A last shot hit him directly in the head, splitting it open.

John Needham saw Vivian lying on the kitchen floor. He saw the .38-caliber revolver in her hand. He watched as she turned her body to face him. In the split second of time he had before making the decision to pull the trigger, twenty years of police work flashed through his mind . . . all the nights spent in the noise and confusion of gun battles . . . days of endless paper work . . . weeks of investigation . . . months of trials without convictions . . . the revolving door of repeated arrests . . . the same faces jeering at him, haunting his sleep.

The final shot exploded from John Needham's gun and ripped through Vivian's body. She lay dead on the kitchen floor, the delicate strand of luminescent pearls still around her neck.

The two uniformed officers entered the kitchen, their guns still drawn. John Needham stood motionless in the sudden silence. Slowly he returned his gun to its holster. There would be no arrests this afternoon.

The elevator doors opened on the fifteenth floor, and Buckley stepped out. She'd heard the gunshots and froze. Instantly she recognized Needham standing outside the service entrance to Vivian's apartment. Something deep inside told her she was too late. Needham walked toward Buckley, intending to turn her away from the apartment.

"You don't want to see this," Needham warned.

"Is she dead?" Buckley asked with a morbid fascination she'd never felt before.

"They both are."

"I need to see for myself. Please."

John Needham stood aside and allowed Buckley to enter the kitchen.

She walked very quietly, wanting to be invisible. A few steps inside, Buckley stopped. At first she did not see Vivian, only the man named Sam who had killed her father. A piece of his head was blown off, blood splattered randomly on floor and cabinets.

Buckley stopped. She had no idea it would look like this, so hideous, so barbaric . . . so gruesomely bloody. She felt an involuntary retching spasm and swallowed back the stinging bile, covering her mouth with one ice-cold hand. She reached out with her other hand to steady herself against the nearest cabinet, determined not to vomit or faint.

She took a deep breath, swallowing hard several times. It was only then she noticed that there was a sickening, almost sweet smell mingled with the familiar bitterness of gunpowder in the room.

Several feet ahead of her, lying faceup on the floor, Buckley finally saw Vivian. Her dead face was a grayish mask, purple around the lips and dark beneath the eyes. As Buckley looked more closely, it seemed that Vivian's mouth was contorted in a ghastly grimace. Around her neck was the beautiful strand of pearls that had left a series of reddish blue marks on her pale skin. Her dark summer suit was barely wrinkled, betraying no sign of the final struggle. However, on her abdomen were dark splotches of blood which had soaked through the thin fabric and dripped slowly onto the floor.

Suddenly Buckley knew how close she had come to ruining her entire life. She had meant to kill Vivian herself this afternoon. She had been fully prepared to sacrifice herself to win vengeance. She had wanted justice so badly that nothing else mattered. As she looked down at Vivian's dead body, she realized in terror that she had become almost identical to the enemy she'd fought against so bitterly. In the midst of their battle Buckley had forgotten the ideals and principles she'd always believed in and thought only of the victory. Just a few short minutes had saved her from the fatal mistake of destroying herself in the name of retribution.

Now it was over. Freedom had a very high price. As she turned to leave, Buckley's eyes made momentary contact with the hawkish, expressionless face of John Needham. She realized no words were necessary between the two of them. Their mutual goals had been accomplished. They would probably never even meet again.

As she walked down the hallway to the elevators, she felt a terrible burden begin to lift from her tired shoulders. Buckley realized she was a different person from the young woman of six months ago. She knew in her heart that she could never go back again, that her life would be forever changed.

It was not going to be simply a matter of picking up the pieces and continuing. She was standing at a major crossroad. The battle for T.J.'s freedom had turned into a much larger journey toward her own adulthood. Now that T.J. was safe and had his first real chance to be happy, Buckley knew she must decide what she was now going to do with her own life. The terrible lessons learned from her father's death and the responsibility of the legacy he'd left her must now become part of that decision. She could not turn her back on them any more than she could have walked away from helping T.J.

Outside, the brilliant afternoon sun was shining through massive white clouds. The sky was as clear as it had been in many weeks. The summer thunderstorm had passed to the north.

Seymour's words echoed in her memory. "If you ever decide to change your mind about advertising as a career . . ." Maybe that was what she'd do. Now that she had personally experienced the extraordinary problems that existed for the children nobody cared about, maybe that was the direction her life should take. Whatever profession she chose, Buckley was determined to remember the children. Someone had to care.